Spiral Mind

By

Janina Arndt

Paperback ISBN 978-1-78705-645-9
ePub ISBN 978-1-78705-646-6
PDF ISBN 978-1-78705-647-3

Published by Orange Pip Books
335 Princess Park Manor, Royal Drive,
London, N11 3GX
www.orangepipbooks.com

To
my Mam, Astrid, for imbuing me with the urge to write and the confidence to trust my characters,
To
my Dad, Jürgen, for showing me the Rathbone films,
And to
Tom, for correcting Sherlock on television.

Contents

It has always been my duty to tell the story. Now it is my burden, because I failed my duty. But uncovering who really told the story is all that I can do. There are too many stories now that need to be rectified. Too many lines barring the truth. Who we really were. What we really were. How we were written...

~J.H.W.

Don't think for one second, that I'm not one of them. I joined their silhouettes long ago. I chose this, and I cannot say that I wanted anything else. But that is irrelevant. My name was in the books. Long before I thought I was born. I am not a new character. I was there from the beginning.

~L.S.V.

Part 1: Explosive Advice

Chapter 1

I fell from the Tower that day. The wind in his coat swept me off the edge. I only saw him in my fall – his brown hair, his long legs and arms, his high, loosely-tied collar, and his face with these piercing grey eyes that caught your recent past as you dropped it. But I held on.

The panorama of London was still clear before my eyes, and Anne Boleyn's cold breath was still in the wind around me as her shadow grew larger on the water below.

The carpet felt sudden rather than hard; the pile of books was scattered on the library floor, screaming for the ladder I should have used. Embarrassment came jumping up my shoulders to swing around in my ruined hair like a dozen little monkeys driving the colour into my cheeks in little cars.

Holmes offered me his hand. 'If I didn't frighten you, I should say you look like you've seen a ghost. May I introduce myself–' He politely helped me up, quickly shoving the hairpin back into my bun.

'Sherlock Holmes, consulting detective,' I interrupted him. 'I could have known it from what John told me about you, but, actually, you've dropped your card.'

A mixture of approval and bemusement appeared on Holmes's face. 'Well observed, Miss Vendalle.'

He picked up his card with a lissome move.

'I mentioned John, didn't I?' I asked.

'You did, but John didn't mention you,' Holmes replied, smirking. Obviously, John wanted to surprise him. I had to smile at the idea. 'No,' he said then, 'John didn't tell me you were coming, but this morning he – I don't want to say panicked – but he was a little confused about the fact that he'd never bought matching clothes in his life.'

I looked at Holmes askance.

'Oh, and your name,' he continued, 'appears last on the book I wanted to fetch. I allowed myself a small peek into the administrative system.'

Holmes effortlessly took a volume out of the shelf I had tried to reach for. The pile of books never seemed more ridiculous. I began collecting my mess off the floor.

All of a sudden, Holmes's voice was so near that I almost dropped the books I was holding, my breath quickening in surprise. His moves were soundless and feline as he helped me pick up the rest.

'What has John told you about me?'

'He–' I started, but broke off too quickly to think about how to nicely paraphrase the words *psychopath, arrogant* and *unbelievably egocentric*, 'John said I might find you to be a...'

'Psychopath, unbelievably egocentric and perhaps arrogant?' Holmes completed the sentence.

'Yes, I – I think that's what he said, yes,' I replied helplessly. Holmes grinned at me.

Hastily, I added, 'But his voice sounded different when he said it, and, if I guessed rightly, it sounded like he admires you a great deal, and...' – I searched for the right words – 'he even made me admire you when he talked of you...'

Holmes's smile grew broader, and for a second I could first see in his eyes that warmth he would save for John. We stood up.

'Miss Vendalle, may I ask you another question?'

'Er... sure.'

'What does L. S. stand for? Sometimes even hacking into a system won't give you full information on what you're looking for.'

I smirked at him. 'Lily Scarlett, but I prefer Scarlett.'

'Interesting.' Holmes smiled. 'Do you have any business left in town, or may I take you home to deposit your luggage?'

'Well, you may, but I reckon you have some business left with the watchmaker.' I had noticed his wristwatch in a front pocket of his trousers.

He began to scan me more curiously. 'Miss Vendalle, you do surprise me.'

Holmes offered me his arm. After I checked out the books I borrowed, we left the library.

'How did your watch break?' I asked when Holmes and I had got into a taxi.

'Electromagnetic waves, a little different in wavelength from our usual light.'

'Infrared or ultraviolet?'

'Infrared.'

'This is impossible.'

'I know.' Holmes smiled at me, but the predominance in his face slowly gave way to that same mixture of approval and bemusement, which must have puzzled him. He looked out of the window again, and I smiled to myself.

The watchmaker didn't look very pleased when Holmes handed him the watch.

'I bet he thought your wife had had a go on it with her heel,' I stated, grinning at the thought as we walked out of the building.

Holmes smiled, too. 'In fact, he wouldn't have been too far from the truth.'

I stopped. 'John said you didn't have a wife.' I bit my lip when I realised how that must sound.

'I don't have a wife, I just consider myself as being married to my work,' Holmes remarked, speeding up.

I tied my eyes to the passing shop windows.

'Oh, and I have to apologise for the mess in our flat. Work doesn't usually tidy up a room as well as a wife could if she wanted to,' Holmes remarked. Perhaps, he wouldn't mind my guinea pigs adding to the mess then, I thought, relieved that one person might take my side against John's military lifestyle.

The few possessions attributed to me were sent directly to Baker Street after John had agreed to take me in. It wasn't much when they found me, but for some reason my guinea pigs had been there. The confusion was theirs as much as mine. I would have to ask Holmes about this soon.

How conveniently fate turns out sometimes, I thought, that John should get together with a private detective... He must have liked the way Holmes was striding about the place, as if he owned London.

We were now walking along the Thames and I could not shake off a feeling that Sherlock Holmes wanted to show the place off. London has a peculiar charm with its many mixed architectural styles – like a church window split into hundreds of fragments, each shape, each colour a gateway into a different period.

The London Eye looked like a dreamcatcher, ensnaring dark clouds, furrowed like brows over the city, while the opulent Somerset House opposed the concrete National Theatre.

It took me some time to realise just how disassembled my brain still was as I noticed only much later that I was on my own. Turning round and round, I lost sight of where I was. More and more restlessly, I tried to fix my gaze to a point somewhere, as the thought of being caught in a time bubble with Anne set me on edge. Would I even notice which was the bubble?

'You dropped your hat,' Holmes remarked with a quiet irony from behind me. When I didn't make a move, he placed the hat into my hand.

'Thank you,' I murmured.

'It's what John would have done.' He walked over to the edge of the pavement to give me some space, pretending to investigate a lamp post. Spotting some carvings at the bottom, he rummaged in his pockets and handed a few coins to a yellow bundle sitting beneath the lamp. I joined him, facing the river without question.

Holmes was looking at the water now, the shimmer of the surface glittering in his eyes. His coat was blowing about in the wind.

'How long are you going to stay with us, Miss Vendalle?'

'I... I don't know exactly. John said he would take care of me for a while, because... the doctors said I should have someone to help me back into life... after all that happened.'

Holmes sharply turned around, his heels screeching on the pavement as he did, walked up to me until there were only inches between us, and started to observe me intensely from tip to toe.

I could see him capture
the small spots of mascara on my eyelids,
the tightness of my bun,
the scratch at the end of my jaw,
my left shoulder sagging slightly
– he took my left hand and turned it upwards –

5

the ten marks on the palm around my thumb,
parallel scars each half an inch long,
the
– he pushed up my sleeve –
white scar spanning my forearm,
the varying colour of my skin,
the tattoo
– he stepped behind me and knelt down –
on the back of my ankle
'Mr Holmes–'
'Sherlock, *please.*'
**– he rose and pulled my open jacket off my shoulder from
behind –**
the bruise on the joint,
the scratches on my back,
my reddened neck,
the heat in it as he touched it, the
fresh, large, stellar scar under my hair above my
right temple...

I knew what he saw; I had tried to figure it out that way,
too. I hadn't, though. The doctors had been at a loss as well.

'When exactly did you lose your memory?' he asked
quietly.

'Three months ago,' I answered, turning around to him.
'Twenty-two seconds – not bad. The doctors needed a little
longer.'

Holmes smirked infectiously. I could see why he and John
got along so well. He didn't give me time to contemplate,
otherwise I would have had time to inspect something that
caught my eye: a strangely dusty cap with earflaps lurking
behind a corner. As it was, I didn't give it much further thought.
With a swift step, we headed down the embankment and turned

into Temple, exiting at Fleet St where Holmes had apparently ordered another cab to wait for us. Yet, when we arrived, and Holmes raised a hand, it simply drove off.

'What's going on here? Don't tell me someone's stealing the cab!'

'Well, I'm afraid so.' Holmes swiftly paced up and down the pavement.

'Couldn't you have known that earlier? John said you knew everything by just looking at it.'

'Yes, I do, but I had expected them to hijack it once we were inside.'

'*What!?*' I exclaimed.

'Well, what do you expect? We're being watched.' His voice had gone really quiet now.

'What were you going to take me into!? Couldn't you at least have warned me about a thing or two?'

Instantly, my eyes fell on a red dot behind some curtain in a tall apartment building across the street. The thought *gun barrel* shot through my brain. At first, I wasn't sure if that impression was fright or reality, but then I saw the small red spot of a laser pointer dancing across Holmes's chest.

'Don't worry, they're not going to shoot me,' Holmes reassured me as calmly as ever. 'I've still got something they want.'

'Are they pointing one at me, too?' I asked softly.

Holmes nodded. 'No sudden movements or you're dead. These are incompetent snipers; they'll aim at your leg and hit you in the back of the head. Slowly walk into that shop; they'll be waiting for us there.'

Turning to the shop, I immediately saw the tall man in the tweed suit and the earflap hat, with a revolver in his pocket. He was closely examining something with his hands – a cap or something of that kind, not unusual in a clothes shop. The only thing that startled me when we entered was that I had seen that cap before. *But where?*

'Good afternoon, Mr Holmes. Would you please follow me?' the strange man mumbled. I wondered why he was stooping constantly; it didn't seem to be part of his natural appearance, but the disguise was rather spoiled by it. I could hear in the way he maintained his voice that it was capable of reaching wide distances. One strand, longer than the rest of his hair, hid behind his ear – the man had a bald patch in the middle of the head, which he was clearly trying to conceal with longer strands, and one of them had fallen out, despite the tonnes of hair gel I could see on it. So the man had had time in the morning, but afterwards something had disturbed him that had made him take off his hat at least once without giving him time to fix his hair. Holmes also observed the man closely as we followed him into the back of the shop and then upstairs. I wondered what else *he* saw...

Finally, we reached a small, dark room. The strange man offered us a seat in front of a desk, behind which he, himself, sat down.

'Mr Holmes, I presume you know why you're here,' he said coldly.

Holmes nodded, just as icily.

'You have failed to comply with our ultimatum. Are we still firm, or do we hold our own brother dear after all?' asked the man.

'You know my answer,' Holmes retorted.

'Very well, then. We will arrange a meeting for you and your brother some time from now if he doesn't change his mind about helping us out. If you refuse, we know other means, but that's not news to you,' the man continued. 'Unfortunately, we'll have to keep the young lady's luggage, apart from this box which arrived at Baker Street this morning. Ericson!'

Another tall man came in, holding the box with my two guinea pigs. He was wearing a black suit and sunglasses. It looked ridiculous next to the tweed. The box hit the desk with a bang, and I quickly bent down to catch a glimpse of my pets. Fortunately, the little rodents looked unharmed, but it seemed naïve to think they weren't involved in some plan. I would have to examine them at Baker Street.

'You may go now, Mr Holmes,' twanged the tweed man as Ericson opened the door. Holmes shot a suggestive glance at me. Together we rose. When I saw his hands moving forward, I immediately turned around, taking the chair I'd been sitting on, smashing it on Ericson's head. Holmes had overthrown the desk, burying the tweed man under it, and within seconds we were in the hall of the upper floor, the door locked behind us. I clutched the box with the guinea pigs, which I grabbed when Holmes had taken Ericson's keys.

'We'll need to climb through the window. They're expecting us to come out through the back, and the front door is senseless anyway,' Holmes advised me. 'We won't be able to take the box with us, but they'll see to bringing it back to you.' His frown opened up a landscape of theories about my pets. Then he turned to me once again. 'So, if you don't mind,' he opened the window, and lifted me up at my waist, 'going first.'

I put the box on the chest next to the window, then pulled myself up by the frame. He held me until I sat firm, but it wasn't until he let go that I noticed – I had to jump approximately eight feet. I had never made such a leap in my life – that I knew of. Strangely, I wasn't afraid. I took a glance at Holmes and jumped.

Again, the ground felt sudden rather than hard. A thought hit me, an impossible one; he could have just let me climb the chest. *No, there must be another explanation, don't flatter yourself...* I shook my head.

This was an impossibly bewildering first day in London. I wondered if it was normal for this city.

What the hell *would anyone want with my guinea pigs?*

The sound of Holmes's feet hitting the ground next to me interrupted my train of thought. He rose slowly, looking back at the window.

'They'll be perfectly fine. This way,' he instructed, as I gave him a questioning look.

I had no idea, what this was all about, and I couldn't persuade myself that this was a good start for my new life, but I enjoyed it far too much not to follow Sherlock Holmes as he dashed down the street.

'But where are they expecting us now?' I asked Holmes.

'We are in the street to the left corner of the shop. I deliberately got out here, because they will have positioned their men at the back, but this is the only side of the house without a way through into the street. Nevertheless, we must speed up a bit, Miss Vendalle, if you can keep it up for some time. They won't take long to find out where we went; I had to leave the window open.'

We started running. When he made only one step, I had to make three to catch up. I envied him for his long legs. They were sharply cutting through the air, never tiring. For someone in his attire, his running was surprisingly elegant, and seemed to cost him hardly any effort. *He must be used to these chases*, I thought.

Houses and shops started to blur. For some reason I wasn't out of breath yet, though I had never expected myself to maintain the pace for very long. We were running at oxygen debt. I hadn't run like that for as long as I could remember.

After about fifteen minutes I had to search for fixed points in the street, like ballerinas do, to compensate for my dizziness, but my legs were not hurting even a bit.

'*Stop!*' Holmes held me back. We were in the shadow of a bridge. 'We'll wait here for John to fetch us. Did you see the small black car on the bridge? That was Ericson's. They've nearly located us already, but we'll be safe enough in Baker Street. I know how to avoid him,' Holmes explained incisively.

'I'm sorry, whom do you mean?'

'Moriarty, he's an old *friend*.' Holmes ground the last word between his teeth. 'He's got something lined up for me, I can feel it, like a plot woven around me. He wants to see me struggle like a bug in a web, but I'm afraid, not for long.' Holmes's voice ceased in a way that made me shiver as he took out his mobile to phone John.

'John, listen, could you please pick us up at Albert Bridge? – Yes. – No, it wasn't, no. – Will you come now!? – No, you don't, she's with me. – Now, don't snivel, she's fine, so will you finally–!? All right, thanks.' Holmes turned to me again. 'Are you all right?'

'Yeah, just a bit dizzy.' I was still panting and leaning against the pylon, yet I was holding my forehead in disbelief rather than exhaustion.

Suddenly, Anne's shadow reappeared. This wasn't the Tower – it meant that she was following me. I wasn't sure whether the water was moving her shadow, or if it was doing it on its own. Her breath next to my very ear flashed ice through my veins. Suddenly, it was gone again.

* * *

I needed to talk, more than anything this instant. Instead I had to drive across the city to pick up Sherlock Holmes *with Scarlett*. I just couldn't believe it. *How on earth he had coaxed a woman into coming with him?*

'The fair sex is your department, Watson,' he quacked in my brain. What has gotten into him again? Scarlett was only just released from the hospital; she wasn't supposed to get into so much excitement before she had a chance to accustom herself to her new situation! I should have picked her up at the station, *I knew it!* With Moriarty lingering about and Mycroft's 'best' men guarding the house, perhaps I shouldn't have told her to come at all. But then no one would have, and I was definitely being *merely* selfless, of course.

I still couldn't believe it. The red traffic lights in front of me were laughing at me spitefully.

Suddenly, Irene Adler popped into my mind. *The woman,* as Sherlock preferred to call her. I had never seen him so uprooted in his physicality as in her presence. *What went wrong with him?* I thought to myself, as the traffic lights turned to green.

The black car was standing across the deck in full length. I could only pray that they wouldn't notice me. But what was this fuss all about? I knew Moriarty liked big shows, but that was a bit obvious, wasn't it? I turned into Cheyne Walk, and parked my car. Next, I crossed Battersea Bridge, went down to Parkgate Road and then into Battersea Park to get to the riverbank unseen. By the time I reached Albert Bridge it had started to rain heavily, making it difficult to spot Sherlock and Scarlett. Under the bridge, someone seized me from behind and dragged me into the shadow.

'Thank goodness it started raining, or you would've been shot on sight,' Sherlock whispered into my ear and let go of me. 'They're aiming at people from the bridge. They haven't spotted their target yet. Oddly enough, there are no reinforcements coming – something's keeping Moriarty. Obviously, Ericson's men have to stay on the bridge, and hold their position. This time it's not only us they're waiting for.'

It was very strange seeing Moriarty's men doing something that wasn't hunting us. Even more perplexing was the fact that we were watching them unnoticed. Sherlock carefully snuck to the edge of the pylon and peered about. In the meantime, I turned to Scarlett.

'It's nice to see you again,' was the first thing that came to my mind, and her beautiful grey eyes lit up as we shook hands.

'It's certainly nice to see you,' she warmly replied. 'I can't tell whether meeting me again is a pleasure after everything that's happened, but I hope I haven't changed too much.'

'Oh, not at all. I 've already told you that,' I quickly assured her.

'Come on, John, she's gathered more battle wounds than you, but, even though it shouldn't, that is what infallibly intrigues you,' Sherlock coolly remarked, not even looking at us.

'How the *hell*...? You presumptuous pile of pomp!'

Scarlett put her lips to my ear. 'I can see why *you two* are friends.'

* * *

John was warmer than I had expected him to be. I felt safe with him, and it fascinated me. His military career was still visible in his short sandy hair, but it was a little too long for a soldier now. The wind took the opportunity to gently lift its tips. When he looked at me an affectionate smile spread over his

13

meticulously fine lips. For the first time, I noticed the peaceful glow in his green eyes. I was still to learn that I would be willing to endure any pain for that glow.

'Thanks for having me,' I said after a short moment of hesitation, stealing a glance at Holmes. I knew that the first memory in my new life would be of him. Even now I can still see his curious eyes before mine.

'Mr Holmes...'

'Sherlock, *please*,' he interrupted me.

'Sherlock, *please*, may I ask how you're planning to get us out of here?'

'We'll go by ship,' came a brisk reply as if there was nothing unusual in his statement at all.

'Sherlock, what is this supposed to mean? I've got my car parked at Cheyne Walk! When am I supposed to fetch it?' John blustered. He looked like this was quite his usual manner of addressing Holmes.

'Mycroft's men will fetch it later on. Come on, our ship's waiting for us.'

A river barge slowly drew near us. The name *Friesland* was painted on its side in large red letters, and a Dutch flag was blowing about at the rear. Holmes seized a large wooden box and stepped onto it.

'Do you expect us to jump!? Scarlett is still recovering from a severe injury to the head! As a doctor, I strongly disapprove!' John cried angrily.

'They'll hear us,' Sherlock hushed us, with a face that looked as if he was about to gag John with his scarf.

'She'll be all right, and we don't have another chance.' With a flying leap, Sherlock Holmes jumped aboard the ship.

At first, I had my doubts on whether I would make it or not. The gap was about four feet, and the ship was moving. John made his first attempt, but stopped at the edge of the box. When he finally managed to cross the gap, he almost slipped off the deck. Sherlock caught him with his free hand. I took a deep breath and I stepped onto the box. If I fell into the water, there'd be no way out for me under the bridge.

'Come on, Scarlett! Quick!' John shouted, and so I braced myself and leapt.

My foot hit a wet spot and slipped.

Sherlock and John quickly seized both my arms. For a very short moment they both held me, and I could faintly feel them tremble. *Or is it me that's trembling?* When they let go, we ran to hide in a narrow gap between two containers, pressing our bodies to the wall. As I waited to see whether we would be spotted or not, I eventually realised the men on the bridge must have seen the barge's empty deck before we entered it under the bridge. They wouldn't give it another thought. I would have to buy a hat to take off to Sherlock Holmes some time.

Chapter 2

The ship was blown up. I'm a soldier, I've seen explosions before, half of which don't deserve to be referred to as such compared to what happened here.

We were flung in every possible direction. I just hoped that we were all still in one piece, although that was naturally no proof of being alive. Yet, in my delirium, I could distantly see Sherlock's coat on the water, his hands still in the sleeves, as well as Scarlett's red bun above her collar.

Would trying to move be naïve? It seemed so, but it worked.

Sherlock's head suddenly shot upwards. I would have thanked heaven that neither of us were in it yet, but Scarlett still wasn't moving.

The sharp stench of burned rubber cut into my nose, but there was something else – probably the freight of the containers, which emitted a very peculiar scent, yet it was completely unrecognisable to me. Perhaps I should have studied Sherlock's blog *On the Identification of Perfumes.*

Suddenly I remembered Scarlett floating immobile in the water. I had to move. *How can I find my way through the burning pieces of the ship?* The colour of the water had vanished under the red of the flames.

Sherlock turned around and spotted Scarlett. He was nearer to her than I was, because he had been hurled into the same direction. As I was struggling, I saw him quickly swim towards her and turning her face up. She was very pale, and I saw blood on her temple. Sherlock's face was also marred with the scarlet liquid. I needed to get to them.

Passing the wreck's remnants very slowly I almost got burnt twice, and the heat weakened my ability to think.

The ship had split between the steering cabin and the containers. When I swam through the gap, I could feel the dead water beneath me. I struggled hard to go further.

'John! She swallowed water!'

I braced myself and moved. My sleeve nearly caught fire, but I quickly drowned the flame. Finally, I reached them. Sherlock held Scarlett's head in his hands to keep it afloat.

'Is she breathing?'

Sherlock shook his head.

'We need to get her up to the shore. I need solid ground to give her CPR,' I ordered.

Sherlock lifted Scarlett up, embraced her limp body and swam away. Swimming next to him, I tried to think of a way to help as Sherlock was struggling against the river pulling at us from different directions.

Scarlett's motionless features clouded my mind. Strands of red hair were floating around her head. Her pale skin looked like wax. I looked away.

Together, Sherlock and I managed to drag her onto the shore. Suddenly, Sherlock twitched. He'd spotted something on the bridge, and instantly rushed in front of us.

'Listen, we have to get behind that wall. They'll see us. Ericson's reinforcements have arrived. Come on, quickly!'

He helped me carry Scarlett to the wall, then he scrambled up the slippery stone. Reaching out for her body over the top, he pulled her up. With one last look at the men on the bridge, I climbed up after Sherlock as fast as I could.

* * *

'No! Stop it! Eamonn! Please!'

They couldn't. *He* couldn't! This wasn't true! Pictures, flashes, faces were chasing each other, hunting each other down in my head, tearing it apart in their cruelty. This was impossible! This wasn't him, this was a man in a mask! *What did he do to me?*

I couldn't see his face even before my very eyes. With the grin of a mask, the man I loved had killed me. For a second, I could feel his lethal lips, before

the vortex of my lost memories swallowed me up.

Turning, whirling, racing –

–distorted – images picking me – to the pieces of – my past–

–guilt of unknown – reason crushing my – conscience–

–and the terror of the – fall – into infinite depth–

– my mind wouldn't survive this.
This was no nightmare – this was madness.

'Scarlett!' John was whispering, but his voice rang in my ears like a siren. At long last, I regained my hold of reality.

'John? Are you all right?' I managed to mutter.

'Yes, yes, thank God,' said John, inhaling the words with his relief. I opened my eyes.

'Mr Holmes!' I cried in shock as I saw the blood streaming down his left cheek. The corners of his mouth briefly twitched into almost a smile – then he looked the other way.

'Sherlock,' he murmured.

18

'John, what on earth happened?'

John desperately looked at me and shrugged.

'Did you save my life?' I asked feebly. He shyly shrugged again.

'Yes – he did,' Sherlock stated with a sudden firmness, turning to me again, 'you're fortunate that he is medically proficient.'

'Oh my God, John. I don't know what to say.'

A smirk. 'You don't have to say anything.' He cleared his throat.

I quickly stood up, ignoring John's protests. My view started to blur, but I ignored that as well. Something about this place intimidated me; the presence of something was crushing my head, and I couldn't stand not knowing *what.* 'We need to get away, please. I can't stay here.'

John had me.

I had begun to falter, and would have fallen before the end of my sentence if John hadn't caught me. Everything was blurry now, as I held on to him, pulling him down. Sherlock's hands came up to support me on the other side.

'Please, just get me out of here,' I stammered.

'Wait a second before sitting down again. I'll call Lestrade; he'll fetch us,' said Sherlock as they both let me down carefully.

When I sat on the pavement again, John still supporting me, the world finally took mercy on me and stopped turning. Sherlock meanwhile talked to Lestrade.

'No, it's not about Mycroft. No. I need you to come to Albert Bridge right away. Yes, it is urgent, she's injured. I'll tell you later who. Now would you *please.*' Then he hung up, shaking his head.

'Do you feel better?' enquired John, who was gently pressing a handkerchief to my temple.

19

'Yes, I do. Thank you, John.' I smiled at him, and when he smiled back I could see the sincerest relief in his eyes.

Suddenly, she had me back. The icy grip of her hand around my wrist made me whirl around. The Queen was staring at me with furious eyes, and the blood bursting from her mouth hit my face to drown me.

* * *

'Scarlett?' She'd drifted off in a daze, her back swaying gently in the wind as if all life had been swept from her body. It was a ghostly sight. Sherlock knelt down next to me, staring at her intently. I expected a long deduction line of what had happened to her in the past, but he didn't say a word. It seemed as though something was stuck in his throat when he opened his mouth and closed it again. When I tried to deduce it myself, my train of thought quickly twirled away. Suddenly, Sherlock rose and looked up and down the Thames. I could see a theory taking shape in his eyes as he stared at the flames on the water.

'What was in those containers, Sherlock?' I asked.

'Nitroglycerine.'

'*What?*'

'Only a few bottles of it, of course, kept in a container at 4°C. Very unusual method of transport nowadays – looks strangely 1890s to me, this scheme. If the police had been to investigate the load, they'd also have noted some tonnes of stolen corn flakes, but I doubt that's what you were asking about.'

I smiled involuntarily.

'Where's Scarlett's luggage?' To my embarrassment, this was the first time I noticed its absence.

'Moriarty's men kept it,' Sherlock replied and frowned at the same time as Scarlett did, now sitting up.

'Oh my, what's wrong with me?' she sighed, vexed. She wildly shook her head, which I would've strongly advised against as a doctor, but she seemed to need it. 'John, could you please help me stand up?'

'You shouldn't be standing just yet–'

She made a clumsy attempt to rise, so I quickly caught her arm and supported her until she was on her feet.

'Do you really think you can stand?' I asked unassertively.

'I- I think I do, yes. I'm sorry for troubling you,' she affirmed weakly.

'Would you mind then if I–' My question became unnecessary when she seized my arm by herself as she started to falter again.

'I don't mind at all, John,' she gasped. Scarlett turned to Sherlock and observed him as he motionlessly stood there, thinking. They had something in common - something which I couldn't make out, but I knew it was the reason why I was drawn to them both.

* * *

'How come you didn't know about the nitroglycerine bottles, Mr Holmes?' I was annoying him, I knew that, but he wouldn't show.

'Sherlock, again, and please, I've been informed wrongly. Lestrade told me the explosives had already been found. Obviously, they've been cheated. Millions in state money for dummies, and they didn't even see. Well, the police are a singular institution indeed,' he sneered.

'What do the police need bottles of nitroglycerine for?' John asked in disbelief.

'There lies the problem. They don't need them; they were looking for explosives being smuggled into the country.

Apparently, these explosives were in slightly historical format, and that was all it takes to fool the highest police officers in the nation. Well done, Moriarty. It was very handy they were hunting us and the bottles at the same time.'

'May I ask, then, how you knew about the nitroglycerine and the bottles?' John looked at me. 'Assuming you weren't conscious already when I asked him that.'

'Oh, you asked him, too? No, I didn't get that, but obviously it was nitroglycerine. It's quite inconspicuous in bottles; it looks like water, and it's scentless. A lot better than dynamite. If I were to smuggle such a load of explosive, I'd choose that format as well. Creative, don't you think?' I finished, while John had nothing left for me except a sheepish look. But in Sherlock's face I could see a resentful smile which made me wonder about the memories he seemed to watch floating on the river.

Finally, Lestrade's car approached. Sherlock didn't turn around. Anne's shadow behind him was gone before I had properly noticed it. Then Lestrade got out of the car.

'Good afternoon, Milady,' said the inspector as he spotted me and shook my hand. He looked at John, who was still holding me in his arms, and raised his eyebrows with a smile. 'You must be the woman Sherlock mentioned on the phone–'

But Sherlock impatiently interrupted him, 'Excellent deduction, Lestrade. We need to get away from here. Moriarty's men are on the bridge. Just get into that car and drive; you can go on talking then.'

Sherlock came over and put his arm around John and me to shove us to the car. John gently saved my head from hitting the door frame with his hand when I got in. Finally, I had John and Sherlock sitting on either side of me and all doors were shut when a bullet hit the car just inches from the window beside Sherlock.

'Jesus!' cried Lestrade and slammed his foot on the gas. But as we were whirling around and then racing down the road, there were no more shots.

'What's this supposed to mean?' Lestrade asked as we turned into another street. 'Only one shot while we were the best of targets?'

'Obvious,' said Sherlock almost yawning now that we had rounded the corner.

'It was a warning for Mr Holmes,' I answered instead.

'Indeed, Miss Vendalle,' he confirmed, smirking.

I leaned over to him, and put my lips to his ear. 'Scarlett, *please.*'

He grinned, then looked out of the window again.

When we got out of the car, I immediately felt a tension in the air of Baker Street as the breeze on my face became a lot chillier than before. Then I noticed the sniper on the roof opposite us.

'Oh, don't worry, he's on our side,' John averred quickly as he saw me looking at him.

'I wouldn't be too sure of that,' Sherlock murmured, unlocking the door of 221B.

'Aren't you two going to ask the inspector to join us for a cup of tea? He saved our necks after all.' I suggestively raised my eyebrows at Sherlock and John, but Lestrade, who was coyly standing next to his car, declined politely.

'Thank you very much, but,' he scratched his head, 'I should be at the police station now.'

'Well then, it was nice to meet you. Thank you for rescuing us,' I added warmly, and in his smile, I could see surprise at this.

'Good afternoon then, ladies and gentlemen,' he replied equally warmly and got back into his car.

'You could be a bit nicer to him,' I reprehended Sherlock and John, who were now taking me to the flat upstairs.

'Yeah, I know,' John admitted, shrugging. He looked disappointed.

'It wasn't Lestrade who saved me from drowning. Thank you, John.'

'It was a pleasure,' he said, winking at me ironically. I started to laugh when Sherlock opened the door.

I had expected a mess, that's true; a real mess, but *this* was beyond my wildest imagination.

'I'm very sorry,' John apologised abashedly. 'I tried to do my best this morning, but Sherlock needs his things where he can find them. I'm still holding out hope that we can change the condition of this flat all the same.'

Sherlock smiled at me most charmingly, and shook his head. I had to laugh.

I suddenly tripped over a wrench and bumped into the messy detective. He caught me on reflex. I was breathing much too quickly, and my pulse was far too high. I looked away as we both let go. John meanwhile put aside the biggest things on the floor that were in his way.

'Excuse me,' Sherlock said suddenly, looking at the wall. I wasn't quite sure whether he was apologising to me or to the wallpaper. Somehow it felt like I was constantly driving his memories of someone else into his mind.

'Come on, Sherlock,' John rebuked him. '*Do* something! Clear up some stuff, *now*! I'm supposed to take care of Scarlett, not witnessing how she leaves here with another scar.'

'Please, have a seat, Scarlett. Your head needs some quiet. I hope we won't be too loud,' he finished, throwing an angry glance at Sherlock.

I was flattered by John's concern. Eventually, I sat down in an armchair off of which John had quickly taken a few books. It was a very nice flat, rather cosy altogether, I noticed, observing it properly for the first time. There was a neat little fireplace, which couldn't possibly pass the fire code considering all the things lying around. A skull surveyed the room from the wooden Victorian mantelpiece, sporting some letters attached to it with a knife. Next to them was an old-fashioned gas lamp, carefully balanced on a blue china vase. Behind it I recognised a small picture frame lying on its front, crouching against the wall, as though to hide its content with all its might. In the middle of the room was a square table bearing a remarkable foreign tablecloth with a beautiful paisley-like tapestry in red and blue on it. Newspapers were dynamically spread across it as well as on the surrounding chairs. Some peculiar little notes in bright yellow and green were sticking to every opportune place for the lazy mood, making the landscape of black letters appear like a meadow with flowers. The floral wallpaper seemed rather offended. The chairs' cushions exhaled their colours, as though to tell the stories of their numerous occupants. There were bulges everywhere in everything, even in Sherlock's jacket as he knelt down, and they all seemed to hide an adventure. To my left a set of crossed Japanese swords and daggers was forbidding the way into the wall, and jackets, scarves, gloves and shoes were disguising themselves as furniture.

Peering through the kitchen door, I could see hundreds of experimental gadgets, flasks, tripods and stands, even a Bunsen burner and a microscope, piled up in test rigs. The whole kitchen seemed to be a laboratory with the units seeming very unlikely to contain food or anything suiting their original purpose. Grains of dust were dancing in the light of the window as occasionally the evening sun came through. I wondered if they had a landlady, when I heard a cuckoo knocking at the door.

Everyone loved Mrs Hudson's 'Ooh, ooh,' it seemed. Sherlock and John's faces visibly brightened, as she entered. I'll never forget her first look at me when she entered the room. It was very telling: John had told her about me, but judging by the size of her eyes I could see his description hadn't altogether been very accurate. Mrs Hudson looked even more confused at the sight of Sherlock and John tidying up the place.

'What is going on here? Did you hypnotise them?' she asked me almost reproachfully.

'Haven't had the time yet,' I replied casually while John laughed out loud.

'Don't believe her, Mrs Hudson. *We,*' he gave Sherlock a suggestive look, 'are completely under her thumb.'

Sherlock didn't look up, rather he kept on clearing the floor with an obviously unusual effort. Mrs Hudson came over to me.

'I'm sorry, I haven't even said hello yet, dear. Welcome to Baker Street!' She gave me a cordial hug, and then invited me down for tea. I didn't have a good feeling about leaving the two of them alone upstairs, taming their dragon's hoard, but I felt much too dizzy to help them anyway.

'See you in a bit, boys,' I said and went after Mrs Hudson.

'Seriously, *how* did you do that?' Mrs Hudson asked, all incredulity, as she brought me a towel to put around my shoulders. 'I've seen John tidy things up a little for girls sometimes, but *Sherlock?*'

I shrugged.

She poured some tea into my cup. 'So?' she dug deeper.

'Er...' I tried to remember what I could've possibly done. 'Tripped over a tool,' I determined after a while, sipping on my tea.

Mrs Hudson raised an eyebrow. 'Anything else? Did you pay them? Did they pay you?'

I laughed so loudly I almost spilled the tea. 'No, no, that's really not it. I hope I don't look like *that*.'

'Well, dear, you're wet all over, and the boys are, too. You'll have to admit that it's not hard to imagine some strange orgy. But I was once a young woman, too. Besides, we've got all sorts round here.'

Mrs Hudson smiled at me knowingly. I felt the need to correct her.

'I'm sorry, but we really didn't do anything indecent, we–'

'I know, dear, that's what we all said.' *Mrs Hudson must've had quite a youth...*

'We were thrown into the Thames when the ship we boarded was blown up. I know that sounds less likely than an orgy, but it's true.'

'I've heard enough strange stories in this house to believe you. Would you like some biscuits?' she enquired warmly.

'Oh, Mrs Hudson's famous biscuits? John's been raving about them! Of course, I'd love some.'

Her smile grew broader. 'Tell me something about yourself, dear. You'll understand that I was a bit shocked to see a young lady when John said he expected an old friend from Bart's,' she explained.

'Oh, right, he didn't mention that I was a woman?'

Mrs Hudson shook her head, grinning.

'Well,' I hesitated, 'I can hardly tell you anything about myself, because–' I cleared my throat. 'I lost my memory. The police found no relatives of mine to take care of me, and when John said he'd take me in, it was quite a relief. He was some years above me in Bart's, he said, and he even visited me in the hospital when I was still unconscious.'

'John is sweet, isn't he? How was your first day here?' Mrs Hudson asked as I tried my first biscuit.

'These are really good!' I quickly threw in, 'Where should I start? Mr Holmes—'

'*Mr Holmes?* Hasn't he offered you to call him Sherlock yet?'

'He did, but—' I swallowed half a biscuit, coughed, and changed the subject. 'He met me at the library, and after that our cab vanished, we escaped some criminals, called John next, and when he arrived, we boarded a ship, which exploded and hurled us into the Thames. Judging by my headache, something hit me, so I passed out, and when I woke up, Mr Holmes said that John had saved my life.'

'Well, I can't take all the credit,' interrupted John, who was suddenly standing at the door. 'If Sherlock hadn't held your head out of the water until I got to you, you wouldn't be sitting here either.'

Now Mrs Hudson was really puzzled.

'I smelled some biscuits, so I came downstairs to recover from the hard work on our flat,' John said hastily, excusing himself for taking a handful. 'Are you feeling all right, Scarlett?' he asked with a warmth in his voice that almost dried my clothes. I nodded.

'Won't you sit down? I'll get you another towel,' Mrs Hudson offered, but John shook his head.

'I'm really sorry,' he looked at me, 'but I have to go upstairs again, and help Sherlock. I'm also really sorry for all the mess. But thanks very much for the biscuits!' he added, just before rushing out of the room.

Sometime later, Mrs Hudson and I jolted up at the sound of a scream. An awful cry from upstairs. At once I threw off my

28

towel, and we ran up to the door, but it seemed to be blocked somehow.

'John! Sherlock! Are you all right!? Can you hear me!?' I shouted, beating the door.

'Sherlock! John!' called Mrs Hudson.

A chuckle came from inside.

'Told you so!' Sherlock said to John while casually opening the door. 'That's ten quid.' He grinned at us. 'Come in, ladies. We've just finished.'

John was still tidying up one corner of the room while Sherlock happily went into the kitchen, which surprisingly now looked like one. They had both changed their clothes and looked as respectable as of old.

Mrs Hudson and I raised four eyebrows.

'Sherlock, how could you do this again? And to *us*? Lestrade's been complaining as well,' reprehended Mrs Hudson.

'It was just a bet,' Sherlock informed us from the kitchen.

'A *bet*?' I asked through clenched teeth.

John put away his things, and came over with a guilty face. 'Listen, I'm terribly sorry, this was really stupid. You're shaking! I'm so sorry. Sherlock, apologise *right* now!'

'I'm *not* shaking!' I shouted at John.

'Oh, you are,' Sherlock maintained, still in the kitchen. It was like I had addressed him.

'Sherlock, apologise *now*!' John bellowed.

'No, I won't. I don't regret it, and she'll be fine,' Sherlock replied, entering the room with a cup of coffee in his hands and sitting down on the couch.

To prove I was fine I sat down next to Sherlock, took the cup from him, and drank up all the coffee. He looked like a horse.

'So, what bet did you have?' I asked sharply, putting away the cup.

'We,' John began, but Sherlock shook his head warningly.

29

I raised my eyebrows. 'So?'

'No, sorry, it would defeat the purpose of the operation to tell you,' Sherlock insisted, getting himself another cup of coffee.

John went into the bedroom to get me another towel and some of his clothes. When he came back, I wordlessly took everything and vanished into the bathroom. I looked awful.

Nevertheless, I undressed, rubbing myself dry, then put on John's dark red shirt and jeans over my own slowly drying underwear.

From the kitchen I could hear Sherlock and Mrs Hudson talking intensely.

John's shirt smelled very good. It felt protective. Though I looked even worse in it than in my wet clothes.

For a second, I had to sit down, because my head was crushing me in. It hadn't been altogether difficult to suppress the pain with other things occupying my mind, but now the pain was back in full force. The bathroom started to spin slightly. I forced myself to splash my face with cold water, and then took another look in the mirror.

I wondered if Lily Scarlett Vendalle was my actual name. It had to be, John would've known it from our time at Bart's. Suddenly, the question as to whether I'd had a relationship with him popped up in my mind. I breathed in the scent from his shirt again. It must be awkward for him if we had.

I unravelled my bun. My red hair unfolded in waves down to my thighs. Unbelievable, how long it had grown. Shrouded in this curtain of DNA, I wondered what it might have stored that my brain had forgotten. In the hospital, I had read somewhere that trauma can change your DNA. It will stop certain genes from exerting their effect.

I had to get rid of the knots in my mane. They might betray something to Sherlock I didn't want John to know. As there was no sign of a comb, however, I just put my clothes in the laundry basket and went back into the living room to sit down on the couch.

Grimly, I looked about the flat, which was now hardly recognisable. All the stuff, the clothes and newspapers that had been lying around, were gone. Even the bookshelf I couldn't recognise before was now easily distinguishable as such, though some of the volumes were still oblique. The floral wallpaper looked fairly pleased.

John quietly sat down next to me. 'Again, I'm sorry, Scarlett, we used to- oh, never mind. I'm sorry.' He shifted uncomfortably.

'It's OK, just don't do that too often, will you?' I said after a while. He looked so very crestfallen.

John shook his head, daring to slightly smile over the matter. Sherlock sat down opposite us in the armchair, finally having his coffee.

'I guess I won't be needed here anymore,' remarked Mrs Hudson looking at us in disbelief before leaving the flat to the three of us.

Chapter 3

Finally, she was here in Baker Street, sitting next to me. I had pictured it differently. Instead of relaxing into a friendly conversation, we sat tensely for a while, without a word. It felt very strange that she was wearing my clothes. She wore them with grace, or rather discipline. I think it was discipline she wore them with. I don't know why, but somehow, I felt very drawn to this. She'd always had a fascinating tension to her.

'So, Mr Holmes, what can you tell us about me?' Scarlett suddenly asked.

Sherlock's mouth twitched into a smile. He put away the cup. This was going to be either incredibly interesting or unbelievably annoying. *Most likely both.*

'Well,' Sherlock cleared his throat, 'Judging by her condition and the way she holds herself, she'd clearly been in a military-like organisation before she lost her memory. Obviously a criminal one, otherwise her records would've been found. There must've been some kind of initiation ritual to that organisation, or another she's had to infiltrate, which is obvious from the systematic scars on her right palm. She's used to enduring pain, as we can see right now from the fact that she hasn't asked for any kind of treatment for the cut at the side of her head which she simply ignores, though it must be rather painful, because it's an inch deep and severely bruised. She's

32

bound to be concussed. Face it, John, you didn't notice, and she didn't complain.

'Moreover, she's got a post-traumatic scoliosis and several scars from severe injuries which suggest that she's been either a spy or an assassin. Also, she's in incredibly good shape even after three months in a hospital, and her skin colour is fairly dark for a redhead, the tan spanning areas someone with her occupation couldn't have gained here, so she must've been in some tropical country. Given the traces of dust I found on the clothes she brought with her, which I took the liberty of taking out of her bag and examining when she came here, I'm inclined to think she spent her past few years in South America.

'Apart from that, her loss of memory is just temporary as it's caused by a traumatic event concerning the man she loved—'

'Wait! What's this supposed to mean?' she exclaimed accusingly.

'Oh, that's very simple. I thought you'd seen that, too. Well, your bun was as perfectly tight as it must've been in that organisation, but your mascara is negligently applied, which proves your muscle memory has not learnt this action yet, so you must've hardly been doing it in your everyday job. Perhaps you applied it only for important events where you wanted to appear feminine — like dates. Now you have a problem with applying your femininity, which makes you shiver while putting on make-up. Clearly, there's been something with her boyfriend.'

Her jaw had dropped when he'd first mentioned it, but now it seemed to tear her face apart by reaching for the floor. Her eyes were open in utter shock, almost bursting by what she pictured before them. She seemed to be pierced by bits of memories, with the pain straining all her muscles. I wondered what was happening to her.

Sherlock saw it first, before her eyes rolled back. He jumped up and caught her before she slipped off the sofa. My reaction would've been too late.

'Did I say something wrong again?' Sherlock complained at my angry look. I shook my head.

'Couldn't you've just said it a bit more gently?' I shot back, as we were laying Scarlett down on the sofa.

He simply looked at her, probably deducing her memories. I gave up waiting for a reply. I hated not knowing what he was thinking; it was vexing how he always expected me to know what he knew, and even stranger that he never learnt that I couldn't follow. When he looked up at me, confusion spread in his expression.

After a moment he barked, 'Why are you staring at me? You're the doctor, do something!'

I was completely dumbfounded, but somehow I managed to stumble into the kitchen to wet a towel with cold water. When I came back, Sherlock was standing at the window. Kneeling down next to the sofa, I gently pressed the towel to Scarlett's forehead, which reminded me that I had yet to tape her wound. Her head felt rather hot even beneath the towel.

'She's suffering from post-traumatic stress disorder just like you did when you came back from Afghanistan.' Sherlock's voice made me start. It had this certain softness to it which reminded me of satin whenever he used it. His perspective on the parallel he drew between Scarlett and I startled me even more.

He kept looking out of the window.

'Anything unusual out there?' I enquired, sitting down on the couch, and feeling for Scarlett's pulse.

'One of Mycroft's snipers got himself into some trouble. I think he's about to blow up the flat opposite us,' Sherlock calmly observed.

'*What the hell*, Sherlock!?' I dashed to the window, but he held me back, pulling us both away from it.

'The glass will break if he doesn't think. Now let's see. What do you make of this, John?'

The sniper seemed completely out of his mind. He was fighting some kind of small box in his hands, but I couldn't properly see if he was trying to open or close it.

'What is this? A bomb in a box?' I sneered sarcastically.

'Exactly,' Sherlock replied with sparkling eyes. 'A tiny explosive device inside the musical box he's bought for his daughter. Neat. Moriarty has outdone himself again.'

'Sherlock, you always say that. What the hell is he doing there now?' I frowned over the sniper's fight with the toy.

'There's a spring inside the box which mechanically closes it at a certain angle to the lid. Now, the bomb is attached to this spring which will set it off if it's moved jerkily. So, he has to remove it without fully opening or closing the box. This is quite the clumsy dance.' Sherlock took a last look at the peculiar scene, then turned around and vanished into the kitchen.

'What're you doing there!? He needs help!' I blustered, but as he came back, he was smiling broadly.

'Come on, John. I already helped him when I texted him the two possibilities where to look for the bomb in his room. He should be able to get himself out of this.'

And indeed, when I next looked at him, he was wiping his forehead. The box lay scattered on a table whereas the room was still in one piece. When I turned around to take a look at Scarlett, Sherlock was kneeling beside her, dipping a tissue into the cup he'd just got from the kitchen, and holding it to her nose. 'What's in there, Sherlock?' This was more than suspicious.

'Oh, just some strong herbs to wake her up,' he replied casually.

Indeed, her eyelids twitched instantly at the smell. She wrinkled her nose in disgust and lulled something that probably meant, 'What are you feeding me!?' before trying to push the cup into Sherlock's face.

With a swift dodge, Sherlock rose again and put aside the strange green liquid. 'I think you could work this out by yourself. At least as soon as you regain your memory,' he claimed with a smile.

I quickly sat down next to her and felt her temperature. She seemed to have already cooled down. 'How're you feeling?'

'I'm okay, but my head has decided to ache now. I'd be grateful for some coffee,' she croaked feebly.

'Of course. Sherlock, will you—'

'Coffee's out. You should rather clean and bandage her wound while I go downstairs and have a little chat with Mrs Hudson. Perhaps she's got some coffee left.'

And gone he was.

The next few days were a bit less excruciating than this one. Scarlett's wounds slowly healed, as I gave her all the medical and, well, other attention she seemed to need. It filled me with indescribable warmth to care for her, to see the soothing effect of my touch. The light in her eyes and the comfort she gained seemed to spread even to Sherlock.

We were still waiting for clues from the Yard about the nitroglycerine affair, as well as for news of Scarlett's luggage. Sherlock wouldn't tell me what exactly had happened to it, or what actually happened to him and Scarlett before I had picked them up. This wasn't the time to talk about it, he told me every time I asked, which meant, so far, there was too much he didn't understand about the business to say anything about it. I didn't want to press Scarlett on the matter either; she didn't seem very

36

eager to speak about it herself. As usual, I was at a bit of a loss about what was going on.

Lestrade showed up for coffee – stolen from Mrs Hudson – once, but he could only tell us that the police were at a loss too, as what else than usual.

Mrs Hudson didn't mind the theft.

After Scarlett had recovered quite well, I decided to take her out to show her around London. I was proud of my city, and grew even prouder of her when the weather kept playing along for an incredible amount of time and almost all the queues were shorter than anyone could have reasonably guessed. Sometimes Scarlett seemed to be chased by shadows that only just vanished when I turned to look, but she brightened soon after and nevertheless seemed happy with our trips.

First, I took her to the London Eye so she could feel the whole pride of a Londoner in their city. On the peaceful ride after the exhausting queuing, I put my arm around her and showed her the Elizabeth Tower and the Houses of Parliament from above, which we'd already seen while waiting, as well as Westminster Abbey and New Scotland Yard at one side, BT Tower, Charing Cross, the Royal Opera House and the British Museum at the other. Patchy clouds were casting shadows on the pulsating city, and from time to time a few clear-cut sunrays would beam down into the streets at their edges. I explained to her where which quarter of the city lies, and she smiled and put her arm around me as well.

Later on, I took her along to Buckingham Palace, which she didn't especially marvel at, but the weather was brilliant and, apart from all the annoying German tourists everywhere, the palace was set in simply beautiful surroundings, she said. After a tour through the palace, which I hadn't seen in ages, we went for a walk in St. James's Park. This really enchanted Scarlett with all the whimsical paths, the glowing green leaves and the enthralling fountains, where sunlight was glistening on the water shooting back into the sky. She had an explicit weakness for the squirrels, I discovered.

We bought something to eat on one of the benches, and the next days we kept exploring the parks of London, starting at Green Park, moving on to Hyde Park, and finishing with Regent's Park.

Since I so often couldn't resist buying her tiny decorative things, because she loved them so much, I insisted on her visiting the Victoria & Albert Museum with me. We must've spent the best part of the day inside that museum. Scarlett was totally captivated by all the colourful exhibits. In the end, I could hardly get her out.

After about a week of Scarlett's patiently wearing my clothes, I decided to drop her at Oxford Street with Mrs Hudson, who I'm convinced had the time of her life going shopping with a young woman for a change. In the evening they came back, laughing heartily and carrying three bags filled to the top with indeed some charming clothes, which Sherlock only acknowledged with an irritated look. Disregarding my current account balance, I easily persuaded them to let me pay for the shopping *because the ladies were oh so happy,* which earned me a peck from both of them. And yet, Scarlett kept wearing shirts or trousers of mine sometimes, as though she needed it, and I happily provided her with them when she asked.

While we had plenty of charming dinners at home, getting to know each other well again after all this time, Sherlock was brooding over his laptop and newspapers in turn. I wondered what he was looking for all that time. He barely said anything at all, and I had a feeling he had more than the usual reasons to keep quiet. Some of them I suspected to be of potentially awkward nature with Scarlett sharing our flat, and so I thought it best not to bother him about it.

Sherlock Holmes, *of course,* kept solving cases apart from that. Usually, I would write them down in my diary as the proper

38

adventure stories they were so I could show them to my children one day.

There were quite a few crimes Sherlock solved, but I couldn't find the time to write up the cases of, like *The Serial Ash Stealer*, *The Second Sprain* or *The Speckled Bond*. I still took notes, all of which I carefully kept in my casebook, along with all additional material Sherlock piled up investigating.

Scarlett was rather interested in the criminal investigations going on, but I tried to keep her out of that business as best as I could, because I was afraid it might strain her mind too much, and since I was responsible for her safety, I saw it as my duty to keep her out of danger. For myself, I tried to abstain from interfering with Sherlock's investigations, but I soon realised sometimes he needed saving, too, so I kept an eye on him not just when he asked me to. I couldn't keep out of *all* the trouble when it stared me in the face.

* * *

It was thrilling to see a mind like Sherlock's at work. He kept dashing about for some hours, muttering under his breath, to then sit down in his armchair without moving for a whole night.

When he was out of his depth, he would play the violin. He played flawlessly, elegantly, mind-bendingly. Sherlock Holmes was an artist. Somehow, I was not surprised.

He seemed to inspire himself as he danced across the room, his music still in our ears. It was as if it propelled his thoughts in a way. Sometimes, he solved two cases in one day.

Now and again, Sherlock would show me the clues he would start with, or the newspaper article that had caught his attention before the client arrived. Even maggots in a dead man's eye couldn't put me off. It was an amazing experience to see everything unfold on that wall as Sherlock's eyes shone when he talked about all the connections. There was a map of London, and around that he had pinned pictures, notes, articles and all pieces of evidence that fancied hanging on a wall. Some pins were connected with a string, and in the end every string led to another until the case was complete.

My wish to help with solving cases grew stronger, but John wouldn't have me in danger. The only thing that remained for me to do was to watch Sherlock working at home, interviewing clients and occasionally even catching a murderer in our flat. It seemed to make him feel proud about 221B being the trap for so many criminals.

One afternoon, the case of *The Mandarin Stone,* as John would call it in his files, was finally solved. There was a ring at the door, which Sherlock had been expecting, quietly wrapped up in his armchair, his hands folded, and his eyes gazing at the ceiling until they focussed on the sound. John and I had just returned for a coffee. Sensing that Sherlock needed help, John hurried into the living room with me on his heels. A moment later a huge man dashed in, boiling with anger.

'Where is my stone!?' he kept shouting.

Sherlock calmly rose and told the man with enigmatic irony, 'I've been to the market. That should be enough for you. It was enough for me to know what you did.'

John just scratched his head, but suddenly Sherlock cried 'Vatican Cameos!' and they both overpowered the man.

The next thing I heard was sirens and looked out the window only to see blue lights flashing. Sherlock inconspicuously fumbled around with man's pocket and gave John a sign to release him. As they did, the man dashed right out, but Lestrade was waiting for him with his officers.

Another man came in – a broad redhead, frightening in appearance, but helpless in his eyes. To our astonishment,

Sherlock produced an enormous glittering jewel from his pocket and handed it to the man, laughing heartily.

'Here you are, Mr Merton!'

'How can I thank you? You saved my life with this stone!' cried Mr Merton in delight.

'Well, I certainly saved your reputation,' Sherlock replied. John and I exchanged bewildered looks, but Sherlock simply offered all of us a chair, and we sat down in front of the fireplace.

'I expect you all aren't quite as familiar with the facts of the story as you'd like. Mr Merton here knows about as much as you,' Sherlock told us, 'so I hope it won't bother him if I start from the beginning. A Mr Negretto Sylvius engaged me yesterday to get a ten-thousand-pound jewel back which he claimed to have lost in a boxing fight.'

'The wretch!' the client shouted.

Again, I exchanged a glance with John, but he was just as puzzled as I was. Sherlock continued. 'His whole demeanour seemed so composed to me that I began by examining him first. I noticed he'd lost money by betting on horses, and so I sent a member of my network of homeless spies – they call themselves Baker Street Irregulars – to find out his hotel room, which I took the liberty of searching myself. I found the jewel wrapped in a mandarin peel, but I left it there to get to the person he had actually stolen it from. A few hours' research into gems recently purchased in auctions led me to Mr Sam Merton here, who is, in fact, a boxer, and legally owns the stone, as well as a mandarin plantation. Just as I expected, Sylvius called me later, telling me he was sure Mr Merton had taken it. Sylvius was clearly aiming at his reputation. For that, I figured, Sylvius must place the stone somewhere to stage Mr Merton's apparent theft, and I would give him the opportunity. So, I told Sylvius to come here today at five o'clock, letting him believe Mr Merton would be here, but told Mr Merton to come later. In the end, I couldn't keep myself from a little joke and swapped the stone for a mandarin in Sylvius's pocket.'

Sherlock was a captivating storyteller. We were all rather amazed at this tale, most of all Mr Merton, and I just wished I could've seen this adventure myself. My mind buzzed at the thought of taking part in Sherlock's investigations.

Chapter 4

Everything seemed to go very well until the incident at Vauxhall Arches. Scarlett had worn me down to take her along and collect data from Sherlock's Irregulars. Strangely, seeing London's more uncomfortable parts didn't seem to diminish her curiosity about the place. If anything, it only seemed to increase it.

We didn't find our contact man immediately, so we had to linger in a corner for some time. At first, I didn't notice Scarlett's gaze riveted to one side, but then I realised there was something in the red graffiti on one of the walls which deeply unsettled her. I tried to calm her down, but it was no use. Again, she seemed to see shadows in almost every corner. Her eyes grew wider with fear, and suddenly she started running. I ran after her, but she was faster. Before I could do anything, she ran into a dark hooded figure, pushing them over in her haste. When I reached them, she had already grappled the person on the floor and took off the hood with a swift movement.

'Seriously, Sherlock could spend a bit more time training his Irregulars,' she sighed when she saw the young man's innocently surprised face.

'How did you know I was one of Sherlock's and not a criminal mastermind?' the lad protested. I smirked at the idea.

Isaac Houston was one of Sherlock's most frequent visitors from the network, and he was a very good, hard-working informant. He gave us expired flight tickets and the address to an abandoned house somewhere in Greater London.

As always, I had no inkling of Sherlock's plans with this, but I didn't have very high hopes that he would tell me anything concrete at this point. The entire journey home, I tried to picture what Sherlock would deduce from this, but couldn't get anywhere.

When we arrived at our flat, Sherlock looked astonished at what Isaac had given us, but wouldn't elaborate. A moment later he went off to Mrs Hudson's.

I took out the medical aid kit and a cold pack for Scarlett and examined her head which she seemed to have hit when she'd bumped into Isaac. To ease the skin, I slowly loosened her hair from its bun.

She smiled at me. 'Don't worry.'

'What? I didn't say anything.' I was confused.

'I know, but I can see in your eyes you think you didn't keep me safe.' Her look was gaining tenderness with every word.

'Well, it seems, you'll only get a nice bump,' I diagnosed with relief, my fingertips resting on her silky red hair. I had forgotten how it felt, but now the memories came flooding back in. When she spoke again, I realised I hadn't moved and quickly let go in abashment.

'I-I'm sorry,' I stammered, embarrassed. I felt guilty about letting memories into my mind that would have pained her.

'No problem, I can't complain. I really enjoy the thrill of the life you two share. How did you come to know each other anyway? I suppose you weren't already living with him when we studied together?' she wanted to know with huge doe eyes.

44

This question stung more than the first one, and I took a deep breath while gently applying a cooling balm to the swelling on her head. She twitched every time I touched it.

'We... er... no, we weren't living together by then. I, um' - I cleared my throat and looked her into the eye - 'I was living with you.'

Somehow the surprise in her eyes was quite a positive one, and a smile briefly illuminated her beautiful face before a shadow of sadness chased it away.

'I'm sorry I don't remember,' she said quietly. 'It must've been a splendid time. Why did I leave?'

Now I wished *I* couldn't remember. Again, it took some time to find the right way to answer. Carefully, I wound a tape around her head, fastening the cold pack to the bump.

'Um, well, you... had someone else you... preferred... to live with,' I finally said knotting up the tape's ends.

'Oh.' She was speechless at the effort it took me to recall those things. 'John, I know this is awkward for you, but I need to know the extent of it. Was I more than a flatmate to you?'

'Yes, no well, yes, you were, yes.' I cleared my throat again. She seized my arm.

'John, were we a couple?'

I laughed in embarrassment. 'Yes, well, yes, that's how awkward it is to me.'

She let go of my arm. 'I'm sorry, I had to know. I'm sorry for making you feel so awkward,' she added, but I shook my head.

'No, it's alright.' I packed up the aid kit. 'Does the tape feel okay, or is it too tight?'

'It's alright, perfectly fine.' Now she cleared her throat. 'John, I— thank you. Thanks for telling me this. Thanks for having me. I couldn't imagine anyone who could care for me better.'

I smiled. 'Well, I hope you're right. I'll go and fetch you some coffee. Hopefully Sherlock and Mrs Hudson haven't been smoking weed.'

She laughed at the idea, but to me it seemed so likely I thought it a rather serious matter. When I went downstairs, Mrs Hudson's chuckles almost made me believe I was right. Her explanation that Sherlock had told her such a funny story wouldn't quite drive the pictures out of my head, especially with Sherlock laughing hysterically at my sight.

* * *

My head was aching quite a bit by the time Sherlock came upstairs. I could hear John talking to Mrs Hudson intensely, his voice not far from shouting sometimes. Apparently, the door was open.

'Have you ever held a gun since you woke up in the hospital?' asked Sherlock in his ominous out of the blue way of starting a conversation.

'*What?*'

'You're still in incredibly good shape even after lying in hospital for a month – a period in which human muscles usually become more or less completely wasted if you only spend them in bed. And judging by your spinal injuries and the severe wound at your temple, clearly an arbitrary act of a person and not one of the wild animals you used to face, you were definitely supposed to spend most of the time lying down. You've been remembering bits in the hospital already, haven't you, Miss Vendalle?'

I had tried to forget things so much, to hide them from myself. The nights when I didn't wake up in my bed but had to creep back into the building avoiding CCTV. The nights when I

46

searched the bag they had found me with. The feverish dreams when I tried the substances I cut out of the lining. I hoped the nightmares would explain everything, but Anne always interceded, took my head away before it could think. I didn't want to remember those days anymore, as the notions of my past were strangling my heart before they could form memories.

'Yes, Mr Holmes, maybe I have, though I don't know what was a dream and what a memory. But no gun, I swear I never held a gun, not that I can remember!'

Suddenly the door banged shut from a gust of wind. I could only see the blood spreading over the floor from behind it, reaching Sherlock's shoes, and heard Anne's devastated cries: '*Mary! Mary!*'

Again, my view started to blur, and familiar footsteps sounded through my empty head. I listened to them intently, waiting to see properly again. There was something unnatural to them, a rebounding thud that didn't sound like footsteps at all – then I realised. It was the echo of Anne's head hitting the ground. I couldn't bear the sound of her dying voice, so I ran to the window and ripped it open. I quickly estimated the height – then I climbed up the sill to jump.

Sherlock pulled me back. His grip was incredibly firm for an injured man – *how do I know that?* Considering my struggle to get free and my screams, he must've thought I was mad.

I could only see a red vortex sucking me in. His hands were everything that could hold me back from jumping. My heart rate rose rapidly, my breath quickened into hyperventilation, and little stars flashed up in my vision. When he finally let go of me, tears were streaming down my cheeks and my mouth tasted of blood. He had placed me back on the sofa. I looked at my hands and I found them stained with blood. Sherlock was standing next to the window, panting heavily, his

47

hands on his knees, blood dripping down from his face in the shadow, staining the carpet of 221B Baker Street.

'You're in even better shape than I thought, I give you that,' he murmured contently.

I could hardly grasp what I had done. The wound on his cheek from the previous case had opened again, and when he came over to sit down opposite me, I could see two bloody bites on his left hand and a stab in his side, caused by a small pocket knife he had been keeping in his jacket. He took it out with a smile now. What appalled me even further were the marks of it through the cloth that suddenly stood out against the blood stains on the palm of my right hand.

'You did know it was there – some bloody good training you've had. Your instinct is brilliant. Bolivia is a lot safer without you,' remarked Sherlock, smirking. Putting the knife onto the table and drawing back his jacket to observe the wound, he was still panting with pain and his face grew pale. I couldn't move without shaking, but I forced myself out of my seat and ran to the door.

'John! Come up here! Please!'

I was a killing machine. A monster. There was no way to change that, no redemption for me. I didn't even know how many people I had killed, how many I had tortured in my life. And now I was a mad, violent creature, unable to restrain myself from hurting the people I loved. I was a ticking time-bomb.

When John came upstairs, he stopped in the door at first, throwing glances at Sherlock and I in turns. He dashed to Sherlock to examine his bleeding wounds.

'God! What happened!? Has he gone far yet?' he asked, opening the aid kit again, which he had left on the sofa before.

'Who?' I wasn't quite sure what he meant.

'John thinks we've been attacked by a burglar,' Sherlock snorted. He seemed rather amused by the whole affair.

'You owe me a good explanation,' John demanded, stapling the stab wound. Sherlock groaned with pain at first, but then pulled himself up and regained his composure.

'Miss Vendalle here has had another one of her visions.'

'Visions!?'

'Visions, indeed. She saw something and then tried to jump out of the window. I held her back and, as a reflex, she tried to struggle free, stabbing me with my pocketknife. I knew you'd do that the moment I saw you observe the flat the day you arrived. A knife never escapes the trained eye.' He smiled at me with a piercing look that nailed me to the door frame.

Clinging to the wood, the memory of my eye capturing the small bulge in his jacket occurred to me and frighten me even more.

Watching John's calm hands tend to Sherlock's wounds helped me cool down.

'Anything else you might add about what you already know about her?' he addressed Sherlock. He didn't seem to intend to get rid of me yet. I hadn't expected that. Even I wanted to get rid of myself now.

'Ouch! Couldn't you be a bit more careful? Anything else, let's see,' Sherlock pretended to think hard, 'Bolivia perhaps. She worked in Bolivia. I asked Mrs Hudson – the drug's from Bolivia. Apparently, it's called Chinchilla's Foot. Miss Vendalle had it in her bag, but none of the doctors recognized the substance. She took some this morning to find out what her memories in the hospital meant, because she'd had a vision that seriously disturbed her. The drug's got a very distinct smell.'

'Wait. You know the smell? Don't tell me you've been high for one of your cases again!' John snapped.

'Of course not, John. You know I keep a blog on the identification of perfumes. Though I can't guarantee I haven't tried this one yet. Anyway, it's quite heavy stuff, and by the state of my consciousness I'd guess Miss Vendalle has kindly injected it into my veins anyhow. Now if you were so kind to excuse me.'

He stood up and walked over to his bedroom door. 'Oh, and John? She sleepwalks. Don't shoot her when she tries to kill you in the middle of the night. And, yes, Miss Vendalle, you *have* been holding a gun since you were brought to the hospital. You only weren't awake at that moment. Goodnight, ladies and gentlemen.'

Then he vanished.

'What the hell was this?' John asked me, dragging me to the bathroom to clean my paralyzed hands.

'I'm a killer! John, let me go, throw me out, I'm going to kill you all! I-I can't stand this, John, let me out!' My voice was shaking heavily along with my body.

'Shhh... Listen to me.' He dried my hands and looked straight at me. 'You're *not* a killer. Not anymore. To me, you're an innocent human being now. And I won't let you go mad.'

Thankfully, I could manage a feeble smile. 'John, what would I do without you?'

He shrugged, putting away the towel. 'I don't know, start a safe and stable new life in the countryside, fall in love, marry, have a family, I really don't know,' he said smiling at me with the most amiable innocence and virtue in his face. It was the fitting piece of the puzzle to the warmth in Sherlock's look for John.

* * *

Scarlett's face had changed with the weight of everything that Sherlock had said. She was branded. Only I didn't know whether by Sherlock's words or by her old life. Her smile seemed broken to me for the first time, as she was utterly shaken with what she had done to Sherlock. When we entered the living room again, she was still shaking at the sight of the blood stains and she kept looking at her hands.

'Come and sit, Scarlett, I'll get you something to eat.'

'Oh thanks, no, nothing to eat, I can't- no, I'm sorry, I can't.'

She looked as though she could still taste Sherlock's blood on her teeth. It was strangling her. I knew about the fear of the monster inside oneself. I had a monster inside me, too, but I had learnt to live with it.

Carefully, I sat down next to her and put my arm around her shoulders. 'Listen, I know exactly how you feel. I'm a soldier. I killed people and I still have nightmares about them. In a way, it is worse not being able to save someone, but as a doctor you can't avoid that happening. It isn't easy to live with, but there are ways to cope. I can promise you that. We could look into options for therapy, for example, and in the meantime, you'll have the time of your life with the thrill of Sherlock's cases. You'll recover in time.'

She weakly smiled. 'As long as I don't kill you both before that happens, I guess.'

Hesitantly, she bent her neck to lay down her bandaged head on my shoulder. 'John, does he often take drugs?' she suddenly asked. 'I mean, like the one I had in my pocket?'

I was truly startled by her sudden concern about Sherlock. Obviously, the scene wouldn't go out of her mind.

'I don't actually know, I have to confess. You can never tell if he's got it under control, whether it's an "experiment" or if he just needs to get high. He always says it's for a case. But it hasn't been very often recently.'

For a while we simply sat there, thinking, and I was beginning to get uneasy, when she finally spoke again.

'John, may I ask you another question?'

'Yeah, sure.'

'Who is this man chasing you?'

'You mean Jim Moriarty?'

'Yes. What does he want from you? Sherlock said he'd got something Moriarty wanted. Is he only after Sherlock, or both of you?'

'That's a very long and not altogether pleasant story. I'll tell you everything some other time. The short answer is that he's a maniac, but also Sherlock's intellectual equal. He's actually after him more than after me, and I fancy Sherlock knows a lot about him that could be very unpleasant for him and his network, but no, I have no idea what else Sherlock has got that Moriarty wants. He hasn't even told me that yet. Typical of him.'

She briefly laughed.

'John,' she said after another while, 'I think I want to go to sleep now. Just give me the key to my room, I'll lock the door, and nothing will happen.' She slowly rose from the couch.

I quickly stood up in case she was feeling dizzy again. 'If that's what you want. Wait here a moment, I'll look after Sherlock for a second. I'll be right back to take you upstairs. You can also sit down again if you want.'

'Thanks, John,' she said, smiling at me a little more calmly than before.

After I returned the aid kit, I walked over to Sherlock's bedroom and knocked at his door.

'Come in, John.' Sherlock had curled himself up on the bed, staring intensely at the ceiling. I could almost see the flowers dance on the wallpaper.

'Sherlock, are you all right?'

'Oh, very much so. This is brilliant stuff; the way it twists your mind it makes me see connections I could hardly have made otherwise. I can almost see through Moriarty's plans as clearly as if he'd shown them to me. You should see this, John.' He turned to one side and looked at me through the mirror on the wall.

'Sherlock, this isn't funny. You'll be out of your mind one day if you keep doing this.'

'Well, this time it wasn't voluntary. You can't say that.'

I shook my head. This man was completely beyond the bounds, and yet I couldn't really reprehend him for it. It was the same every time. I should have someone slap him out of his druggy dreams next time. Instead, I went out of the room, leaving the door open and after a second came back with an ice bucket, pouring it over his head before he could react.

'Hey! That's not fair!' he shouted, a little befuddled, sitting up to wring the water out of his sleeves. Then he simply lay down in the wet bed again and curled up his face into his grumpiest expression.

'Come on, we all know you have to get clean again, so why not start with a little bit of water,' I replied, smiling proudly at my prank.

'John, I'm flattered by your concern, but it's really not necessary. I've got it all under control.'

This was too much for me. I grabbed him at the shirt collar and pulled him up to my very nose. 'No, you have *not* got it under control! Even Scarlett's concerned. Now get yourself some other clothes!'

When I let go of him and he rose to his full height, he threw a long, intense gaze at me before swaying out of the room.

For a short moment, I was unable to move as if he had transfixed me with a harpoon like a dead pig, but I shook my head and went to look after Scarlett. I had taken far too much time with Sherlock, I had totally forgotten about her state when I came back. At first, I didn't really look at the living room, as I decided to make her more tea, but walking into the kitchen my brain reconstructed the picture my mind had just captured of the spot where she had been sitting earlier. It was empty.

'Sherlock!'

I ran down the stairs as fast as I could. Sherlock didn't follow.

'Mrs Hudson! Have you seen Scarlett?' I called hastily as I bumped into her at the door.

'No, dear, I haven't seen anyone here,' she innocently replied.

'Damn it! Sherlock! Will you finally come now!?' I shouted.

'Sorry, not in the mood,' he answered, and as real anger rose in my chest I rushed out of the house before *my* inner monster could seize the chance to kill anyone in it.

The night was very cold. The icy wind cut into my face. I had no clue where to go, so I just ran down the street. If Scarlett had done anything to herself then I was to blame for it, and I had no idea how I was going to live with that. Perhaps she had gone to King's Cross where she'd first arrived?

I turned into Marylebone Road. *I should've really had a look if she had taken her luggage with her,* I thought, but then I remembered that Moriarty's men had taken all her stuff. At least they had kept the rest of the drugs away from Sherlock.

The street was too crowded; I couldn't see very far down it. *Did she really take this road? Too many people, there are too many people.* I turned into Luxborough Street instead, as it runs parallel to Marylebone Road. *Should I turn left here or at the next opportunity? Is this Paddington Street already, or Nottingham Street?*

My head was a real mess. I was so disoriented that I ran straight into someone the next moment. I forgot to apologise, and didn't even react when he said my name. Only when he called me a second time did I realise and turn around sharply.

'Dr Watson, I have something for you,' he addressed me in a low, quiet voice. He handed me a huge box, shot a menacing glance at me, and vanished before any thought about a bomb in the box had crossed my mind. The bang nearly blew my brains out.

* * *

'Mr Holmes.' I was indeed astonished when I recognised his tall black figure in the doorframe.

Sitting around had driven thoughts into my mind, and my desire to dig into my forgotten past increased. I had gone upstairs to have a look around the small chamber next to the second bedroom. It was rather absorbing with all the old trinkets lying around. John's old photographs were very touching. I had even found some yellowish pages of his diary. *Has he noticed they are falling out?*

'You do have a worn mind, haven't you?' Sherlock asked, slowly approaching me.

'I'm afraid so. Why do you ask?'

'You simply won't manage to call me Sherlock.' He smirked.

'I'm sorry. I really don't know why, Mr Holmes.'

'Well then, *Miss Vendalle*, what have you remembered so far?'

Every ounce of me screamed at his question, and the sound of the book slipping out of my hands and falling to the ground echoed in my thoughts.

'Mr Holmes, I can't-' I began to rock uncomfortably on the seat as I tried to stop the memories from coming.

55

'Miss Vendalle, it's invaluably important that I know all you know.' His low, incisive voice cleared my mind of all dizziness. He was firmly clutching my upper arms with his large, bandaged hands, chaining my eyes to his.

Pictures of a steep slope racing by under my feet came to my mind and the feeling of heavy black boots dragging me down, my burning throat and a gun in my gloved hand appeared in front of my inner eye.

'Miss Vendalle.' Sherlock drew my chin upwards to make me look at him again. The feeling of the bandage on my skin sent a shiver through me, reminding me of the feeling of guilt I felt when I woke up in hospital.

'What do you see?'

I opened my mouth, but was unable to speak.

'*What do you see?*' he asked more harshly now.

'I-I... I see grass, a hill, I'm running up that hill... My boots are too heavy. I'm holding a gun. I'm not just running, I'm on the run.' I closed my eyes, but Sherlock shook me until I opened them again.

'Is someone following you?' he asked sharply.

'I- I don't know, I- yes, Yes, I think so.'

'Who?'

'I don't know, I don't *know*!'

I wriggled myself out of his grip and ran out of the room, throwing myself against the door to close it behind me. For a moment I could only hear my hasty breath, but when I had just managed to calm down a bit, Sherlock's voice behind the door made me start.

'Thank you very much, Miss Vendalle, now would you please let me out? I've already read John's diaries – I don't have to read them again.'

With a weary smile, I let him out.

'We're getting there,' he comforted me, smiling warmly. He went over to my bedroom, unlocked the door and placed the key in my palm. 'Never leave a key in a lock, and never leave a lock unlocked. Good night.'

And off he went.

Chapter 5

When I woke up, there was a continuous ringing in my ears. Blood was on the pavement. I tried to scream, but I could hardly open my mouth. Burnt papers were scattered all over; I figured a bin nearby had exploded.

Then I noticed the box on the ground next to me. It innocently lay there, hardly a scratch on it. It *had been* the bin then. *What a coincidence*, I almost thought, when Sherlock popped up in my mind, correcting me, 'The universe is hardly so lazy.'

'John!' He sounded almost worried. Kneeling down next to me, Sherlock quickly took off the bandage on his hand and wound it around my head. 'Can you hear me?'

Astonishingly, I couldn't tell if the slight quiver in his voice *merely* came from his being out of breath, but it made me smile either way. I tried to nod.

'You've gone quite far in the short time you went away,' he panted.

'Scarlett! Did you find her?' I shouted as he helped me sit up.

'She only went upstairs and had a look at your diaries,' he calmly explained.

'What?' I just mouthed, staring furiously at my strange companion. 'You knew that all along?'

'I sort of figured that when I saw the footprint with a tiny bloodstain on the doormat pointing in that direction. I bet her past is even more awful than yours, seeing as she seemed quite enchanted by your military diaries.'

I sank back to the pavement.

'No, no, no, John, you need to get off the street. I don't want to drag you,' Sherlock ordered. I realised that I had actually been thrown off the pavement. He pulled me up by my sleeves and casually picked up the box.

'Oh, good, they're still alive. John, you're a doctor, fix them up when we get home,' he announced as he peered into a box.

'What the hell have you got in there?' I blustered, taking the box from him to have a look myself. 'Seriously? Guinea pigs? *Seriously?* Since when do you have pets?' I asked in disbelief.

'They're Miss Vendalle's. If you weren't so horribly orderly, I'm sure she wouldn't have hesitated to mention them to you. They might make a wonderful piece of evidence against Moriarty,' Sherlock murmured with a triumphant smile.

'You're kidding me. Honestly, you've got to be *kidding* me!'

'I'm not. Ericson gave them to us earlier when we had the pleasure of meeting Moran. We had to abandon them on our flight, but obviously they wanted us to have them. They're going to be a brilliant experiment! Ah, it's Christmas, John!'

After my initial shock, the fire in Sherlock's face calmed me down. It was just like the first time I'd seen him solve a crime. As he started to investigate the remains of the exploded bin, it occurred to me that I wouldn't even have been here, if he had just told me that Scarlett was still in the house.

'Sherlock?'

'Mmh?'

'Why did you let me go and search for Scarlett, even though you knew she hadn't gone away?'

He turned around to me again, and looked at me half-puzzled that I didn't know myself, and half-insecure on what to say. The latter half quickly vanished into thin air.

'I had to interview her without you standing by. You're pulling her out of her memories when they could be immensely valuable to us.'

'Don't tell me you've already got a theory!' I interrupted him with so much anger that I even astonished myself.

'Of course I do, but that's not the point.'

'Really, what is it then!?' I shouted. *Is that jealousy?*

Sherlock looked as startled for a moment as I felt. 'It is,' he continued after a moment, 'that if Moriarty's men are keeping her luggage, and bother to bring her pets to us halfway through London, there's something he wants with her.'

I was truly baffled. *What on earth would Moriarty want with Scarlett?*

'Pressure point, John, obviously.'

'I didn't even ask.'

'Oh, come on, John, look at your face.' Sherlock shook his head and turned to the bin again. 'Only a small explosive device. Either a warning or the bin contained something that needed to be destroyed.' He began scratching together all the singed papers lying around. 'What do you make of this, John?'

I had a look at the remnants of paper that the fire had spared. 'It's a magazine.'

'Precisely. *The Strand.* August issue. You've got one up at the flat. Damn, where did you put it? That's the trouble when you tidy up, nothing is in its natural place. How can people live in such horrible order?'

I started to laugh at the wonderfully puzzled expression of my friend. 'Come on, Sherlock, let's go home. My headache's quite bad and I don't really know what you want to make of this stuff here. What was the purpose of blowing up a magazine? I mean, it can only be a warning then.'

'Wrong! There was something inside the magazine; here's a stain, and there is a lump... Might be a memory stick. I have to go and analyse it. Come along, John,' he said incidentally, and started walking.

Suddenly something in the street caught Sherlock's eye. I followed his look, and there was a small red light on the asphalt. It was ticking. Still ticking.

'The bomb detonated too early! It was supposed to explode unseen,' Sherlock realised in fascination. 'The neighbours on this side are on holiday, those on the other side are old enough to be deaf enough not to hear the bang, and for the rest it won't be loud enough to alarm them! Brilliant!'

Sherlock's mood was indeed brilliant on our way home. Lost in his thoughts, he paced down the street, too quick for my aching head. Everything started to blur around me and suddenly something tall, thin and cold appeared in my way, which upon closer inspection felt very hard as well when my head clanged against it.

* * *

I had just gone downstairs to get myself a glass of water. Surely, nothing much could have happened in the meantime?

You can easily imagine I got the shock of my life when Sherlock came in, carrying John, motionless in his arms.

'Sherlock, what happened!?'

'Two.'

'What!?'

'Nothing, just counting.' Sherlock cleared his throat. 'He walked into a streetlamp,' he said as he went into his room. I followed him closely.

'How could you let this happen?' I reproached him, pulling the duvet out of the way.

'Well, I didn't see it!'

Sudden anger had flashed over his face which seemed to be at himself rather than at me for asking this. I had learnt to read his strange moods in his expressions over time, and at least to an extent I felt I could say I understood him.

Sherlock carefully laid John on the bed, one half of which was completely wet for some strange reason. I quickly shoved a pillow under John's head.

Memories of their past together seemed to flicker over Sherlock's face when he pulled the duvet over John. Peculiarly touched by both embarrassment and affection, I went into the bathroom to get the medical aid kit and a wet towel. Sherlock hadn't moved a bit when I entered the room again.

'I'll sleep on the couch,' he only said quietly.

I've never seen a better friendship in my life. In fact, it was the most perfect correspondence of two souls you could imagine. Sherlock's voice changed when he talked to John; there simply was a tinge of affection in it that would melt the Japanese blades on the wall without making them lose their sharpness. The words would still cut the air, but unable to kill, unable to destroy; they were the preserving force, and I do believe that every word he exchanged with John was preserving his life.

As John was taking his time waking up, I decided to begin treating him. I cleaned the wound on John's head below the bandage, which I'd already changed. I put a plaster over his nose. I cooled the bump on his forehead and the one on the back of his head. Sherlock watched all of my moves; it seemed as though they were calming him down as well. Suddenly, his bleeding hand came to my mind again.

'Show me your hand, will you?' I said to him. He was holding it behind his back. At first, he gave me a startled look while the lack of interpersonal knowledge was curling the bridge of his nose. He extended the hand without a word. He wanted to pull it back the instant I touched it, but I managed to grip it firmly. I carefully wrapped another tape around it, leaving his cold, round fingertips uncovered.

'Thank you for fixing John up,' he murmured suddenly.

I looked at John again, who seemed thirty years younger with his eyes closed and a slight, peaceful smile on his lips, 'I hope he'll be fine.' All of a sudden, I was scared he could have lost his memory, too.

Suddenly, his eyes fluttered open.

'Sherlock? Scarlett?'

He remembered our names!

'What happened?' He blinked several times, trying to sit up wearily. 'Are you crying? Are you all right? Did you insult her?' he babbled.

'Maybe.' Sherlock broadly grinned at John.

'Mr Holmes said you ran into a streetlamp.'

'Well, I suppose that was the long dark thing that suddenly stood in my way... Have you fixed me up already? Thanks a lot, that's very nice of you.'

John's smile was redemption to me. The way the tip of his nose went up when he smile, as if reaching for a switch to light up his eyes, seemed to cage the monster inside me. I took a deep breath.

'You two haven't been sobbing at my bedside together, have you?' he asked in confusion, looking at Sherlock and me in turn.

'Of course, we haven't,' I replied, throwing a curious glance at Sherlock, who looked even more irritated than John. I had to grin.

'Good,' John said, checking if his nose was broken, but still looking at us like we had gone mad.

'Well, you two still have to tell me the reason why you went outside at all,' I remarked, thinking through the events of the evening.

'It was because of you,' John answered with his eyebrows raised at my ignorance.

'Really? Did you decide to get rid of me after all?'

'No! I thought you'd left for good when I didn't see you there after I came back from Sherlock's room. So, I went looking for you,' John explained, giving Sherlock an accusing look.

'But he knew,' I started, but broke off when John shook his head. 'Don't ask. It's senseless with him anyway.'

'But what on earth made you run into a streetlamp then?'

'First, someone gave me your guinea pigs. Then a bin exploded next to me, so I wasn't totally able to concentrate on the way home, which resulted in my walking into the streetlamp. Sherlock, where have you got the box and the magazine?'

'Wait, someone gave you my guinea pigs? A bin exploded? Are you making something up to make it less embarrassing for yourself?' I blustered.

'No, he isn't. I had to leave the box in the street, John. You were heavy enough that I couldn't carry you both. The magazine's here in my pocket,' Sherlock said calmly. 'Just give me a moment, and I'll fetch the guinea pigs as well.'

I rushed after him.

'They're still alive, don't worry. I checked,' he assured me. Then he opened the front door. There the box lay innocently on the doormat.

'They really do want you to have them,' Sherlock remarked as he picked up the box. 'I had to leave them some hundred yards from here.'

I instantly peered into the box. My pets were cuddling in one corner as if nothing had happened.

'You still haven't told me how you found John. Why would you go looking at all if you let him go without a word?' I asked Sherlock on the way up.

'It was clear he was somehow heading towards King's Cross, as he had no better clues, so I figured out the route he might intuitively take and went after him, because, as he had been away so long, I knew he wouldn't give up soon. Moriarty has already abducted my brother, whose presence I can perfectly dispense with, by the way, I thought it might not be too safe on the streets far from Baker Street for John,' Sherlock explained, and opened the door.

When we entered the flat, Sherlock immediately threw his coat over the couch and went into the kitchen.

'What are you doing there?' I asked, passing the open door on the way to John.

'Analysing something,' he briefly shot back, protective goggles on his nose already, searching for something on the table's chaos.

I shrugged my shoulders over the consulting detective's obsessive nature and left him to his fate, hoping that he wouldn't blow up the house as well. There had been enough explosions already.

'John, can I bring you anything?' I enquired when I saw his pale face.

He was sat up in bed, holding one of Sherlock's books in his hands. 'Oh, this is so embarrassing! Scarlett, I should be asking *you* those questions,' he sighed with disappointment. I smiled at him kindly and sat down next to him, carefully placing the box on the bedside table.

'What are their names?'

'Sorry, what?'

'Your guinea pigs. What do you call them?'

A brief laugh escaped my mouth. 'Oh, right. Their names are Benedict and Martin, but I only call them B and M, because of the collars I got them with the letters on. Couldn't find any with their whole names.' I shrugged.

'Could you introduce us?' John said with a benevolent glow in his eyes. I chuckled. He had an extraordinary talent of lightening the atmosphere in a room.

Carefully, I seized the box and seated myself in a way that we could both look into it, while John hesitantly extended his arm for me to lean against it. Then I pulled my pets out one after the other.

'The curly caramel one here is B, and the sandy one that looks like a hedgehog – that's M.' I lifted the small golden letters, which were attached to leather collars, into the light and dazzled John with the reflection. He laughed, squinting.

'Sorry,' I chuckled, and stopped. 'I think they like you.'

'Hello, there. Nice to meet you,' John addressed them most respectfully. 'What makes you think M looks like a hedgehog?'

'I guess that's because of his nose, and the crowns in his fur obviously,' I replied fondly.

'Ah, right. *Obviously*.' John didn't exactly look convinced, as his face scrunched up exactly like that of the guinea pig.

'I wonder what they did to them. An implanted camera would be a bit too simple, wouldn't it?' I scanned every corner of the box.

'Yeah, and for an explosive device they don't need guinea pigs,' John reckoned, also intently staring at my pets.

66

'John, what is he analysing?' I wanted to know, nodding at the kitchen door after a while without a clue.

'He found something inside the burnt magazine. He's trying to figure out what it was before it blew to smithereens.' He paused and looked away for a moment. 'Scarlett, if you want to leave, it's OK, just tell me.' John's voice sounded desperately tender.

Of course, I wanted to leave, and of course, I wanted to stay. I knew what was left of me well enough to see I was going to...

'She'll stay. It's obvious,' Sherlock informed us from the kitchen.

'How did you know *this* time?' John blustered.

'You can easily tell how stubborn she is from the times she clenches her jaw when something doesn't quite yield her inclinations.'

The swoosh of the Bunsen burner suddenly sounded very loud in the bedroom.

'How does he always see such things when I can't?' John pursed his lips in dismay.

'You see different things,' I told him after a moment.

He smiled into himself sarcastically. Then he looked at me. 'Do you mean that?'

'Sincerely, yes.' I squeezed John's hand and stood up. 'Goodnight, John.'

He kindly smiled at me. 'Thank you, Scarlett.'

'For what?'

'For staying with us.' John's voice seemed to be burdened with weight when he said this, but the warmth in it wouldn't quite give way under it.

I was a burden; I knew that well enough, but somehow it felt wrong to leave. To feel John's warmth, I realised, I would go to world's end. How could I leave? Sherlock was right after all.

'Goodnight, Scarlett.'

For a moment, we didn't move at all. Perhaps, we were expecting the other to say something or do something, but neither of us did. Eventually, I went out of the room, closing the door behind me.

Sleep didn't come easily to me at all that night. The thought of dreaming of Anne or waking up to see her eyes staring at me would not let me rest. After about an hour of lying awake like this, I decided to go downstairs, get a drink and check up on John. When I opened the door to the kitchen, though, a strange sight met my eyes. It took me a second glance to see that Sherlock was experimenting. The only light in the room came from the Bunsen burner, its flame chasing theories over Sherlock's face. Staring keenly at the sticky substance he was extracting from a coal black lump, his eyes seemed to become portals to a higher world.

'Mr Holmes?' He didn't answer; he was totally absorbed. I had to smile. 'Sherlock?'

'Not now, John.'

Very carefully, he put a drop of the substance in his pipette onto a Petri dish, keeping the gap in the lump open with a pair of tweezers. After that he dipped a steel rod into a small flask, then into the gap, put away the tweezers and took the Bunsen burner to hold it out in front of him horizontally. Then he held the stick into the flame. With a hiss, the flame grew crimson.

'Damn it!' Sherlock put everything down.

'Lithium,' I said quietly. He turned to me, surprised.

'What did you say?' His voice was at its lowest pitch.

'That just sort of slipped out of my mouth, but it's obvious, isn't it?' I replied a little insecurely.

'How would *you* know?' he asked, frowning in astonishment. The corners of his mouth twitched downward for a millisecond.

'I studied medicine with John, didn't I?' I knew that was no explanation, as I couldn't remember anything from that time at all, but I couldn't think of any other reason why I should know this.

Sherlock shook his head. 'That's impossible. The access to such information in your brain must be totally blocked, considering how hard it is for you to remember that time period. How did infrared light break my watch when you met me?'

At his incisive command, my train of thought rushed past my brain and out of my mouth. 'Small stains of soot on your pocket, glass doesn't burn to ash, there was an invisible layer of polish on the glass, which absorbed the infrared light, heating up the glass, the metal frame and, underneath it, the lithium used in batteries, causing it to expand and shatter the glass.'

'Correct.'

'Really?'

Sherlock didn't answer me. Instead he mumbled to himself. Eventually he spoke, 'It's like red threads laid out for you that you can figure out on command. Someone planted information on you that must fit into a bigger puzzle. So much effort for such a simple purpose.'

'What is your theory?'

'You're being led to solve a case.'

'What does that even mean?' I was starting to lose control over myself. My hands had formed firsts which I only noticed when my nails dug into my palms.

Sherlock just walked around the table, shoving around his mess. 'Can't tell you.'

'Are you serious?'

'I said I can't tell you, isn't that clear enough?' All of a sudden, he sounded regretfully menacing.

'Does that mean you don't have a theory?' I shot back.

A slight tinge of helplessness passed over his face before his features hardened again. 'I always have a theory, but it's no use talking about it, before I've eliminated every other possibility. One should always look for a possible alternative, and provide against it – first rule of criminal investigation.'

He had pulled himself together again, but I had seen the mask lifted. His shovelling around of things wouldn't wipe that away. Something made me feel afraid of myself again, and I had to know what at any cost.

'Mr Holmes, you have to tell me,' I insisted firmly.

He went on looking for something in his chaos. Suddenly, my fist hit the table with a bang. He froze.

'Sherlock Holmes, tell me what's wrong with me!'

His eyes moved around quickly. Then, he went to wash his hands at the sink .

With clenched teeth, I grabbed him by the upper arm and turned him around, forcing him to face me. Normally, I would have let go quickly when I noticed the violence pumping through my veins, but I forgot to with all the thoughts wreaking havoc in my mind.

'It's not your fault,' he whispered suddenly, 'that's all I can tell you.'

The sound of his whispering voice seemed to elevate me into another sphere. I was completely taken aback by the range of emotions rushing through his words, like a river. He had struck a nerve. I only noticed my grip around his arms had tightened when he carefully placed his large, taped hand on mine. A shudder went through me when he deliberately lifted each of my frozen fingers off his arm, one by one. The bandage was slightly damp still, but it seemed ages ago that he had washed his hands. He moved on to the other side, lifting each of my fingers by their tips with his own. He didn't want to detach me from him, but from myself. He didn't let go but took my whole hand and turned it upwards to once again take a look at the marks on my palm. Then he carefully let go and looked straight into my eyes. It seemed as if he was reading novels in them.

'What a case...' he murmured, turning to the table again. After a moment, he turned off the Bunsen burner. I registered the tap, still running with water.

Sherlock seemed to have the same thought, because he immediately went over to turn it off. It was nearly pitch black in the room; the only source of light coming from the stairs. It didn't seem to trouble Sherlock in the least. His swift movements brushed a soft breeze against my skin. He closed the door, then ruffled papers. Something was dripping.

I wanted to ask what case he meant, why recognising a lithium battery in the analysis was something to swear at, and most of all, why on earth he wouldn't tell me how I knew about the chemicals. Suddenly he put his hand on my mouth, drawing me close to him and gripping my wrists firmly to hold them behind my back before I could react.

Immediately, all my senses went into overdrive. All my muscles tightened, my breath grew more rapid, my pulse elevated, and adrenalin shot fire through my body. I almost couldn't think anymore, trying to struggle free instantly.

Sherlock was stronger than me. I could feel it was taking him all his strength by the way his hands were quivering from the strain. A strange smell went up my nose, it almost made me pass out. I tried to scream, but it was muffled beneath his large palm. I was truly panicking. The choking sound of my voice and the stench burning in my nose and eyes made me hyperventilate. The ground seemed to vanish under my feet.

And that moment, Anne's head rolled down, hitting my feet, staining the darkness with blood.

'Lithium!' The sound of Sherlock's low, incisive voice seemed to lop off my own head. Abruptly, he let go. It felt like my head was tumbling down to the floor before I hit it.

'Lithium, alkali metal, symbol Li, relative atomic mass: 6.9 units, atomic number 3, two shells, detection: crimson flame.' The words just passed through my mouth, like a button had been turned on.

All of a sudden, I saw myself pacing down a corridor in a castle, pictures rushing by me. Something was inhibiting my steps, something soft but thick and heavy. Silk. A dress. I couldn't run. I would trip. I would fall.

'Lily!' I was jolted back into the darkness of the kitchen. Sherlock's hands were clasping my face, as though he knew it would fall apart otherwise; I could but faintly feel his quick, warm breath on my skin. I hoped he wouldn't have to blow the dust off me that I'd collected from the historical scene of my vision.

'Sherlock?' I croaked feebly.

'Thank God, John would've killed me...' he sighed.

When he let go of my face, his hands were trembling. I could feel his legs at my side as he took a deep breath. When I sat up, my face was suddenly very close to his. I didn't see it. I could only perceive it by its scintillating tension as he held his breath. Neither of us moved.

'What did you see?' he asked quietly, although excitement must've been boiling up inside him. I started to breathe quicker, trying hard not to go into shock as I recalled my vision. My thorax slowly began to sink back to the ground.

Sherlock caught me by my arms and held me up again, so my face was as close to his as before. 'What did you see, Lily?'

The sound of my first name sent a wave of shock through me.

'I saw... There was a castle. I broke into it. I ran up a spiral staircase. There was a glass bridge out of a window, I ran across it. I entered a chamber that didn't exist; it couldn't exist! It was floating miles above the ground. I opened a safe. How did I know the code? Then everything burst into a red flame, and I fell. Suddenly, I was in a corridor. I tried to run, but my dress wouldn't allow me.' My head fell back, bending my throat – I was empty.

'That'll do for a start, Miss Vendalle,' said Sherlock, taking my hand and helping me up.

'No, it won't, Sherlock,' I retorted, grabbing his arm firmly once again. 'You will tell me, right now, why you did this! Why was the lithium a bad sign? What was that horrible stuff you tried to gag me with? Who the hell I am?!'

'Experiment, only the battery, no idea, the key.'

It took me a moment until I puzzled out his answers. They didn't say a lot. All I could gather from them, apart from the fact that Sherlock hadn't intended to abduct me, was the following: the memory device that had been blown up had no data left for Sherlock to analyse, with only the battery being left and possible having corrupted the metal poles in the storage. The substance he had used on me was completely new to him, so it was part of his current investigations, and ... *What did he say?*

'Sherlock, what am I the key to? Whose key?'

'Again, it's better not to tell you. Go to sleep, and whatever you do, make sure you keep yourself in one piece at any cost tonight, will you?' His words made it sound like my life would depend on this. I nodded.

73

'Goodnight,' he said with a sudden, artificial smile. Sherlock opened the door and pushed me out. The door banged shut before I could turn around. With a shrug but without fear, I went upstairs, locking the door behind me.

Finally, I was calling him Sherlock.

Part 2: More

Chapter 1

The next morning I didn't know what was real anymore. My memories of the night were confusing and totally impossible. First, I checked if I was still in one piece as Sherlock had advised me. It seemed so at a glance, but somehow, I didn't trust my eyes. When I sat up, the room turned with a jerk, and I was hanging from the ceiling. Someone had tied my arms and legs to the bed and transfixed it to the left corner of the ceiling. *Am I finally going mad or is that blood weighing down my head like lava pumping through my veins? If I'm not going mad, is it really my own blood that will kill me at last?* I decided it was not a death after my taste, so I took a look at the mirror on the wall next to me: I was sitting perfectly upright and the bed was on the floor. Only, my face had a strange complexion.

Everything started to blur

Fog rolled up   in the middle of the room
A veil of heat took away my

                        senses
Anne appeared in the mirror behind me to

                     take away my mind, I
had to stay in one piece
             I would lose

                 One piece…

I was screaming when I woke. My head was aching terribly, and it still felt unbelievably hot in the room. At least it wasn't upside down anymore. I dashed to the window and flung it open. It was rather late already judging by the approximate position of the sun behind the clouds. The fresh, incisive London morning air cooled me down. When I touched my face, though, it still felt like a volcano about to erupt.

Clutching the window frame, I tried to inhale the colours of the view over the roofs. The bluish black of the Victorian age iron, the sandy façades, the dark red brick walls, the grey of the sky, the coal black of the industrial revolution, the white of the window frames. London felt like freedom.

Suddenly, I noticed I was still wearing the clothes John had lent me yesterday. I went into the shower room and had a morning shower. When I was finished, I discovered John had been so attentive as to provide me with another of his shirts which lay on a stool next to the window.

Afterwards I tied my hair to a bun again, not without Sherlock's deductions about it passing through my head. As I was about to leave the room for breakfast, a scratch just above the door handle caught my eye. It had clearly been caused by a knife, and there were black marks on the wall next to the door. Finally, I saw the tiny piece of paper behind the mirror.

Hello, darling princess.

'John! John! Sherlock!'

I ran down the stairs so fast I almost flew, crashing into the living room with a loud bang. John immediately came over and embraced my shaking body.

76

'It's all right, it's all right. Just calm down and tell us what happened.'

John sat me down on the couch. Sherlock was sitting in the armchair opposite me, drinking a cup of tea. I was still shaking with the horror of the note behind the mirror. What frightened me even more was the sudden recollection of a voice calling me *darling princess*.

'Someone was in my room last night,' I stated when my mind finally uncoiled.

'I thought so. Who was it?' Sherlock asked, calmly stirring his tea with a spoon.

'*What?*' John wasn't quite as calm. 'You knew that and let her go to her room alone? Not even checking up on her? You bastard! We're supposed to help her back *into* life, not out of it!'

'Anyway,' I said before they could start a fight, 'I didn't see anyone, but there's a small cut in the door and some black marks probably from shoe soles next to it. There's a note, too.' Another shiver went down my back.

I couldn't bear to say more, but Sherlock seemed to understand. He went upstairs to fetch it.

'Hello, darling princess,' he slowly read, back in the living room, with an irritated expression. 'Who would call someone that? Clearly, your boyfriend was a bit of a dreamy sad dog, though he seems to be as eager to make you remember him as we should be, only that he knows too much and we too little. He and his companions were totally silent.'

'He and *his companions*? What the hell, Sherlock? Oh, sometimes I could...' John's teeth were clenched.

'I had to do it. I knew they wouldn't kill her, and we badly need the information they left,' Sherlock explained, holding the piece of paper against the light. 'There's a watermark on it,' he turned and turned the paper. 'U-MQ-RA. UMQRA. John, could you please search my files for that?'

77

I stood up and walked over to him. 'I think it's a pattern, like a stripe of letters. There's an edge of another letter where the paper is cut off.'

Sherlock looked at it intently. 'I see... You're rather good.'

'Sherlock, you've got more explaining to do,' John threw in. 'What did you find in the lump yesterday evening?'

'A lithium battery. The data has been totally destroyed or stolen,' Sherlock swiftly replied. 'Wait! John, you're brilliant! Can't get a better man to inspire the genius!' He dashed into the kitchen with a triumphant smile.

'Here we go again,' John sighed. I sat down next to him and leaned my head against his shoulder.

'A brain also needs a heart, John,' I told him gently, and he smiled to himself.

When John Watson put his arm around me, I felt like deep within the core of the Earth everything was fine, and it was through his gift that I could sense it. I knew exactly how badly Sherlock needed him, because I needed him exactly the same way. There was something about his smile that always made me return it. His shoulder never felt hard and his arm never heavy, and in his embrace, I was never guilty, nor bad. He looked at me askance, scanning my face for marks before softly touching my chin, turning my head to have a look at the bump. My bandage had fallen off during the night and I hadn't bothered to put it back on.

'You really need to cool this again, otherwise it's going to give you hell.'

He tenderly placed his hand on my cheek to most carefully run his fingers through my hair, separating strands in order to examine the bump more closely. I smiled at him.

'Hah! Found it!'

Oh, Sherlock also still existed.

'Found what?' John asked, as though he was just about to eat Sherlock for lunch.

'The magazine, it's in the magazine! Obviously! What we need is in there; the phone was a red herring! It was just the carrier of the explosive device.'

With a radiant smile Sherlock came back into the room, swiftly sitting down in the armchair, unfolding the magazine with the burnt edges and holes. His eyes were scanning the paper with a speed that almost made me dizzy. Their jerky, yet precise moves, the tense focus in those grey portals were riveting my eyes to them in the most agitating way. When a pleased smile lit up his cheeks, they spread goose bumps all over my body.

From then, I was torn.

'Adultery!' The charge was immediate. Anne's scream seemed to make my skull burst. I caught a glimpse of her wrecked body behind the chair, hardening mine until I felt it crack. Before I passed out, I faintly heard my fragments clink glasses with the window.

* * *

'Scarlett!'

She'd risen from the sofa, her mouth and eyes wide open. Her lips turned blue and she collapsed in the middle of the room. Her eyes were wide open as she was holding her head and shaking. She was completely unresponsive. I rushed to lift her up.

'Help me, Sherlock! What are you doing over there?' I blustered as he paced around the corner in which his chair stood, taking in every atom of it.

'She saw something, right there behind my chair, and then there was this sound like glass clinking together!'

He froze at the window, staring intently at the flat opposite. The small glass doll from the sniper's broken music box hung from the window on a red wool thread, clinking against it as she moved about in the wind. It took me a second to see the horror: the doll was beheaded.

'What's that supposed to mean?'

'It's a clue, right into the heart of Moriarty's cobweb,' he murmured, with an unhealthy fascination in his eyes.

'But why should Scarlett go into shock at its sight? What's *she* got to do with Moriarty?' I knelt down to check Scarlett's pulse.

'He's using her as bait,' Sherlock stated, a quiet grip constraining his voice.

'*What!?* A bait for whom, for what, what for?' I reproached him in utter rage.

Sherlock ignored my protest. 'He's trying to plant information on her, but I don't know how. Damn, he knows more than I do. Maybe his network was in contact with the organisation she was in.' He kept walking through the room restlessly, his hands at his temples.

'Scarlett, can you hear me?' I asked, turning back to her. I held her head up a bit in hopes that she would be able to let go of it. Her hair was still knotty from the night. How could I help her?

Finally, she opened her mouth to speak. 'Where is she?'

At once, Sherlock stood still.

'Who?' I asked her. She hadn't quite woken up from her daze yet. There was some dreamy veil about her pupils, an emptiness I couldn't properly fathom.

'Anne,' she stammered. In an instant Sherlock was kneeling next to her, gazing into her eyes.

'What happened to Anne?' he asked in a clear and calm but urging voice.

'I... It was all my fault. I didn't know. I should have died in her place. I should have been Queen. My head... my head...'

The skin on her face became so dangerously tight that my throat felt strangled.

'Scarlett, wake up!' She started to writhe and cough. I bit my lip.

Sherlock was equally petrified but then an idea formed in his eyes. Something made him hesitate at first, a repulsion I could not explain. I flinched when he shouted, 'Lily!'

She woke up with a jolt.

'What happened?' she panted breathlessly, staring at the empty fireplace.

Sherlock and I just looked at each other in confusion.

'You said something about–' Sherlock began.

'Don't say it,' I warned him.

'But maybe she can tell us more.'

'Just tell me what I said. You already know everything about me anyway,' she told Sherlock with an inexplicable look.

'Almost,' he replied, his lips thrillingly dancing on the edge of a smile.

'Oh, come on, I already feel much better. Will you tell me now?'

I shook my head, but Sherlock just wouldn't shut up. 'You talked about Anne Boleyn.'

And, of course, she went into shock again.

'Scarlett, wake up!' I had caught her this time, and now I was softly patting her cheek.

'Oh, come on, John. She's just pretending. A brilliant doctor you are,' Sherlock laughed.

Scarlett sat up with a grumpy face. 'Did you have to spoil it immediately?' she complained with a smile. 'Sorry, John. Just a little revenge for your bet...'

'Hey! That was Sherlock's bloody idea, not mine,' I rebuked her.

'I still don't know what it was,' she shot back. 'What have you been counting? I kept track – you're at fourteen, and I'll find it out the hard way if you won't tell me now.'

'The times you called me Sherlock.' I spun round.

'It's over, John, she's doing it every day now.'

'And you didn't bother to tell me!?' I blustered.

'I'm sorry.' Scarlett looked at the floor.

'It doesn't matter,' I snapped, 'now I'm angry at *him*!'

'Sorry, nevertheless. But my acting wasn't quite so bad, was it?' She smiled proudly.

'Not at all, he totally fell for it,' Sherlock replied, still chuckling.

'Oh, you bastard!' I growled at him.

'It's OK, John. We all love you. But I think I do need some coffee now. Could you get me some?' Scarlett asked with her hand at her forehead, not quite as amused as before.

'Sherlock?' I snarled, and he went without a word.

'What did the doctors say about your panic attacks in hospital?' I asked Scarlett after a minute.

'Why, they had no idea. No deficiency, nothing physically detectable. They told me to get a therapist, though, because they thought it was linked to my PTSD,' she explained, still sitting on the floor opposite me.

'And just this once, they were right,' Sherlock stated, coming back from the kitchen.

'What? Do you conjure coffee now?' I complained, annoyed at Sherlock's early return.

'Wish I could,' he grinned, helping us up and then handing us the coffee while we sat down, 'but no, I just happened to have made some spare coffee shortly before she came downstairs.'

I put away the cup in my hand and stood up. The only thing that seemed reasonable to me now was to cool down her head again. I'm not a psychiatrist – I couldn't help her with what she had seen, or shield her from things that might frighten her, but I could make her feel more comfortable physically, and hope it would at least ease her pain in some way.

In the kitchen, I took a cold pack out of the freezer and fetched a new tape. Somehow, the silence in the living room disturbed me. Even aggravated me. I had expected them to talk as normal people would, and I had also expected them to annoy me by laughing about me, because I'd fallen for Scarlett's fibbing, but this unanimous silence... truly got on my nerves. The idea that they didn't need words to communicate – like me, the puny little doctor – made me so angry I wanted to throw away the aid kit I was holding. But my arm stopped after I had raised it.

There was a message on the floor next to the bin. It was made out of red thread.

XOXO – ED

'Sherlock! Come here, quick!'

He appeared in an instant. 'What is it?'

I pointed at the writing.

'Oh.' First, he pulled out his smart phone and took a picture, then proceeded to kneel to carefully examine every inch of the thread and the floor beneath it with his magnifying lens.

'Three years old. Has been sewed with already, but was ironed afterwards to straighten it,' he stated after a moment.

'Who would iron a thread?' I asked in confusion.

'It's someone who was very keen to shape the writing perfectly. There are loads of bends in the thread, which suggests something like a buttonhole. Oh! The *bastard*!'

83

Without another word Sherlock rushed to seize his coat from the rack. Turning up the collar he gave a groan and chucked it into the corner. 'The bastard,' he muttered again through clenched teeth. He dashed about to see how they'd gotten in. I carefully snuck over to check whether my suspicion was correct. Indeed, the thread had been removed from his top buttonhole.

Whoever had broken in was by far the most audaciously barefaced criminal we'd come across yet. The name Moriarty popped up in my mind, but he couldn't possibly have anything to do with this. *Did we have two break-ins last night? Hardly likely, but hadn't Sherlock said Moriarty was using Scarlett as bait?* I must've misunderstood that. It was as preposterous as twins being the solution to a mystery in a crime novel...

Chapter 2

A few days later Sherlock was still stuck in front of his crime wall. When I came in, he was scratching his head as he glided over the numerous notes. Suddenly, he ripped off one note and went straight to the window. Holding it against the light, he gave a gasp of excitement.

'UMQRA, I suppose,' Scarlett threw in abruptly. He didn't turn around, but I could see the impact of a smile from behind.

'You really *are* rather good,' he murmured casually, then took his phone and called a cab.

'*Where* are you going?' I barked.

'We're going to the morgue. I need to analyse these two papers, and – there's been a break-in. They took two corpses. Minnie just texted me. Steven was the last to lock the doors. Oh, this is going to be *so* interesting!'

Sherlock thrust some jackets at us and stuffed the papers into his pocket before vanishing down the stairs.

'*We?* What about Scarlett? I can't leave her alone now that people are looking for her!' I hollered after him.

'She's coming with us!' Sherlock called back as Scarlett hastened to the stairs, but after a moment's thought, I stopped her at the top.

'No, this is not going to work. We're staying here!' I decided.

But Sherlock just looked up. 'Don't be silly! The game is on!' And despite my groaning, we were dashing after him, of course.

'How do you know it won't be driven by a criminal like last time?' Scarlett asked as we waited for the taxi. Sherlock didn't even look up from his phone.

'They're busy elsewhere right now.' He smiled into himself.

The cab arrived. I opened the door for Scarlett, but Sherlock rushed in first without a word. With a sigh, I beckoned Scarlett to get in, and stuffed myself next to her.

'To St Bart's, please,' I said after an awkward silence and a questioning look from the driver as Sherlock simply wouldn't look up from his phone.

What the hell is going on with him again? One moment he was ecstatic, the other he seemed to vanish in languor. It was something that held his mind in its grip, making it immune to outer influences. He kept shuffling pages and pages on his phone, searching for something. His eyes had this sharp precision that made his face even more aquiline.

We arrived at the morgue just a few minutes late and ran into Minnie, whose hair was in a chaotic disarray.

'Oh, there you are. The bodies are upstairs. Should I get you some coffee?'

Scarlett shook her head. 'No, thanks.'

'Black, two sugars please, I'll give it to him. I don't need one right now,' I told her.

On our way up, Scarlett kept studying the halls and stairs we were passing. There was something about her observant look that strongly attracted me to her. Maybe that was why I could stand living with a high-functioning sociopath...

When we entered the morgue, Sherlock immediately began reading the files, and within minutes half of them were littered across the floor.

'This is not what I need. Minnie!' He chucked the rest of the papers to the floor.

'Coming! Here's the coffee,' Minnie piped from in the hall. She coyly scuttled through the room and handed Sherlock the cup.

'I didn't say I wanted any coffee,' Sherlock remarked with an irritated face.

'John said to make you one. I can also give it to Steven,' Minnie stammered helplessly.

'Oh, no, it's fine. I didn't say I *didn't* want coffee, did I?' Sherlock smirked and took the cup. 'Oh, and would you please do me a favour and have a look at the engineer now,' he added with a charming smile.

'O-Of course,' Minnie stuttered in astonishment.

'Very kind of you,' Sherlock purred, bending down to shuffle around some papers on the floor. Minnie's eyes grew larger and larger as the detective started crawling on all four.

'You can close your mouth now, Minnie,' he dryly stated after a moment.

When she scuttled out, she nearly bumped into Steven who came stumbling into the room.

'Er- er- there's - a - problem - downstairs - There's a problem downstairs. Have you seen Minnie anywhere?'

'She's not going to help you,' Sherlock retorted, sipping his coffee.

'What- Why?'

'You offended her.'

'No, I didn't.'

'Then how do you explain that she just gave me coffee with a bloody toe in it?'

'What?' Steven's expression grew more and more inexplicable.

'She told you not to dissect the engineer yet,' Sherlock replied, scanning the papers on the floor.

'Yes, but—'

'But you did it anyway. Why don't you go buy a new coffee machine now?'

'*What the—?*'

'Oh, for God's sake, while she was making coffee in your room, the toe dropped out of a plastic bag on one of your low shelf boards - any kind of box would've kept its contents or fallen off entirely, which Minnie would've noticed. She had placed the cup below the shelf, because there's the only free space on your desk, and turned around to the coffee machine to fill another cup when the toe dropped into the cup she placed on the desk, which is evidenced by the coffee stains on the back of her lab coat. She didn't hear the splash. Now how would you explain that other than by the sound of an old roaring coffee machine?'

Steven seemed to be thinking hard whether or not he should strangle Sherlock on the spot. His nostrils widened as he took in a breath before pursing his lips.

'You aren't going to tell Minnie I already dissected Hatherley, are we clear on that?' he hissed at Sherlock.

'Of course, I'm not telling her,' Sherlock reassured him with a superior smile. 'I only kindly asked her to dissect him before she left here a minute ago.'

'Oh, you- *You-*' Steven took a deep breath before rushing out of the room.

'You make a new friend every day,' I said when the door banged shut behind him.

Sherlock chuckled contently as Scarlett laughed out loud.

'What have those two been up to before we came here then?' I asked as Sherlock began picking up some of the papers.

'Oh, they just stole another corpse for me,' he replied casually.

'Isn't one skull enough for your flat?' Scarlett remarked ironically.

'Well, yes, but we needed to ensure this one wasn't going to be stolen by Moriarty's men. It's in the fridge at Salvatore's restaurant. Steven might have forgotten to properly lock the door, but then again, he mixed up the two bodies' tags, one of them being the most important one to Moriarty. He can indeed be useful to us sometimes,' Sherlock smirked. 'John, would you mind picking up the rest of the papers?'

Of course, I minded, so I gave Sherlock a very hard stare indeed, but he just raised his eyebrows and went over to one of the desks. With a sigh, I bent down.

'James Barker. Ted Baldwin. Who were they?' I asked him, with a look at the photos in the files, which made my stomach turn in a fit of unease.

'Two of Moriarty's assassins, killed by MOD men last month. They took Baldwin – Barker resides at Salvatore's now.'

'But why would they steal them? They haven't gotten sentimental now, I assume.'

'There must be something inside their bodies that would give information away that could seriously endanger Moriarty's plans. An implanted tracker or memory stick. Could be either about his whereabouts or some of his consulted crimes.'

'And you don't know what it is yet?'

'Not yet. Minnie said they only got here yesterday, and she hasn't examined them yet. We'll do it either today or tomorrow, but we must be quick.'

'Guys, did you hear that?' Scarlett suddenly asked. She had paused her activity, and was listening intently.

'Yes,' Sherlock said, slowly rising from the desk. He carefully walked over to the door and listened. With a sudden move, he snatched his mobile from his pocket. After a moment, his face hardened.

'There's trouble downstairs. Minnie texted me. She managed to sneak out of the building, saw two men with masks.' Sherlock thought for a moment, then turned around and suddenly all the shutters went down at once, and the lights went out.

Chapter 3

The darkness was intimidating.

'John? Where are you?' I asked.

'I'm over here. Can you reach the desk to your left?'

I turned around to reach out, ran my hand across some metal drawers and eventually got hold of the wooden surface of the desk.

'I've got it, where am I supposed to go?'

'Face the desk, and then go left until you find a cupboard below it,' John directed me.

As quickly as possible I felt my way through the darkness. 'I think I've got it. Which drawer?'

'Let me do this.' Suddenly, Sherlock was standing next to me, lighting the way in front of him with his phone. I slapped my forehead. Sherlock fetched the lock and dashed over to the door.

'You agree we're safer in the dark, don't you?' he asked, turning off his phone.

'That was you?' I complained.

'Of course! Now, get away from the door as far as possible!' he ordered.

'John?'

'I'm here, mind the slab,' he answered me.

Sherlock had turned off his phone now. The noises from outside came closer and closer until they became two pairs of footsteps. I nervously stumbled in the direction of John's voice, feeling my way around the slab. Then I stretched out my hands and suddenly felt John's face. Unconsciously, I let my fingers glide over his cheeks. He had closed his eyes.

A loud bang shook the room. They had hit a door, but not the one to our room. At the sound John instinctively pulled me under the desk. He put his arms around me protectively as we crouched between two cupboards.

'Sherlock, get down!' he hissed trenchantly.

Sherlock didn't answer. He halted near the door. *What is he up to?*

The seconds stretched into torturing minutes. The noise from outside the door grew louder; they'd gone back into the hall. We heard voices before a shot rang through the air. The voices ceased, but the steps came closer to our door. Sherlock was still standing there like a statue; I wanted to seize him, drag him away from there, but John restrained me with all his might.

'He's got a plan, believe me,' he whispered into my ear when suddenly we heard the sound of a lock pick scratching at the door.

When the lock gave a sighing click, nothing more than a silent ray of light spread on the floor, slowly broadening until a just as terrifyingly silent shadow appeared in it. When I gasped, John's hand flew to cover my mouth, quivering violently. Then, with a smooth step, a black figure entered the room. It stood still for a second, spreading menace with its presence.

Then a scream – but from the intruder. I could see Sherlock drawing back a pipe as the man shrank away from the blow, but with his next move he caught the pipe as it whooshed through the air. Sherlock dodged the blow – the pipe hit the other wing of the door – and Sherlock caught the man by the throat, dragging him half into the shadow.

First, there was a gasp, then another scream, and the man dropped the pipe. After a moment of heavy breathing, the black figure struggled free from Sherlock's grip. A fist rushed through the air landing right in Sherlock's face – a gasp – stumbling steps. John could barely hold himself back.

The black figure rushed over to the files on the opposite table, but Sherlock was on him within a second, slamming him against the desk. Both men struggled with each other for a while. Sherlock's back came in the light as he tried to keep his grip firm around the wriggling arms of his opponent who suddenly whirled around, grabbed the pipe and thrust it forward.

Sherlock's scream turned my stomach. The pipe had hit him in the stab wound at his side. With a groan, he sank to the floor.

'Well, dear brother, I did expect you to be in better shape,' remarked the black figure, casually switching on the light.

'Mycroft!' John yelled as he sprang out from under the desk. 'How could you? He's your brother!'

He ran over to Sherlock, kneeling down next to him. I rushed after him in utter astonishment. Blood had started to spread over the detective's light grey shirt. He was biting his lip in pain.

'I need a compress, quick!' John ordered.

'Where are they?' I asked, halfway through the door.

'Forget it! I'll fetch them. Open his shirt and press a tissue to the wound until I come back.'

Before I could say a word, he furiously hastened past me. At first, I just stared at Sherlock's brother, who was actually supposed to be detained by Moriarty's men, and... *My God, his brother!* My eyes went down to Sherlock, who was curled up on the floor, his blood dripping down.

'You bastard!' I hissed at the intruder.

My hands were shaking when I opened Sherlock's shirt. It was me who had injured him in the first place. My pulse went up button by button. To my surprise I was completely calm when I saw the wound; I couldn't tell whether it had gotten deeper because of all the blood, but it was certainly larger. I fetched a handkerchief from the desk and pressed it gently to the wound. Sherlock grabbed my wrist. I knew I was hurting him, but I had to stop the bleeding.

'It's OK, Sherlock, you'll be all right. John will be here in a minute,' I tried to soothe him. Eventually he let go and closed his eyes.

By the time John returned, the handkerchief was soaked, and my hands were covered in blood.

'My God,' he said when I took off my hands. 'I hope he won't require stitches...'

He gave me a new handkerchief, then carefully cleaned the wound and covered it with a compress that he fastened with leucoplast. I went to throw away the bloody rags he had handed to me. I had Sherlock's blood on my hands again; it made me tremble as I walked.

'Is there a water tap somewhere by any chance?' I asked helplessly when I couldn't spot one in the room.

'The toilets are down the hall to the right,' John informed me.

I went to wash my hands. I could barely look at my face; guilt kept thrusting out a fist at me from behind the glass each time my eyes met my reflection. With a shudder, I dried my hands and ran back to John who was now yelling at Mycroft.

'You bloody bastard! This is a serious injury! We don't even know if he'll get internal bleedings! You could've torn his kidney! What the *hell* were you thinking!? This is not about sibling rivalry anymore here, *do you understand!?*' He roughly grabbed Mycroft by the collar and pushed him against the wall with a bang.

Mycroft took his mask off to reveal an unimpressed face. Somehow, he reminded me of an ostrich. 'How was I to know he had a little scratch already? May I ask who did that?'

A shudder went down my back, but John only snarled at Mycroft with disgust.

'You mind your own business,' he hissed. He let go of him and turned to Sherlock, who was trying to stand up. I rushed to help, supporting him from under his arms while he pulled himself up at one of the desks.

'Easy, Sherlock, easy. You won't get anywhere like this,' John tried to convince him, but Sherlock was trying so hard to stand straight that it would've been more effort to get him to the ground again. Together we made sure he didn't fall. After some moments he let go of us as seemed capable of standing on his own, even though not very securely.

'John, we need to go to Salvatore's, now. Call a cab, please,' Sherlock croaked, gasping in pain in between the words.

John looked at him askance, considering whether the detective was fit to estimate if he was able to stay on his own feet. Eventually, he got out his phone, shaking his head. I noticed Sherlock squint the moment John turned around. He tried hard to keep up his countenance, but the pain came back hard on his face now. I went over to quietly support him again.

'Thank you,' he murmured with a concerned look at John, who was now talking on the phone.

Suddenly, Mycroft chuckled.

'What is so funny here?' I barked at him.

'Oh, nothing, nothing at all,' he twanged.

Sherlock squeezed my shoulder. 'Don't bother talking to him, you won't get anything out of him anyway. I know why he's laughing, and no, it's not what you think. It's completely irrelevant.'

I gave him a hard stare. I wasn't totally satisfied, but when I saw how he looked at his brother, scanning him fiercely, I suddenly noticed a glimpse of fear coming up in Sherlock's eyes. There was something wrong, and I had no idea what.

When John came back, I quickly let go of Sherlock.

'They'll be here in a minute. Let's get you downstairs,' he said to Sherlock, who simply smiled and walked cautiously out of the room.

As we followed him, we saw a shadow through the glass door at the end of the hall. When we drew nearer, I gave a cry.

It was the body of a man lying on the steps, shot between his eyes.

John rushed over to me and put his arms around my shaking shoulders.

'Jesus! Did you shoot him!?' he shouted at Sherlock's brother.

'Oh yes,' replied Mycroft, turning up his nose. 'He was a double agent. Pity, he had a lot of talent.'

* * *

Out in the street, the cab was already waiting for us. There was something suspicious about it, perhaps it was the driver's open glare or the headlights flickering slightly.

'Sherlock, let's take another—'

But in he went, despite my words, as he always did, so we went after him, Scarlett following me into the back while Mycroft got in the front. The car sped off before I could even finish my sentence.

Suddenly, Sherlock put his lips to my ear. 'Listen. If anyone in here makes a sudden move, protect Scarlett. Do you hear me?'

Totally bewildered, I found myself nodding.

Sherlock's remark strained all my muscles for the rest of the drive. On the one hand, I wanted nothing less than to turn my eyes away from Scarlett, but on the other hand I dreaded that I might miss the 'sudden move'. I kept my eyes sharp for any twitch that might cost our lives.

In the meantime, Sherlock, whom I could only spare anxious glances at from time to time, kept scanning his brother and the driver meticulously. Once, he looked up to the ceiling above the two. He was searching for something either on them or on this cab, which was why he got on it despite the suspicious circumstances. What could Mycroft possibly have to keep from his brother?

The journey seemed to have no end. *Is Salvatore's really that far from Bart's?* At first, I thought this must be the tension of Sherlock's warnings. After what seemed like ages, I allowed myself a look outside and noticed we were taking quite the detour. The driver took us down the Strand right to Admiralty Arch. Charging more for an unnecessary loop way wasn't quite the style of crime Moriarty preferred to follow.

I gave Sherlock a questioning look, but he only put a finger to his lips. Scarlett, meanwhile, naïvely smiled at Trafalgar Square passing by outside the window.

A few moments later we turned right into Cockspur Street. The cab stopped in a back road to its left. I thought this was it, but the driver only turned up the headlights a few times. Too late did the thought of it being Morse came into my head. He then stopped and turned the cab around. Sherlock smiled complacently with a tint of admiration in his eyes.

Scarlett gave me a questioning look, but I just shrugged.

The car stopped about fifteen minutes later. When we got out, I could hardly believe my eyes: we were at Salvatore's.

I said before that we were being abducted, although I threw aside the thought at that moment, too. And Sherlock knew all along, as always, and he didn't tell me what was going on, as *always*, but this time, he should have told me...

Inside the restaurant, I was immediately aware of a strange tension in the room as though each guest was either held at gunpoint or a hired killer. Looking at Scarlett, I could see a cold rigidity in her eyes impeding her movements.

Sherlock strode over to a table in the back and sat down. We followed suit.

'What are we doing here again?' I asked him.

'I want to know how my dear brother escaped,' he said, turning to Mycroft with a smirk.

'Well, it wasn't easy, if that's what you want to know. Though, I never thought you'd care. Clearly not an advantage, but then you never listened to me anyway,' Mycroft grumbled.

'Will you tell us already?' I growled at him.

'There's really not much to it apart from getting your hands dirty, which I detest, but then since my dear brother couldn't spare the time to get me out...' Mycroft threw a disapproving glance at Sherlock.

'Enough of this! Everyone has resentments. We know that, but two show-offs are definitely not making that better. Either you tell us now, or you tell us *now*,' Scarlett interrupted.

Mycroft seemed to be taken aback by her fierceness. Finally, he sighed. 'Fine. If you're so eager to ask, Miss...'

'Vendalle, I'm—'

'John's ex-girlfriend at Uni, I know. Obvious.'

'Mycroft!' I shouted. Sherlock, who was sat between me and Mycroft, grabbed my arm and stopped me from jumping.

'You can brawl with him later, though I wouldn't recommend it,' he coolly pointed out. Then he drew me closer to him and whispered, 'Don't touch him. You understand?'

I hesitantly nodded. The Holmes brothers were yet another mystery I never expected to solve.

Mycroft, in the meantime, ordered a cup of coffee. The rest of us weren't in the mood to really drink.

'In fact,' he finally began, 'the only thing it takes are some willing participants. I knew there were about ten men guarding the house they kept me in, and from the stains on his wrist and the darkened fairly visible arteries on the back of his hand I could see the one guarding my 'cell' had a little weakness for a special kind of drug, not very common in Europe. He was clearly still taking it, so I assumed he must be getting it from the black market. It came in handy, therefore, that I frequently let my agents check on that sort of business. I told him I knew where he could get the stuff a little cheaper. He took the bait immediately, stupid bloke. I gave him a little note, and eventually when he got his day off, he went there. There, my people were waiting for him, telling him they'd get new stuff in a few days. But that was not the only thing they told him. I had planned that scenario before, and the idea was to convince him that one of his superiors shared his addiction, and that in order make himself a little popular for a promotion, he could only win if he invited him to have a little drink.

'Of course, the guy totally fell for it. I could see he had taken a lot when he came in the next day. He was still a bit drowsy, in fact. Before that I hadn't missed the chance of taking in the other guard for me, Morgan was that second guy's name. I told him he should be careful with Gulton, the first bloke. Of course, I also told him Gulton was planning to get him out of the way in order to get promoted, because their superior actually preferred him to Gulton, so he got a little frightened. They kept me in such a small house with so few people, I got to know them sooner or later. Morgan had a little 'crush' on Miss Fletcher, the cook they'd hired. She was totally ignorant of the business they were up to, though; they were always careful to keep her out of the way. In fact, she was the best cover for the hideout, because she was sociable and authentically wiped all suspicion from the neighbours' minds. By the time I figured out all their schedules, and knew which day Gulton was on guard at the back door, I had arranged two little meetings. Gulton would try to get promoted, and Morgan would get his rendezvous. I faked a note from Miss Fletcher so Morgan would get the impression that she knew everything and was still 'deeply in love' with him - all that useless gibberish. He fell for it. Since he was on duty, he sent her back a note telling her to come down to the room adjoining my cell.

'She did, of course, but by the time she arrived, Gulton had already tried to get his superior high, which immediately got him searched. The superior gave him a good reproof and assured him he was going to report him to "the boss". For that he needed Morgan, though, because he was closest in the building and best acquainted with Gulton. I knew they had other agents testifying at such reports, because it had happened before to one of their men who had failed to trace someone - an illustrious person of some kind. Morgan was then called upstairs and Miss Fletcher arrived at my cell with quite a surprise. I told her to release me by orders of Her Royal Majesty, the Queen, and due to the questions she'd been asked by the neighbours about her strange employers and the screams at night, she all too inclined to believe me. They'd had to give her the key to the front door of the house, or she would've gotten too suspicious to take the job. Since there was a whole lot of trouble going on upstairs, the front door was only guarded by a camera that the superior was definitely too busy to watch now. He wasn't going to his room for a while anyway. Apart from that, Miss Fletcher passed through the front door unnoticed every evening, so I knew no alarm would go off if she let me out. And that's what she did. I told her to disappear immediately, to leave London as soon as possible, and then I disappeared myself. I nicked a mobile from an old woman and got in touch with my assistant, who was kind enough to pick me up and provide me with some food and a mask. I had expected you to be in the company of Moriarty's men by the time I arrived at Bart's, which is why my entry might have been a little rough – for that I offer my apologies,' Mycroft finished, tucking his hands under his chin like Sherlock usually did.

Sherlock now looked at his brother with cold indifference.

After a long, awkward silence, I finally decided to call the waiter and ordered some baked beans for a second breakfast. Scarlett said that she'd like some, too, but the Holmes brothers wouldn't have a bite.

'Digesting makes me slow, too much blood in the stomach and too little in the brain,' Sherlock used to say.

At least there were two of us eating, so it wasn't too awkward. I mean, regarding the food; regarding the conversation, well, there was none for quite some time.

I was used to the disapproving looks between Mycroft and Sherlock, and them currying favour with each other's arrogance, but for Scarlett this was an entirely new experience. Eventually, I tried to break the North Pole ice, which had miraculously found its way into Central London – who said CO_2-emission caused climate change?

'What now, Sherlock? Can we see Barker?'

'Shut up, John!'

I saw fear in Sherlock's face; only a trace of it in his angry expression, but I knew exactly how it looked. I had done something stupid – I knew how that looked in his face as well. The moment I realised, the hired killers had already risen from their seats and surrounded us. Four tall men appeared behind us. Before I had time to move, a gun pressed into my back, preventing me from doing so. Four pairs of cold eyes in marble faces. We slowly raised our hands.

'Easy, gentlemen,' murmured a man who appeared to be in command, pushing the gun harder into Sherlock's back. He flinched.

Scarlett's eyes grew larger and larger with worry, and her fists were quivering. I could see she was about to jump up and punch someone if it hadn't been for our opponents' choice of weapon.

'Mr Holmes, would you be so kind as to follow us?'

Sherlock smiled grimly, but I could already see his victory dawning on the left corner of his lips. The man led him into the kitchen. The other three remained with us.

'You may put down your hands now, but not one wrong move! No speaking or she dies first,' snarled the guy behind Scarlett. We sat in an awfully straining silence, only interrupted by clinking dishes and extraordinarily loud water taps.

Suddenly, there was a slap and a groan of pain. It was Sherlock's voice. My muscles contracted.

Another slap, silent this time. Then we heard a harsh voice being raised, but it was so muffled we couldn't distinguish a word.

The scream that followed turned my stomach.

Scarlett clutched her mouth.

What are they doing to Sherlock? What do they want?

* * *

I didn't know a voice could cause so much pain in my gut. The echo of Sherlock's scream faded in my head, taking the horrible images of his distorted face with it, only to be replaced by another scream that tore the silence. It wasn't Sherlock this time; the voice was hoarse and a bit higher than his, only lowered by age.

John seemed to know that voice; his head went up with a start, bitter realisation in his face. I wanted to move, to do something, to soothe John in any way. I only slowly lifted my hand near his, but immediately the man behind me grabbed my arm, pushed it into my back, and slammed my head on the table. Then he thrust his gun into my temple.

John winced, staring at me in horror. He had seen me dead – I could see it in his eyes. Slowly, the icy cold touch of the barrel on my skin reached my senses. My head was throbbing while my veins were pumping against the metal circle on my temple. How ironic, the circle as a sign of endlessness...

Sherlock screamed again. A commotion followed. Loud bangs. Bumping and rumbling, shouts and gasps of outrage.

Suddenly everything went quiet. For quite some time, we could only hear a low, muffled voice. I closed my eyes to try and catch a word, but failed. I opened my eyes when I heard a strange clinking sound. To my astonishment John was almost smiling.

Before I could give him a questioning look, the kitchen door was slammed open and Sherlock came out, blood matting his face and hair, but wearing a broad grin. He straightened his suit and brushed the dust off his sleeves. I blinked in disbelief.

'Would you please show us outside, gentlemen? You can also go looking for another job if you want to disobey your orders, I'm only forwarding them to you. Get moving or I'll do to you what I just did to the others, and I'd highly recommend having a look at what happened to them before I'd opt for that if I were you.' Sherlock was slightly out of breath, but when he started talking as fast as a racing car to show off, you couldn't tell he'd been disturbed in any way.

The agents detaining us virtually shrank back and vanished into the kitchen. My arm could finally unfold, and I could breathe when I straightened up.

'Jesus,' John sighed.

Sherlock came over to us and shoved us both towards the door while Mycroft came ambling after us.

Chapter 4

'What the hell, Sherlock!' John blustered when we were outside. We were making our way to the Underground station at Oxford Circus. 'Could you just for one second not be a drama queen and explain what's going on!?'

Sherlock and I both smiled at him.

'Later, we've got some business to do now, haven't we, *Mycroft*?'

His brother looked at him in astonishment. 'Oh – yes,' Mycroft replied coolly.

On looking at Sherlock's smeared face again, I pulled out another handkerchief I found in my pocket, and gave it to him. He took it with a grateful smile, and wiped off as much of the blood as he could manage.

When we entered the station, a strange smell tickled my nose. Before we got on a train, I fetched myself a bottle of water from a vending machine. Wetting another handkerchief, I stuck it to Sherlock's bleeding temple where it stayed until we got on the train.

We had nearly a whole carriage to ourselves, except for the old lady sitting perched into a corner. I could feel John buzzing with energy, threatening to explode, but I could tell from Sherlock's expression that he would not yet say a word.

'Sherlock, will you finally tell us what happened? How did you get out of there? Who were these men? Apart from the obvious fact that they belonged to Moriarty, of course. Will you just for once not be all mysterious and talk?'

He would not. When Sherlock looked at John, shaking his head with a superior smile, he was not being a drama queen. He was acting.

His presence suddenly didn't feel natural anymore, but slightly fierce. In a remote corner of his eyes, there was terror. Sherlock knew John wouldn't see it, but he didn't anticipate that I would. I wondered whether Mycroft saw it. *What kind of brother is he anyway?*

* * *

Since I couldn't get any information out of Sherlock, I stared at the ceiling and wondered where we were going. We were on the Bakerloo line towards Harrow & Wealdstone, which usually took us to Baker Street Underground station. After the strange route we had taken to Salvatore's, I didn't let myself believe that's where we were headed at all. I looked at Scarlett. She was pale but alert, squinting her eyes slightly as if there was something she wanted to conceal. Mycroft looked overly interested in the walls of the Underground tunnel and Sherlock was studying his brother. I couldn't possibly suppose he had missed him, so what was wrong there? *Certainly, they hadn't brainwashed him in Salvatore's kitchen? Not that one would notice any difference.*

I wondered if he was injured further than his old wounds and the ones they'd inflicted upon his head. It must've been a horrible pain when he had screamed, and that didn't seem to have come from the cuts and scratches in his face. I winced at the thought.

Intuitively, Scarlett's hand was on my arm. 'Everything okay, John?'

I wanted to kiss her hand. I wanted to kiss her, apologise for every little wrong word I had used, for not having had the courage to go after her when she had left me back then. Instead, I gulped and barely had the strength to say, 'Yeah, I'm fine.'

She looked at me for a long moment, and with a knowing smile said, 'Good.'

She seemed to understand exactly what I was thinking. I didn't dare to take her hand. She was a different person now. I had no right.

Sherlock's words rang in my head, 'There's been something with her boyfriend.'

I was afraid I might bring her trauma back if I tried to win her affections again. I couldn't bear to be the reason for her memories distorting her face.

To my astonishment Scarlett ran her hand down my arm and secretly placed it on mine. I slowly turned my hand around to take hers, but then I flinched at the pain when her cold fingers touched the burnt spots.

'Sorry!' she exclaimed, attempting to pull back her hand, but I held it firmly in mine.

'It's all right, they're actually cooling, that's... er... very good... of them,' I stammered, and she smiled.

* * *

We got off the Tube at Paddington station.
'What are we doing here?' John asked.

107

'I need to talk to Billy. He'll have to come round to 221B for tea some time,' Sherlock announced with that strange artificial smile I had seen on him a few times already. It seemed very unlikely for him to invite anyone for tea right now.

'Who's Billy?' I asked.

'Bill Wiggins, chemist, head of his homeless network, if you want to put it like that,' John answered.

'I see.'

A few minutes later, we entered a side street. Some yellowish bundle was sitting in a corner, playing with a spray can.

'You go' some spare change for me, Mr 'olmes?' mumbled the bundle, poking Mycroft with the can. He disgustedly frisked aside.

Sherlock chuckled.

'Tea on Friday at seven, my flat. Some flowers would be welcome, Billy,' Sherlock instructed the boy casually, but with a stern look in his eyes. He secretly placed a banknote in a bundled-up pocket and squeezed the boy's hand.

Billy nodded. 'All righ', sir. Thank you, sir. Have a nice day,' he called after us.

Before we got on the Tube again, Sherlock seriously went into a phone box just to argue with someone on the line for a few minutes. When he got out, he constantly texted someone all the way to the platform. He even got on a different compartment than we did. When I decided to go over, John held me back, saying that Sherlock knew what he was doing.

The ride was long, though it only lasted four stops. I noticed Mycroft's fingers twitch from time to time. He had something of a strangely composed air about him anyway. There were stitches around his ear, almost invisible in the shadow of his hair, and very small purple spots around his nostrils. *Stitches... why?* A very unlikely means of torturing someone. *Brainwashing? During his imprisonment?* It seemed rather logical, but why the stitches in that particular spot? There were much more convenient spots to get to the brain. *Impairing his hearing sense?* Didn't seem to have had that effect. I couldn't make a thing out of it. Then there were the spots around his nose. *Has he been exposed to enormous cold?* But that would leave larger traces.

Then it hit me.

His hair was dyed! I could see the slightly lighter hairline in one very small spot. That wasn't necessarily strange. Although, the dark red shade he had chosen to dye his hair with looked rather unfashionable for the M.I.6.

M.I.6? I had to think again how I had got that impression. There was nothing in his general appearance that could've told me that, so I tried to remember what I had last observed.

His pocket! There was a card sticking out of the jacket. Undoubtedly, it was a well-sewed, expensive leather pass with a tiny corner of the M.I.6. emblem stamped on its cover. Very careless of him to let it stick out like this. *Could it be fake? Is Sherlock's brother a criminal? How do I know the sign?*

Anne's face suddenly appeared next to Mycroft's. Smiling, she pointed at her head, at his, at mine.

I closed my eyes before I could drift into a daze again.

'You all right?' John asked instantly. I didn't open my eyes, but seized his arm and laid my head on his shoulder. Carefully, he lifted my hand and placed around my shoulders.

'You can keep my head if I lose it, John, all right?' I said with quiet fear.

He mirrored the frown in my face, and thought for a moment. Then, he said, 'Sherlock already has a skull. I don't think we need another one.'

I burst out laughing.

109

When we finally arrived in Baker Street, Sherlock had become very weak. He was pale and sweat was pouring down his temples. When John wasn't looking, I would support him sometimes. He gratefully took my arm, but the tightness of his grip was telling.

Once in the flat, he sank into his armchair.

'John, get the aid kit. Now, please,' I urged with an anxious eye on Sherlock.

John hurried away, and I knelt down next to Sherlock. His was breathing heavily. I opened his jacket. The blood stain on his shirt was freshly wet. I opened it up for the second time that day.

The wound was larger than I had expected. It had burst open. I took out a handkerchief and carefully wiped all the blood around it. Sherlock twitched, but didn't say a word. John was taking too long, so I pressed another handkerchief to the wound. Sherlock groaned with pain, but I didn't move my hands.

The fact that I'd done this to him no longer pained me like it used to, but the sound he made sent chills down my spine. When I looked at his face, jaw clenched, lips parted and nostrils widened, my pulse painfully went up with fear, but I knew I had to wait for John.

Mycroft, meanwhile, went to get some coffee from the kitchen.

When John came back, I stood up to wet a tissue for the cuts in Sherlock's face. I heard a strange noise coming from the kitchen. A look through the door showed me the most preposterous expression on Mycroft's face, but it disappeared from his face as fast as it had come up, so I quickly went to the bathroom instead. With several compresses in hand, I went back to John, who had busied himself with treating Sherlock.

Carefully, I dabbed at the cuts and scratches on Sherlock's face. One was very near to his left eye. Worried it might swell, I told him to hold a cold pack to it. His eyes were half closed, but he managed to raise the pack to his temple.

'I really hope he doesn't have internal bleedings,' John averred when he was done closing the wound again.

'Shouldn't we call an ambulance?' I asked. John shook his head.

'After today, I certainly don't trust any driver with Sherlock's life. Moriarty might have infiltrated every car in London! There's nothing we can do for the moment, since he's too weak to move. Sherlock?'

His hand with the cold pack had slipped off his face and his eyes were closed now.

'Sherlock!' I said a little louder.

He tried to speak, but couldn't. I took his head into my hands, and held it up.

'Sherlock! Stay awake! What's wrong with him, John?' I cried frantically.

'I don't know, because I don't know what they made him take,' John replied, feeling Sherlock's pulse. 'It's like he's falling asleep...'

Together we moved him to his bedroom.

'We need to get him into a recovery position, so he doesn't choke on his own vomit,' John instructed.

'What did they do to him?' I asked desperately.

'I wish I knew. They must have drugged him with something, but I can't find out what it was without the right equipment.'

John quickly scanned him again. After a beat, he resolved, 'I'm phoning Lestrade – you wait here with him.' And out he dashed, the phone in his hand, ready to dial.

'Sherlock, come on! You can't just fall asleep.' I nudged him. Blood dripped on the side of his pillow. He was so pale.

John was quietly, yet agitatedly talking to Lestrade, but I could hardly distinguish the words.

Everything seemed to fade away. Only the blood on the pillow remained. I forgot where it came from. He had too many injuries. We had no idea how bad his injuries actually were. *All the blood... Sherlock...* With a jerk, he began muttering in pain.

'Mycroft... not Mycroft...'

I laid my hand on his forehead, his skin hot underneath my fingers.

Queen Anne appeared, furiously rushing towards us with murder in her eyes. I couldn't –

move, wouldn't be able to – move... in time!

Everything was turning

But I *had to* stop her

Faintly, I could perceive a gun in her hand

and a sharp clicking sound –

In an instant, I covered Sherlock's head with my body. Then I heard myself scream.

John was next to me after a split second. 'Scarlett, oh my God! Is everything all right? Did you see something again?'

I still couldn't move, and somewhere I felt a burning pain. 'The gun, she's... got a gun...' I stammered as John lifted me up. 'I heard it click.'

'No, Scarlett, that was just my watch. I reset it— Oh my God!'

I had turned around. There was a bleeding wound in my upper arm. A grazing shot. *How is this possible?*

'Where is she? Where did you see her? Get down! Get out of the room!' John shouted, quickly pulling Sherlock off the bed onto the floor.

Shortly after me, he dashed into the living room and went to fetch his gun. When he came back, he hastened over to Sherlock's bedroom and closed the door behind him. I couldn't stand leaving him there, so I followed him before anyone could stop me and knelt down behind the bed next to him. His gun was ready to fire. But there was no one to be seen. And the window... was still in – *one piece*... Turning to the door, I screamed again. The bullet was stuck in the keyhole.

'John! She's in here! She must be!'

'Sh! There is no one there,' John had to convince himself, but actually he was shushing me, so I wouldn't attract attention rather than because he thought this wasn't real. He was terrified. His jaw was clenched, and his lips were trembling.

We both perceived a breath being held in the room, a breath that wasn't ours. When we dared to look under the bed, there was complete darkness. *Is there someone on the other side?*

Then with a sudden impulse, John leapt onto the bed and

fired. Silence. No scream. Nothing.

John exhaled. 'Nobody there... It's just the blanket... Hanging lower down than on the other side...'

I sank to the floor in relief. 'Oh... Oh my, John.'

When he came back, I rose and wrapped my arms around him.

* * *

Scarlett was shaking all over. I tried to hold her tightly so she would stop, but her convulsions were too strong. Stroking her back, I noticed I still had the gun in my hand. Throwing it onto the bed, I noticed Sherlock was still sleeping on the floor.

'Sorry, but we need to get him up. I don't think he'll be pleased if he wakes up down there,' I remarked, and she shyly laughed.

'I'd like to see his face though,' she joked, if a little wearily.

We were still chuckling when we lifted up the consulting detective together. When I shrugged my shoulders, Sherlock's head nodded in sleepy agreement, and we laughed out loud until our tension had somewhat dissipated.

'I think we should carry him to the sofa. Who knows what's in here? He won't be pleased there either, but better grumpy than shot,' I stated with a smile. Scarlett nodded Sherlock's head again, and we brought him over.

When we had laid him down, I suddenly thought of his brother. 'Where's Mycroft?'

'I don't know. When did you see him last?' she responded.

'No idea. It was all so hectic,' I murmured.

While Scarlett settled into my armchair and closed her eyes, I went to have a look around the flat, but Mycroft was nowhere to be seen. I was just twisting my mind over all the places he could have gone to in London when suddenly he stepped out of the kitchen with a steaming teacup in his hands.

'Hope you don't mind my getting something to drink. Was there any trouble? I heard shooting.'

I could barely keep myself from shouting at the arrogant bastard! I dashed forward and slammed him against the door frame.

'John, John, calm down,' Scarlett insisted quietly. 'Let him drink his tea first, or someone will get seriously hurt.'

114

Begrudgingly, I did as she said. Mycroft enjoyed every moment sipping his tea in slow motion.

'You don't offer seats here, do you?' he remarked dryly in between.

Scarlett grabbed my arm and pulled me down into my armchair when my breath grew more rapid. Then she sat down on my lap.

'Sorry, we're one seat short, but you can certainly sit down in the kitchen, seeing you've already made yourself at home in it,' she retorted, and I had to smile at her nerve.

With a snort, Mycroft disappeared as he was bidden.

When I sat down next to her, Scarlett leaned her head against mine. For a while we just sat there, recovering from the shock. I pulled a tape out of the aid kit and wrapped it around the wound in Scarlett's arm. When I tenderly twitched at the knot to adjust its ends, she smiled.

'It looks just like a pair of fox ears.' She got up, picked up a pen and sitting down on my lap again, she carefully drew a fox's eyes and snout beneath the knot. The whiskers grew especially long. I chuckled at her being so child-like.

'Be careful, John Watson, or you'll also get whiskers,' she threatened cheekily.

'No, thank you.' I laughed.

She threw a mischievous glance at Sherlock, pursed her lips and then pointed the pen through the kitchen door at Mycroft.

'I bet *he'd* look pretty fancy in fox whiskers,' she finally decided, but in the end, she just put the pen away.

'Do you think she's still in the bedroom, John? Did you lock the door?' she suddenly asked.

'I, no, I didn't.' He went and locked it immediately. 'How she got in there is beyond me, though.'

'But you believe me, John, don't you?'

'Of course, I do. There's alarmingly real evidence.'

With all my mental might, I tried to work out where the bullet might come from. *What would Sherlock say?* The window was intact, so the shooter had fired from inside. We had checked the whole room, even under the bed though. Even behind it there was nothing at all, only the blanket. The case was straightforward: the blanket must have fired the shot.

'You haven't, by any chance, figured it out already, have you?' I snarled at Mycroft the next moment. He was still busying himself with his tea alibi.

'What? Your inability to protect your friends, or my brother's drug problems?' Mycroft sneered with satanic butter in his voice.

'You bastard!' I bellowed. I wanted to stand up and strangle him, but Scarlett was still sitting on my lap.

'Let him say what he has to say. I want to know whether that's why Sherlock's sleeping. And if there's something we can do,' she argued.

Her care about him always frustrated me in two ways: firstly, it reminded me that *I* should be taking care of him, and secondly, it made me uncertain about how much she cared about me. Mycroft gave me a slimy smirk.

'I presume he's been taking drugs recently – I'd say not more than a few days ago. Out of curiosity this time, I think, since it's one I haven't smelled yet. *She's* tried it as well.' He pointed at Scarlett. 'It might have affected his condition in a way that he couldn't stand today's struggles, I find it very unlikely for a single use. That means he's taken more recently. John, you didn't get him away from it. You failed a few times to rescue both Sherlock and this young lady here from harm. I would spend some thought on my attitude if I were you, Dr Watson,' he concluded with a taunting smile.

If I ever thought I'd stop being offended by any remark of either of the Holmes brothers, I was mistaken. But I was also mistaken about something else at that moment. *About several things actually,* Sherlock would have said. And again, I was offended, despite the fact that I was only hearing his voice in my head. Typical.

For two long days Sherlock was hardly conscious. When he was awake, he was delirious, barely able to feed himself. I tried to wake him with the strong herbs he'd woken Scarlett up with the other day.

I asked Mrs Hudson a thousand things about drugs, which she only reluctantly answered; nothing that we could use for Sherlock's treatment. When I asked her about the 'strong herbs', though, she suddenly began acting strange. Not only did she stammer whenever I spoke to her, she also shuffled me out of her flat quite abruptly, as if she was embarrassed about something, but I couldn't put my finger on it. I had too much to worry about to give much thought to why she freely talked to Sherlock about drugs, but wouldn't give me the same information when he was in trouble. Even afterwards, I wasn't quite sure whether what happened the next day was related to the subject, but Sherlock would have seen it coming.

Thanks to Sherlock's non-existent help with chores, I was forced to add the shopping and, therefore, leaving Sherlock and Scarlett alone in Baker Street to my list of worries. In the shop, of course, the queues were endless, and I had a row with the machine, taking me the whole of three hours to get back. Then, as I finally went upstairs, I distinctly perceived a strange smell coming from Mrs Hudson's flat.

'Mrs Hudson! Is everything all right in there?'

I knocked, but no one opened. I knocked again, harder this time, but as the smell was getting stronger, I just kicked the door.

Mrs Hudson was sleeping on the table, still in the same clothes as yesterday, and from the kitchen a small, diaphanous cloud emerged.

I ran to the oven. A tray full of coal black ex-biscuits calmly started to fill the kitchen with smoke, but there were no flames yet. I quickly seized some towels and opened the darn thing, pulling out the tray, which was so hot I only felt a stinging pain – and flung it onto the stove. Then I switched off the oven and opened the window. By this time, I was coughing heavily, and when I looked at my hands, pink bubbles were forming on my skin. There was something pungent in the smoke which made me wonder if Mrs Hudson had baked the strong herbs into the biscuits, but when I saw the smoke sneaking into the living room, where the old lady was sleeping, I put the thought aside and closed the door tightly with some towels before I woke her.

'Mrs Hudson, you need to get up!'

She blinked in bewilderment a few times, as she slowly rose from her stool. 'Ah, John... what's that smell? I didn't... did I... Oh my, the biscuits!'

I kept her from running into the kitchen, but took her arm and gently guided her upstairs.

'The smoke needs to get out of the room first. I took care that nothing will burn. You can just sit here and rest,' I told her as I seated her in an armchair. Then I made her a cup of tea.

'Thank you, John. I can't believe I almost cooked the whole house, I'm so sorry... I have no idea what's got into me! Such a thing never happened to me before! But I can't think of what made me fall asleep... Thank you so much, dear,' she croaked.

'Well, no problem, Mrs Hudson, as long as I'm there to put out the fire,' I answered warmly.

In recompense for this strange little episode, Mrs Hudson kept bringing us food.

In order to kill some time Scarlett helped her to properly clean the oven after *The Adventure of the Coal Biscuits*.

Mycroft, in the meantime, took a strange interest in the furniture in our flat, which I tried to counteract by snarling at him whenever he touched things. Not being a psychopath, I had trouble to even imagine what might be going on his head. *Who does he think he is anyway?* It was as if someone was reading our whole private life without asking, and I could only prevent him from prying into a very limited number of events. Even more worrying was the fact that this kind of power was usually employed by someone on my side, who was now sleeping on the bloody couch, unable to defend us, or to see through things.

On the Friday which Sherlock had invited Billy for, something finally happened. I had just *absolutely unintentionally* spilt some of my tea on Mycroft's trousers, for moving the skull on the mantlepiece, when Scarlett called me over. She had spotted something on Sherlock, I could tell from her voice, but so could Mycroft. There was something unnatural about the way he was looking across from the kitchen... It took me some moments to recognise it, but there was curiosity in his eyes. I should've known by then, that something was wrong with him, but I didn't. *As usual.*

Scarlett had knelt down next to Sherlock, examining his right forearm. Her body was blocking my view, so I went over and knelt down beside her.

'Look, John. There's a red mark here, like a large pin prick. No encrusted blood on it, so this must be its actual size.

And then there is this glowing about it from under the skin. There's no inflammation around it, yet there is this reddish tinge.' She carefully wound her fingers around the spot. 'It's warm, John, warmer than the rest of his arm.' Tightening her grip, she frowned. 'There's something inside his arm, something round and hard, but very small. It's buzzing. I think it's a tracker!'

At first, I couldn't believe it, but when I felt it myself, there was no doubt in my mind. *Was that what had caused him so much pain in the restaurant?* I shivered at the thought. *What is it for? Is it a bug? Certainly not a camera, but who needs to see our faces? Did they drug him alongside planting this? And why is it glowing? They could've concealed it a lot more easily...*

'I should remove it,' I decided.

'No!' Scarlett grabbed my arm. 'I think he agreed to this on purpose. Otherwise, wouldn't he have told us to get rid of it immediately?'

She was right. Even if he'd been forced, he would've said something. *Is he being reckless again, playing the game to get high, or is this to his advantage? Is he cooperating with someone?* Surely Mycroft would've known, but he simply jumped on the drug affair. *So, he doesn't know...*

Scarlett seemed to be jumping to the same conclusions, observing him with care.

'Right,' I mumbled. Then I stood up and walked over to the kitchen to get myself some tea. Mycroft's eyes followed my movements. I had a feeling I should not drink *his* tea. Trying not to make anyone notice, I poured the rest of his former alibi into one of the lab plants and made a new pot of tea.

Scarlett was still kneeling in front of the sofa. She had Sherlock's face in her hands and cautiously inspected the side he'd been lying on. She frowned. Lost in thoughts, she ran her fingers through his hair fleetingly. Then she stood up. I was a bit taken aback, but after a moment I remembered I had made the second mug for her.

'For you,' I said when she sat down in my armchair.

'That's very nice of you, but I'm not actually thirsty,' she excused herself, a little embarrassed.

'Come on, you need to drink something to warm you up. I can see that, I'm a doctor. But I'm also human, and I'm too lazy to bring this back into the kitchen now,' I urged her. She took it with a smile.

The sun was setting already, and soon enough it was dark. We said nothing for a long time. I realised I had forgotten to punch Mycroft when he'd finished his tea. Actually, I felt punched myself.

Since we weren't alone, I didn't dare ask Scarlett what she'd been doing with Sherlock's head; it was none of my business anyway. Then again, I remembered Mycroft's remark that I had failed to protect Scarlett and Sherlock. It could be argued, Sherlock wasn't really mine to protect and it wasn't entirely my fault that he was lying injured on the couch. Only now that he was incapable of protecting himself, I didn't feel entirely free of responsibility.

I felt even more responsible for Scarlett's safety, though. She wouldn't even be in the midst of this danger if hadn't been for me. Thinking about it, I noticed I had only failed protecting either of them while trying to protect the other. *What if I have to decide between them? What if my decision is fatal to one of them?*

I couldn't cope with my thoughts, so I stood up to make more tea when something pinched me on the way.

'Ouch!' I got pinched a second time.

Only then did I realise I was standing next to the sofa, and Sherlock's eyelids were twitching angrily. Nobody could see it at the moment, because Mycroft was studying a bookshelf and my leg blocked Scarlett's view. Clearly, he didn't want them to notice he was awake. I wondered how long he had been awake for. In any case, it was his plan not yet to reveal it to anyone, so I just walked on and said, 'Probably just a lost mosquito', when Scarlett asked. I had to get her and Mycroft out of the room somehow, so I could talk to Sherlock. But I had a strange feeling when I thought of putting Scarlett and Mycroft together into one room. So, separately. I wanted to ask Sherlock how the *hell* I was supposed to manage this. I wanted to ask him a lot of things actually. A fact that stirred a surprisingly large amount of anger in me.

I was still running over possible ways of getting them out of the room when I found Mycroft already gone.

'He just went to the bathroom,' Scarlett explained, 'and I thought perhaps I should go up to my room and change before Billy shows up. I feel a little hot in this.'

'Of course,' I smiled to myself.

For a moment, she seemed to linger at the door, unable to leave. Then she said, 'John, I don't know, how to phrase this... Please don't think you failed to protect me, or Sherlock. I take all trouble gladly alongside you.'

A weak blush overcame my face. I could hardly believe I was not to be smashed by the weight falling off my shoulders. She took my hands and looked at them.

'They're getting better, aren't they?' she observed happily. I could only nod. Then she looked at me askance.

'What is it?' I asked. She just reached out and ran her fingers through my hair.

'It's damp,' Scarlett replied after a moment. Then she felt for hers. 'Is this sweat? Or do you have such damp air in here sometimes?'

'Usually the air is rather dry here,' I answered.

'Hmm. Well, then it must be sweat. Do get yourself another shirt as well, will you? I'll check the heating in my room.'

And off she went.

Then I remembered I actually had to talk to Sherlock, too. I quickly fetched two new shirts and brought one upstairs.

'The radiator is turned off, John. It must be the one downstairs. But thanks a lot.' She squeezed my hand as she took the shirt.

'You're welcome,' I replied hastily, and rushed back to Sherlock.

'Couldn't you have been a little quicker?' Sherlock groaned when I turned to him.

'You bastard! You were acting the whole time! You bloody malingerer! Now I want to hear a good defence!' I snapped.

'You'll get one, you'll get one. Help me up first,' he moaned. Shaking my head, I gave him a hand to sit up.

'I wasn't acting the entire time. Since you spotted the tracker already, you might think they injected something with it. Not true, they drugged me before I made the bargain for them to insert the tracker in my arm. I'll tell you the whole story later. I only woke up when you carried me to the sofa. They didn't give me enough.' He put his hands under his chin. 'I need to know what happened during the last seventy-two hours.'

I gave him a brief account of the events in the bedroom two days ago. Sherlock listened intently, his fingertips together, his eyes fixed on the door to his room.

When I finished, he declared, 'This makes things a little more complicated than I expected. Still, we need to keep up act. This is a trap, and I need it to work, John. When Billy comes, let him know about the plan. He'll have two boys with him to instruct. Try to keep Mycroft on this floor, but keep him at a safe distance from Scarlett. Do you have your gun?'

'Yes, it's over there.'

'Fetch it and keep it in your belt. Get some clothes to cover it.'

'But it's boiling in here!'

'Do as I say, or you might get yourself killed.'

I begrudgingly complied. When I came back, Sherlock had more instructions for me.

'You'll order pizza for dinner and take everyone into the kitchen. Keep the window open; never turn on the stove. Keep the kitchen door closed, but all others open. Let Mycroft sit at the window. You sit next to Scarlett. When you hear commotion outside, try to conceal it as long as you can; talk louder. I'll be backing you.'

A chill went down my back. *Why won't he tell me the whole plan?* But as I began to get furious, I heard steps coming down the stairs, and I knew he didn't have enough time. In an instant, he back to 'sleep' again.

'Is he all right? You look concerned,' Scarlett observed on entering the room.

'No, no, he's, um, really fine - actually...' I stammered, while getting pinched rather forcefully. Trying to conceal this second ominous mosquito attack, I continued with a sheepish smile, 'Shall we order pizza for dinner?'

'That'd be nice. Unless the pizza service is also infiltrated by your fan - what was he called again?'

'Moriarty,' I replied gloomily, 'and no, I hope not, but if it makes you feel better, Lestrade promised to be here after finishing work, so I can ask him to bring the pizza.'

She chuckled. 'Yeah, better safe than sorry.'

While I was talking to Lestrade, who was a bit annoyed but understood the circumstances, Mycroft finally came back from the toilet. I hadn't noticed he'd been gone for so long until I saw his cranky face again. It must've been nearly twenty minutes. *I guess he read my mind and actually did take a newspaper along*, I thought to myself.

Then I beckoned everyone to sit down in the kitchen, hastily putting Sherlock's test rigs off the table. Mycroft wanted to sit down at the door at first, but I quickly sat Scarlett down on that chair when he pulled it out.

'Very considerate, thank you,' I remarked with a most perfectly polite smile. Then I pulled out his chair for him, and laid the table.

Finally, we were all sitting in place and the game was on. The bell rang when we were about to have an awkward silence. But it wasn't Lestrade.

Billy was standing at the door with one of his shaggy companions. They were both breathless.

'They took Isaac! An' they're coming 'ere! Le' us in, le' us in!' Billy cried when I stepped out. I took them both inside immediately and locked the door. As Sherlock had instructed, I didn't take them up where everyone could hear.

'Who's after you? Where did you lose Isaac?' I asked the boy.

'A' Camden Lock. They jus' grabbed 'im. They're armed to the teeth, looked like agen's,' panted Billy, while the other one was just shaking. 'A' firs', we though' they were jus' normal police when they told us to stop sprayin', bu' then they recognised us or somethin', an' star'ed chasin' us. They 'ad guns, bu' they didn' shoo'. I swear they wan'ed to catch us alive! Finn fell once; he thinks 'e's broken 'is arm.'

The boy held his arm out for me to check.

'It's just a sprain, nothing too bad. Now, do you have any idea who they work for? Did they say anything?' I asked.

'No, we couldn' understand wha' they were sayin' once we were runnin'. They 'ad in-ear phones. Bu' they defini'ely don' belong to the police. We know those already. Sherlock told us to follow some o' Moriar'y's men a few times, bu' they didn' belong to the ones we've seen either. Sherlock said 'e 'ad somethin' impor'an' – wha' is i'?' Billy wanted to know.

'I don't know either,' I told them. I explained what I could from the snippets of a plan that Sherlock had provided me with; that he was only pretending to sleep, and why it was important that nobody should overhear our conversation. And of course, that they weren't, by any chance, to give away anything of what I had just said.

The bell rang again just as we went into the flat.

'Seriously, Lestrade! One minute earlier!' I growled. The boys looked at me askance.

'Pizza service,' I explained ironically but of course none of them got the joke. I gave a sigh and told them to go into the kitchen to introduce themselves. Shaking my head, I went downstairs and opened the door.

Once again, it wasn't Lestrade.

126

Chapter 5

I rushed down the stairs when I heard John scream. A man in a suit and sunglasses was cowering over John's motionless body. He immediately raised his gun at me. To my astonishment, I was totally calm, but the man wasn't; his left hand was twitching. There were stitches at his neck which suggested a recent operation. He must've been taken a considerable amount of analgesics that he stopped and was now nerve-wrecked. That could work to my advantage.

I raised my eyes in shock, staring at the empty space behind him. 'Oh my God, be quiet, just be quiet,' I stammered helplessly.

The man turned his head for a split second, which was all I needed to kick the gun out of his grip and strike his throat with the side of my hand. Before I could reach for the fallen gun, the man came at me again. I tried to kick him in the stomach, but he managed to catch my foot mid-air, sending me sprawling to the ground.

Meanwhile, John was slowly regaining consciousness, groaning and moving on the floor. My head was pounding from the fall, and at first, I just tried to struggle free, but then I realised, my hand was closer to the gun than the man's. I only had to distract him, so I wriggled and lashed out with my legs as hard as I could. At the same time, I painstakingly reached out for the gun. When I was close enough, I spat in the man's face, grabbed the gun and fired.

Please! Don't let him be dead, don't let me be a killer again, I heard myself thinking. I had only aimed at his shoulder.

When I opened my eyes again, I exhaled in relief. I had hit just where I had aimed, however, that wouldn't stop the man from coming at me. The moment he took his hand off the wound, I jumped up and knocked him out with the gun.

Breathing heavily, I bent down to a terrified John. He immediately grabbed my outstretched hands.

'Scarlett, are you all right? Is he dead?' he stammered as I helped him up.

'I'm all right, he's just unconscious. We need to tie him up,' I explained, laying my hands on his cheek to move his hair away from the wound at his temple. The blow must've knocked him out straight away.

'Come on,' I said after a moment, closing the front door. We carried up the heavy agent, and disposed of all his weapons. We tied him to a chair in the living room, next to Sherlock who appeared to be having bad dreams.

* * *

I tried hard to remember the plan. My aching head wasn't willing to spit it out quite easily. Mycroft at the window. All windows open. No, all the doors. *Was the kitchen window supposed to stay open?* We were supposed to stay in the closed kitchen. Commotion. *Didn't he say something about commotions as well? Was I supposed to conceal them? Well, this would be a good opportunity... What is going on outside, for God's sake?*

The kitchen door was open, naturally, since Scarlett hadn't known about the plan when she had come to my rescue. The window was clearly still open, too. *Decoy. That guy was a decoy!* They were coming through the back door. Then it dawned on me that he was alone. Scarlett looked at me, my realisation

128

mirrored in her own face, and we both dashed into the kitchen. Mycroft was calmly standing at the stove, drinking another cup of his coffee.

'You should take a look outside,' he remarked coolly, 'there are people climbing up your house.'

That was a bad joke if it was one, I thought. I had better check that, seeing as Mycroft wasn't given to outbursts of humour usually. Taking out my gun, I slowly approached the window and peered down the wall.

It *was* a bad joke. There was no one there, at least not on the wall. Yet in the backyard there was a group of agents making a fuss.

'These are your men, Mycroft! What are they doing there?'

For the second time that day somebody hit me in the face.

I shook my head. Hit back. When I opened my eyes, I saw an agent with a bleeding nose in front of my kitchen window. Seriously. He appeared rather startled at his broken sunglasses, so I knocked him out, and pulled him in.

'What's this supposed to mean, Mycroft?' I blustered. Scarlett calmly walked over to tie the second guy up in the living room.

Mycroft just shrugged and said, 'I'd take a look outside again, if I were you.'

With a growl, I did. I just couldn't see anyone on the wall. Then I heard a quiet scratching noise above my head. They were coming from the roof!

I whirled around and pointed my gun upwards, only to stick it up the first agent's nose above me.

'Should I say hands up now, gentlemen?' I remarked dryly. There were four of them, in harnesses, roped up at the roof. 'Next time you should invite yourself a little more politely. Now you would you be so kind as to get down to the ground? I'm not offering to use our stairs. One wrong move and I will shoot you down, are we clear?' I beckoned them to go past me.

But then Scarlett screamed, and in an instant, I had a foot on the back of my head.

Seconds later, they were swarming into the flat. I scrambled to my feet, but to my horror found that my gun had been tossed to the other end of the room. Meanwhile Sherlock, the bastard, was still pretending to sleep. *Very helpful.*

Speaking of bastards, where is Mycroft?

Gone. *The bastard,* as I was saying.

I knocked out the next agent trying to enter the window, and then rushed into the living room.

First, I saw Scarlett being held at gunpoint. There was blood on her face. I was confused, at that moment, but when my eyes moved slightly to the right, confusion became a helpless understatement: Mycroft was also being held at gunpoint. By his own men.

The word 'mutiny' crossed my mind. I fumbled for my gun. It wasn't under my belt. The next moment, Billy and Finn jumped out of the bathroom, carrying four guns. They pointed them at the agents.

'Nobody moves!' Billy cried. That gave me time to ask questions.

'What's going on here? Who hired you?'

Nobody moved, not even their lips. Stupid blokes. One little James-Bond-reading kid next to another.

I took one gun from Finn.

'Mycroft, will you finally tell me what this is about!?' I bluffed at him, but his face was frozen. It seemed to totally fall out of character when one of the agents spoke.

'So, he fooled you, too,' he said so quietly I almost didn't understand.

Can this get any more confusing?

'All right, gentlemen, I think we need to explain why we're here,' said a suave female voice from between the black figures. Agent Smallwood turned around.

We didn't shoot. She was as calm as if we were at her gunpoint. A second later, there were steps behind us as the next load of agents arrived in the kitchen, hurriedly sticking more guns into our backs.

Agent Smallwood was one of Mycroft's top assassins, and she was apparently the one leading this scurrile operation.

'Drop your guns, please,' she demanded with a smile. 'Now that we know you're not aware of Mr Holmes's plans, we won't arrest you unless you continue to interfere with us.'

'I'm sorry, which Mr Holmes are we talking about?' I complained.

Agent Smallwood smiled at me dismissively. 'There's only one Mr Holmes in the room, Dr Watson.'

– – – – –

Confusion. Perplexity. Bewilderment. *Understatement!*

Sherlock was lying on the couch, *still helping a lot*, and Mycroft stood by the wall with his hands behind his head, and not moving anywhere.

'Dr Watson, this is a matter of the highest delicacy. It is top secret, by the way, so should you speak to anyone about this, be assured there will be consequences,' Agent Smallwood announced ominously. 'I take it you've heard of Killer Evans, Dr Watson?'

My head was going to burst any second now.

Of course I had heard of him, even before I met Sherlock. The murder of the Garrideb brothers, owners of the Garrideb, Garrideb & Garrideb Bank, had caused quite an uproar in the media. James Winter, their secretary, had allegedly shot them in their office, but the police later found out it was a killer by the name of John Evans, who had undergone plastic surgery in order to impersonate the secretary. Naturally, it wasn't the police who had figured that out. I later discovered the evidence on Sherlock's phone and Lestrade admitted he'd helped him. *So?* There was nothing illegal about that, and I couldn't see Killer Evans anywhere in the room.

'Dr Watson, you may not have heard, but that same Killer Evans broke out of Pentonville Prison and went undercover some time ago. We know he's had repeated contact with James Moriarty, and finally joined his network under the codename 'Morecroft'. Do I need to explain the matter any further?'

- - - - -

How on earth?

'It all fits!' Scarlett threw in, 'the fake M.I.6 badge, the dyed hair, the stitches on his face.'

Yeah, how could I not see that, I thought ironically.

'Why didn't you mention any of that in the first place?' I asked her, *a trifle* upset.

'Sorry, I'm not Sherlock Holmes. I didn't know what to make of it.'

'Well, I hope you don't mind our arresting this man now, Dr Watson,' declared Agent Smallwood then.

'Not at all,' I growled.

When the agent in front of the killer approached him, Morecroft seized him.

'Do I need to state the ransom?' he snarled, and slowly inched towards the door.

'Do you think I would give you up for the life of one agent?' Smallwood shot back.

'Oh, yes,' he murmured with a sinister smile, and vanished through the front door.

'After him!' Agent Smallwood shouted. As quickly as they'd come in, the agents rushed out of our flat.

Rushing after them, Scarlett and I found a baffled Lestrade, holding four pizzas, in the midst of the flock of Smallwood's agents passing through the front door. He held up four pizzas.

'Didn't realise you were throwing a party,John,' he said with huge eyes. 'I would have brought more, you know?'

Chapter 6

Back in the living room, Sherlock was already sitting up. *Already.*

'Sherlock! Finally! How're you feeling?' Scarlett exclaimed, immediately kneeling down in front of him.

'I'm all right, but that's not the matter right now. Lestrade, you've got your car with you, I hope. We need to get to Belgrave Road. I'll explain things on the way,' Sherlock instructed, getting up to fetch his coat.

'What about the pizza?' Lestrade complained.

'In the car. That's why I said pizza to John,' Sherlock remarked, without making things any clearer, as he was wont to do. 'Lock all the windows. We've got no time to lose. I'll take care of the stove,' Sherlock commandeered.

'What about the stove?' I asked. It was still very hot in the flat, but the stove was off.

'Morecroft placed sulphur pieces out of my test rigs under the cooktops of a gas stove, John. Even you should know what happens when you turn it on.'

'So, he *was* trying to kill us!' I exclaimed.

'Wha— How? I don't get it!' Lestrade complained.

'The sulphur will melt and react with the oxygen in the flame. The result is SO_2 – a toxic gas. The hot temperature in the flat quickens the molecular movements and therefore the production of the gas as well, which would then react with the mucosa to produce acid in our throats,' Sherlock explained.

'But what's Moriarty's point in just sending someone to kill us all off? That's so not his style,' I protested.

'It's not his style, because that was not his point,' Sherlock retorted, scratching yellow chunks off a cooktop. 'His point was to get information. While everyone struggled with excruciating pain, Morecroft would've kidnapped one of us. Presumably me, but I'm not one hundred percent sure. I am sure, though, that this would not be his last attempt, since it failed. John, come over here and help me search the room for bugs. Quick! It must be here. That's the only place where he was alone. Ah- There it is! Hello, Jim!'

Sherlock had discovered a tiny camera behind a book on a shelf, waved at it, and then crushed it between two heavy books. During our search, I found two bugs, Lestrade three, and Scarlett found two cameras and one bug. Morecroft had been thorough indeed, but the method was a little obvious for my taste.

'Billy, what did you find out about the secret base?' Sherlock enquired when we were finished.

'I''s under No. 2, 10 fee' deep. You can only en'er i' in a lif',' Billy shouted from the bathroom.

'Brilliant,' Sherlock enthused, a spark in his eyes.

We put all the devices into a box and had Billy jump up and down on it thoroughly.

I gave Billy and Finn two of my jackets while Sherlock had to give one of his to Scarlett. I gave her a handkerchief to wipe off the blood in her face.

'Are you all right? Do you have a headache?' I asked her when we descended the stairs.

135

'A bit, yes,' she admitted, 'but it's not too bad. You look a little more shaken. I hope you're not concussed.'

Her concern warmed me gently. 'No, no, it's all right,' I objected, but now that the adrenalin subsided, I felt a little less steady on my feet.

* * *

Lestrade had parked his car at Seymour Place. We threw away his parking violation ticket. I was glad when the doors were all shut. At last, Sherlock was going to explain it all. He was sitting in the front seat next to the Detective Inspector, while in the back of the car I seized John's hand for safety. Billy and Finn were crammed into one seat next to me.

'No. 2 Belgrave Road. But not the one in Pimlico, the one in Barnes,' Sherlock announced and Lestrade turned on the satnav.

'Oh, Lestrade, would you just be so kind as to send one of your police cars to Camden Lock?' John asked suddenly. 'Billy and Finn lost their friend Isaac there. Some of the agents were chasing them.'

Lestrade nodded from the driver's seat as we started on the pizzas.

When Lestrade hung up, I couldn't hold back the questions anymore.

'Sherlock, will you finally tell us what happened at Salvatore's? What were you aiming at the whole time? Why didn't you tell us Mycroft was an impostor?'

And finally, he opened up. 'When Morecroft attacked me at Bart's, I already knew it wasn't my brother. Mycroft is *way* less agile. He may be smarter than me, but he doesn't want to do my job, because it requires "leg work" as he likes to call it. The immediate conclusion that it must be an impostor attacking me seemed inescapable, I'm afraid.'

John put his face in his palm while Sherlock continued, 'I hoped I could get more information out of Moriarty's agent, so I decided to keep him for a while. Moriarty sent him to me, because Mycroft has indeed escaped as we noticed when we saw Moriarty's men on Albert Bridge the other day. They're still looking for him now; otherwise they wouldn't have given Morecroft so much time. By the way, Mycroft solved the case of Killer Evans, I just did the running, so this was the perfect opportunity for Morecroft to get revenge.'

'But how do you explain that his voice sounded exactly like Mycroft's?' John threw in.

'Pitch, timbre and speaking habits can be imitated. Drama school is indispensable for agents these days, and British drama schools excel. I've taken advantage of that myself already. Though Morecroft's imitation could not exactly copy the original; it was enough to fool you, because you heard what you expected. Your first impression of Mycroft's face was in an instance of extreme stress, which will have manipulated your perception. His voice reminded you of Mycroft's, but although it wasn't *exactly* the same, you had no reference data to compare it with immediately. You got used to his imitation and stopped questioning it.'

'What about the story he told us of his escape? He couldn't possibly have made this up! And how did he manage to do all the deductions? Only Mycroft could be so annoyingly clever!' John enquired suspiciously.

'Well, about the deductions: they weren't any. You might remember that he belongs to Moriarty's men, and Moriarty is aware of Scarlett's staying with us, as well as of her criminal past and her life before that, which he's now using against us. With rather horrific consequences, if his plan is what I think it is.' Sherlock's voice frighteningly died away. 'In any case,' he continued, 'you can rest assured, whatever he said, he learnt from Moriarty. As for the story of his escape: he *didn't* make it up.'

We all looked at him in astonishment.

The consulting detective just smiled and went on. 'As I said, he'd been sent to substitute Mycroft before he could contact me after his escape. What story could be more convincing than reality? If Mycroft had come along and interfered with Morecroft, he would have told everyone the same story, and everyone else would be inclined to believe the person they had heard it from first. The authenticity of the deductions was unsurpassable. Yet, you could have noticed that Morecroft was careful to avoid mentioning any exact address or escape route, which Mycroft would have done to secure the place immediately.

'Unfortunately, Mycroft hasn't informed his men about his escape yet. Apparently, he hasn't had a safe chance so far. Of course, the secret service also at some point realised Morecroft was an impostor. Since I seemed to play along, they thought I was cooperating with him. *Idiots.* They took us to Salvatore's and gave a signal with their headlights along the way as you might remember. This set in motion the restaurant's infiltration and there they interrogated me about what I was trying to do, but they didn't believe a word. They still don't trust me. I bet my brother has told them nice little tales about me. Anyway, they wanted to arrest Morecroft right away, but I tried to convince them that I should keep him. My trying to have him on the loose totally convinced them I was cooperating with him. Can you believe all that stupidity!?

'They drugged me to arrest me, but Salvatore distracted them, so they didn't give me enough. They interrogated the poor man instead. Finally, I brought up the idea of a tracker, so they would think they had control over me, but I'm now actually able to lead them to Moriarty, once I get the chance to. They agreed to it. You've seen the result. Then finally, Norina of the Irregulars jumped through the open window and we managed to overwhelm them. I had contacted her earlier, in case anything went wrong at Salvatore's.

'I knew they would be coming after us to fetch Morecroft, but until then I made sure I would gain all the information I needed. If I had told you about Morecroft, they might not have let you go, and you might've acted strangely in front of him. So, I kept it to myself. Since 221B is currently surrounded by the secret service, I had to make them think they had incapacitated me until a good opportunity for an arrest could come up. When it came, I still had to pretend to be sleeping, because otherwise they might have arrested me alongside him. They're supposed to believe they've got me under control for the moment. Otherwise they'll mess everything up.

'To explain my plan, I expected them to come down from the roof, because the posts Mycroft put there could be of enormous strategic advantage to them in getting up there unseen. So, I tried to present them Morecroft on a silver platter at the kitchen window. I hoped they would just snatch him, but apparently, they mistrusted you as much as to send a decoy and question you, too. Well, all in all it almost worked out. I really hope they'll do their homework with him.'

We were all a bit baffled. John forgot both how to move and the fact that he had a piece of pizza halfway down his throat. Lestrade was mopping his brow. I had one more question though.

'I assume John has told you about the bullet in the lock on your bedroom door? Do you have an explanation for that as well? Seeing that Morecroft wasn't your brother, I think it might be fair to suspect him?'

John gave me an approving look. Sherlock chuckled.

'I wouldn't be so sure about my brother's integrity even if he wasn't an impostor, but you're right: it *was* Morecroft who shot you. I checked the evidence while we were searching for bugs and cameras. John told me someone shot you from inside the room, because the windows were still in one piece, but both of you hadn't spotted anyone, except you in your vision. And this is the interesting part.

'When he shot you, he had to be visible to you. There was no hole in the curtain, none in the blanket, so he didn't hide anywhere there and shot you then. So, you must at least have seen a part of him. The angle of your wound would prove that, since you were cowering behind the bed. As the number of suspects was very small, Morecroft must have been aware that if you actually perceived someone shooting you, he would be the first to be suspected. He couldn't have risked that. However, he knew you have visions occasionally, and more importantly, he must have known you were about to have one at that exact moment. We can safely assume he knows what triggers your visions, and how to use it to hide behind the images your mind creates.

'Now, about the actual events: I observed the amount of dust under my bed – dust can tell you everything. It had drastically reduced compared to its state a few days ago. It wasn't clean though, which excluded the possibility of Mrs Hudson having cleaned it. So, Morecroft must have been hiding under the bed when you were in the room. I suppose neither of you could account for his being anywhere else at that time?'

We both hesitantly shook our heads.

'I see. And knowing my state, I can assume, without being presumptuous, that you weren't too unoccupied with taking care of me. Thanks for that, by the way. It was very endearing, at least from what I could tell when I was pretending.' Sherlock smiled amiably at us.

'Oh, you bastard,' I growled, still angry that I hadn't realised.

'Anyway, I wasn't pretending when the shooting happened,' he insisted. 'Morecroft was lying under the bed, waiting for you to give a sign of distress that would signal your having a vision. On this cue, he jumped out and shot the lock so the vision would leave a more visible trace. Frightened out of your wits, you would've been unable to tell whether what you were seeing was real. He would still be able to leave the room as you couldn't turn the key any more with the bullet in the lock.

'As you know now, he planted a lot of cameras in our flat, and it is obvious he used one to observe your movements. The blanket was a perfect cover, as it touches the floor on both sides of the bed.

'Now, after he'd fired, he hid beneath the bed again, and followed your movements on his phone. He could see you were about to look under the bed, and so crawled out as silently as possible, to hide behind the blanket on the other side of the bed. When he saw you had fallen for his trick and wouldn't look again, he quickly crawled back under the bed, always moving when you moved, lifting the blanket when you let it down, taking cover in your acoustic shadow.

'The moment you fired into the floor, he was already back under the bed, and absolutely sure that you would now be haunted by Anne Boleyn shooting you. In an unobserved moment – and due to the shock he had inflicted upon you – he managed to slip out of the bedroom and into the kitchen, where he got rid of the dust on his suit. I found a few lint balls in the bin. Did I miss anything?' Sherlock suavely raised his eyebrows.

John cleared his throat.

'I don't think so, no,' I replied, bewildered but relieved that my visions were not yet able to shoot me after all.

141

'Right, and where are we going now?' John asked when he finally managed to swallow his bite.

'You remember the note about our darling princess?' Sherlock said. His deep voice cut into my conscience.

The words triggered something in me – utmost happiness, turned into utmost despair. Suddenly, my throat felt sore and tight, too tight. I closed my eyes before Anne could show up again. John noticed my exertion and immediately put his arms around me to soothingly stroke my back. Slowly, I began to relax.

Then, Sherlock continued, 'You discovered the string of letters on the paper. You were right – it was just a word being repeated. We read UMQRA while it actually said RAUM Q. *Raum* is German for 'room', and *Raum Q* is a secret base in Belgrave Road.'

Our jaws dropped.

'Agents, smugglers, etc. can rent it for important transfers,' Sherlock explained. 'Moriarty uses it as an assembly room for top secret meetings. It was built in 1870 by a German officer called Isbert von Hoffmanstal. He had orders to infiltrate the UK with German spies. A little more recently, the room belonged to the late James Barker, one of the two bodies I tried to examine this morning. After his sudden death, it was taken over by Sebastian Moran. Today it's not booked, so I hope we can have a look around.'

'All right, here we are, ladies and gentlemen,' Lestrade announced a while later as we turned into Belgrave Road. John helped me out of the car, eyeing me closely to see if I was all right. I smiled at him.

Taking Sherlock's advice, we left the car where it was in case we had to get out of here quickly. Billy and Finn lead the way to a darkened corner next to No. 2. It was a small, strangely

142

pink house next to a threateningly high and savage looking hedge.

'I''s under the garden. There's a secre' passage under one of the tiles, leading over there,' Billy explained. We instantly began our search on all fours. A few minutes later Finn had found it. Sherlock helped him lift the trap door. A sigh of disappointment escaped us: under the door there was another one made of iron with a combination lock.

John scratched his head. 'Well, Sherlock?'

'Shut up, I need to go to my mind palace.'

'What the hell is he talking about?' I whispered into John's ear, while Sherlock raised both his hands to his head and tightly shut his eyes.

'It's a way of memorising things by picturing himself storing information in a house. Well, he's got a palace. What else would he get himself,' he replied, raising a brow.

Finally, Sherlock gave a short 'Ah!' only to bend down and dial the numbers 051113. The door clicked.

For a moment, we weren't sure if it was open or preparing to blow us up, but Sherlock just lifted the trap at its corners and went in.

Following him, we climbed down a narrow tunnel on an iron ladder. John went before me, so he could catch me, *and probably* because he was curious.

At the end of the tunnel there was a rather large, but empty room with two lifts waiting. It was very cold. Sherlock pressed a combination of buttons, and one of the lifts opened. It was very small, so Lestrade decided to wait for the other one with the boys. In fact, the lift was barely big enough for three people. When the door closed, I found myself tightly huddled up to Sherlock and John. I could feel them both breathing at my chest. For a moment, I felt like bursting into fragments to avoid the creeping memory of a guilty feeling taking my breath away.

Finally, the lift swung open.

'Welcome to Raum Q,' Sherlock said with an air of victory about him as we entered it. The room had brick walls and, to my astonishment, six windows with a view of a dark forest to the left and right. Inspecting them more closely, I could see there were high definition photographs behind the panes.

'This is to make hostages believe they are far away from civilisation,' Sherlock explained when he saw me examining them. 'Of course, no one is held here for very long.'

The floor was made out of salmon-coloured linoleum, and there were two large, white tables at one side. Next to them, a darkened passage led into a hallway. Sherlock busied himself with a white box which was hanging from the wall above the tables, containing papers. John had found a loose brick that sadly didn't conceal a secret cubicle.

I just watched them. After all, I felt grateful they were still alive, pondering how lucky we were – when suddenly...

The floor creaked quietly.

The walls echoed furtively.

The bricks whispered cryptically.

'Hello, Mr Holmes.'

We whirled around.

A woman of ravishing beauty emerged from the shadowy passage behind the wall. She was wearing a very short black dress consisting of a diaphanous, fluttering layer of silk, and a tight leather one beneath it.

Her shiny dark brown hair was tied up in an elegant knot. Sherlock looked as if he were struck by a lightning bolt. And I was certain she could throw them.

'Hello, Miss Adler.'

Part 3: The Storyteller's Shadow

Chapter 1

Apparently, we were seeing a ghost, judging by the look John was giving her.

Miss Irene Adler, I would later learn, had been executed by a firing squad in Asia a year earlier. She was a German agent, and the only woman ever to beat Sherlock Holmes. How she had managed to escape her execution remained a mystery.

In any case, she was standing right in front of us now, approaching a completely motionless Sherlock. Her steps echoed through the room.

'Scott,' she exhaled as she ran her finger along his jaw. 'What have you been up to?'

His mouth twitched. He was so tall next to her, gazing down in utter titillation. Her piercing eyes enslaved him while her presence seemed to burn him from the inside out.

'Solving your puzzle,' he murmured suggestively. His deep velvet voice sent chills down my back.

'Glad to hear you succeeded,' she replied with a luscious look. It seemed like she was ready to devour him in one bite if she were a tigress. And I was sure she could turn into one.

Instinctively, she ran her hand over the part of his jacket that concealed his stomach wound.

'Haven't been so careful lately, have we?' she asserted, flashing a look at me.

I could barely contain myself, John had to hold me back. *How could she possibly see the connection between his wound and me?* Apparently she knew his gait so well, she could tell that he was hurt in that spot, but how *the hell* did she know about me?

Sherlock was smiling. Just smiling. It seemed as if this woman was his cocaine substitute.

They immediately had an intimacy about them which made us feel like intruders. And yet, I couldn't turn my eyes from them.

She took his left hand. The two bites were still clearly visible.

'Have you been taking drugs together?' she asked soberly.

Wildly, I shook my head, blushing.

'Have you got some information for me?' Sherlock purred as if he were asking for a kiss.

'I have information, yes, but I don't yet know whether it's for you,' she remarked casually. His gaze was embracing her.

'Are you expecting me to beg?' he asked, raising his eyebrows. Suddenly, her face was only inches from his.

'Twice,' she said, lowering her eyelids.

I sensed it was some sort of allusion by the way Sherlock's eyes blazed at it. Taking a short look at John, I noticed he was moving his lips in silent amazement, yet he didn't dare interrupt them.

Yet, a moment later, Miss Adler sharply turned to us. 'You've got questions, I perceive. Dr Watson, the watermark on the paper of Raum Q was my idea. A little extravagance of mine since my great-great-grandfather built this place. That's the puzzle I've given Mr Holmes. I knew he'd come across a note from here sooner or later. I know a lot more about the goings-on here, *Miss Vendalle*, which is why he asks *me* for information,' she concluded with a menacing glance at me. 'Doesn't look very good for her, I've seen her files.'

146

My muscles tightened, my eyes narrowed. John squeezed my hand.

'Where are her files?' Sherlock asked, his voice clearly stimulated.

'I don't know,' she flirted innocently, 'maybe over there in the safe. It's behind one of *those* bricks.'

John rolled his eyes. The brick he held was from the opposite wall.

'Of course, there are a lot of loose bricks here; there are a lot of clients, but they all use them differently. Yours wasn't used at all yet, I see,' she observed, turning to John, while Sherlock was already walking over to the spot she'd indicated. *Do I really need to be astonished at the fact that he knew the code to the safe as well?*

* * *

It was *her* safe.

'I nicked those papers yesterday, out of the table leg here. Jim's never been fond of the brick idea. But with the table he was thorough. He put combination locks even under the legs, but they're concealed by a perfectly normal foot,' Irene explained, nonchalantly. Sherlock made a move toward the table, but something on the paper caught his eye.

'What is it?' asked Scarlett.

'You're not seeing this, you're not going to see this. John, stop her if she tries,' he harshly addressed us.

Scarlett froze in my arms. She tightly shut her eyes, and I only hoped that a panic episode wasn't to follow.

Suddenly the lift swung open, revealing Lestrade, Billy and Finn, their hands in the air.

Slowly, a black figure came into view from the shadow in the lift.

'Here they are, Miss Adler.'

'Thank you, Johnson. You can leave them to me now,' she answered, taking out her gun. 'We don't like police in here, Mr Holmes. Why did you bring him along?'

'Because he's the only detective in London who's not in any of the pictures on your phone,' Sherlock replied, smirking triumphantly.

My eyes almost popped out of my ears! *Did- did he just not exclude himself? Oh, perfect, now I'm stammering in my thoughts already.*

'Fair enough, I give you that,' she retorted, raising her gun. 'That's just another reason to get him out of the way.' On scanning Lestrade more thoroughly, she noticed with amusement, 'his wife sleeps with her physiotherapist.'

I hadn't even been trying to figure out how...

'Obviously. Only a bat would be too blind to see that,' Sherlock shot back.

That made me a bat, then.

'In any case, I can guarantee you Lestrade will not utter a single word about this business at the police station.'

Lestrade pulled a face that said he was not so sure, but Sherlock continued, 'I fully trust him. Lately, he's been delivering pizza rather than solving crimes anyway.'

'All right, gents.' Irene slipped her gun into her pocket again. 'Johnson, you can tell the others it's fine.'

The man vanished into the lift.

'Best believe I'll be taking precautions that he doesn't speak. Mr Holmes, I'd be very careful with these pages if I were you. I can't guarantee they're complete, but they already say a good deal,' she added then.

Scarlett uncomfortably rocked back and forth, biting her lip. I put my arm around her shoulder.

'What business have you had with Moriarty recently?' Sherlock asked Irene all of a sudden. She grew pale, but no less confident.

'Trading pictures,' she retorted, 'to my own advantage, of course. It's none of your business, you can't keep me from doing this.'

'I never said I meant to,' Sherlock replied, 'but it would be tempting for me to try...'

'No! You will do nothing of the sort!' An elusive shadow passed her face.

'I see, you're not doing it voluntarily. It's blackmail, isn't it, Irene?' Sherlock clutched her arms. 'He's got something on you, hasn't he?'

Irene struggled free. 'It's none of your business. Get on with your cases,' she shot back and turned around.

Sherlock knelt down to carefully examine the table legs, but he found only one other combination lock.

'There's nothing in here, judging by its weight. Has he got another safe anywhere in this room?' he asked Irene.

'Not a personal one that I know of. He occasionally uses those of other clients, and changes their combination. Of course, he knows every combination in the room since Colonel Moran took over,' she answered.

'Are you trying to tell us the highest class of criminals in London is at his disposal?' I enquired, just *slightly* upset.

'Oh, yeah,' she scoffed. 'Look at you, worrying for London's criminals.'

'Does this mean,' Scarlett interjected, 'that I belong to the highest class of criminals in London?'

'You did before you lost your memory,' Sherlock replied in his unbelievably unabashed way.

'Sherlock!' I shouted. He just kept examining the room.

'What? You can't spare her everything,' he mumbled, knocking on the floor. 'George, would you mind checking the windows?'

'He means me, doesn't he?' the DI snorted, a little annoyed.

'Billy, Finn, go and search the passage,' Sherlock ordered next, and the lads vanished.

'Scarlett, whatever's in these files, they're not about you anymore, all right? You are a completely different person now, do you hear me? You're innocent,' I tried to soothe her. She attempted a grateful smile.

'You'll cure me, Dr Watson. If anyone, it's going to be you.'

I could only hope I wouldn't fail her.

'There's another lif' a' the end o' the passage,' Billy reported when the boys came back.

Finn nodded energetically. 'I"s much bigger than the other two an' i"s go' twelve secre' compar'ments inside. They ask you questions so they'll open.'

'You've gotta explain this righ', Finn,' Billy interrupted, 'they've go' displays, each of 'em. An' when you touch 'em, they ask stupid things like, Where's the sixth Thatcher, or wha'ever... I don' even know wha' a Thatcher is. Mr 'olmes, do you?'

The boys looked at us with huge eyes.

'Maggie Thatcher,' I started, but Sherlock waved me aside.

'Later, John. Go on, boys.'

'Anyway, we couldn' answer none of 'em,' Finn protested.

'And you shouldn't *try*,' Irene averred threateningly. Shooting looks at each of us, she continued, 'The locks only open if the person who initiated the security question answers it. It works via voice recognition. If you were to give a wrong answer, nothing would happen, but if you answer correctly – it would blow up the whole lift. Rather expensive rubbish for my taste, but Moran thinks he's being clever. Nothing has gone wrong yet, but if it does, he'll have to rebuild the whole lift, and then do what with the builders? Kill them all off? I keep telling him off, but he won't listen. It's too bad I sold this room to Barker anyway, but then I didn't expect to live another two weeks.' She gave Sherlock a gaze that spoke volumes in a language I couldn't understand. But *he* did.

Shaking my head, I said, 'Sherlock, how long do you want to stay here? You might not notice these things, but it's getting rather late now. In fact, it's half past midnight. We all need rest.'

Lestrade nodded in agreement. 'I can't find anything around here anyway.'

Irene chuckled. 'You're not used to much, are you?'

'No, they aren't,' Sherlock confirmed from under the tables. 'You can go home. I guess Mycroft's men will have returned to their posts now, so you'll be safe. I'll come back later, I'm not yet finished. Billy, Finn, will you stay here?'

The boys thought for a while.

'Yes,' Billy replied then, 'bu' can we stay 'ere for the res' o' the nigh', too, Miss Adler? We'd be gra'eful to sleep under a roof.'

Irene checked something on her phone. 'You need to be out of here before nine o'clock. Make yourselves comfortable,' she said casually.

'Right.' Lestrade cleared his throat. 'I'm driving you home. Are we going?'

'Yeah, All right. Sherlock, you're not going to give me the files by any chance, are you?' I asked.

'Definitely not. You can see them tomorrow,' he replied, not even looking up. 'Make sure she stays in one piece. That's most important right now.'

I frowned. A shiver went through Scarlett.

'Yeah, whatever that means.' I agreed quickly. We followed Lestrade to the lifts.

'John, who was that woman? What *on earth* is she to Sherlock Holmes?' Scarlett asked after we'd gotten into the car.

'Oh... Irene Adler. That's er... difficult to say. He just calls her *The Woman*, but that says as much as it says nothing at all. I never quite understood what's going on between them.' I admitted, raising my eyebrows. 'When I met him, I thought he was completely unable to feel any kind of emotion, let alone love for any kind of person; I think love is a mystery to him. When he met Irene, you couldn't say he *had* fallen in love, but you couldn't say he *hadn't* fallen in love either... He's a complicated cat.'

'But cats do fall in love, don't they?' she suddenly said after a moment. I had to smile, but her easy understanding of Sherlock's nature made me slightly uncomfortable.

'I wonder what they're doing down there now,' she murmured.

'I wonder what Sherlock thinks they're doing,' I snorted.

'Oh, come on, guys! The boys are still with them,' Lestrade complained.

'All right, all right,' we gave in.

For a while we sat in silence. I suddenly had a feeling we were being followed while waiting for the traffic lights at the southwest end of Shepherd's Bush Common. When I looked out of the window, I just about caught a man hiding in the shadows across the street. A car pulled up next to him, and he got in.

'Are we being followed?' Scarlett must've seen it, too.

'Lestrade, could you maybe take a little detour? I don't want to make it too easy for them,' I announced, but then the car drove off into the next back road.

'I think *they're* taking the detour,' Lestrade remarked dryly. 'I only wish I knew what to make of it.'

A few minutes later, we arrived at Baker Street.

'Thanks for driving us,' I said to Lestrade as we got out.

'It seems I've become your personal chauffeur,' he replied with a hearty laugh. 'That's what you get for being Detective Inspector!'

We were all laughing now.

'At least it keeps you in touch with the local crime scene,' I maintained, smiling.

Lestrade granted me a fair point there and bade us both goodnight.

* * *

That night, I couldn't sleep.

So, there were files about me and Sherlock didn't want me to see them. *Does he think it might impede my regaining my memory? Is the information dangerous to know? Could he possibly care about my wellbeing in any form?*

John had made me a hot cup of tea, given me a long hug before saying goodnight. Now, I lay awake in my bed, constantly afraid of any strange presence that could appear in my room.

They had already managed to break in without us noticing. Not even Sherlock had done anything about it, and now he wasn't even here to possibly do anything.

Whenever something creaked or knocked, I nearly screamed. Sitting up straight and turning on the lights offered temporary relief. I was constantly checking every dark corner suited as a hiding place before I lay down again.

Sherlock had given me this strange advice again. *What did he say...?* 'And watch out she stays in one piece.' *Watch out! He'd said this to John!*

In an instant I was up and running down the stairs.

'John!' I called quietly, knocking at the door. He was there in a second. 'Sorry, I couldn't sleep, I'm so worried.' I whispered. He just embraced me.

'Don't worry, I couldn't sleep either,' he replied warmly.

'Can I sleep down here?' I asked a bit insecurely.

'Of course. You can have Sherlock's room,' he answered, walking me over.

'Thanks so much, John.'

'No problem. Do you need anything else?'

'No, thanks.' I smiled.

We were standing at the door. After a moment, I realised I was still holding John's fingers in mine. He smiled before he let go.

'Just call me if you need anything. I'll lock the door again. All the windows are bolted, and I've got my revolver next to me, all right?'

I nodded and went over to Sherlock's bed.

Lost in thoughts for a moment, I let my fingers glide over his pillow. When I heard John close the door, I spun around.

'John?'

'Yes?' The knob was still in his hand.

'I need *you*, John.'

He cocked his head.

'I want to see your face when I wake up from a breaking-in,' I said jokingly. He smiled in surprise.

'I don't think this blanket is large enough for the both of us. Go and get yours,' I added with a wink.

He chuckled, already turning to fetch it. Once he'd locked the door, he lay down next to me.

For a while, we just shuffled around awkwardly. There was the odd embarrassed smile, inhaling to say something, but stopping before the first word. In the end, we turned away from each other to exhale.

'I'm sorry,' I said suddenly.

He frowned.

'It's probably too late to apologise, and now I don't even know what for, but I hope you can accept it,' I insisted.

He just shook his head, his face barely able to conceal all that he was bursting to say but bit back.

'It was mostly my fault anyway. Don't think so badly of yourself. It's all different now, anyway. The past is not worth worrying about when you face murderers every day.'

I laughed and laid my head on his shoulder as he wrapped his arm around my back.

'Thank you, John,' I whispered, and before I knew it, I fell asleep.

* * *

At 6 in the morning, the doorbell rang. We had barely been sleeping four hours.

Who the hell is that? I'll kill Sherlock if he's forgotten his keys, I thought, getting into my dressing gown. I grabbed my gun and quickly headed downstairs. When I opened the door, I didn't know whether to question my sanity or laugh out loud. I did the latter.

'*What the hell, Sherlock!?*' I panted when I was finished. 'You went on the tube like that!?'

'None of the cabs would take me.' He pursed his lips and raised his nose at my still questioning look. 'Yes, she took all my clothes and ran away. I had to take the curtains as you can see. Wasn't easy, Billy and Finn were using them as sheets, and they would've killed me if I'd woken them up.'

Still, I could hardly believe my eyes when Sherlock Holmes strode past me, wrapped in a striped curtain from neck to toe. He went up the stairs like a king.

I burst out laughing.

'It's not actually *that* funny,' he grunted when I caught up with him.

'Did she take your keys, too? Were they in your pocket?' I asked, unable to wipe the grin off my face.

'No, I forgot them,' Sherlock retorted, and my grin was gone as quickly as it had come.

'Goodness *me!* What happened to *you?*' Scarlett bit her finger so she wouldn't laugh as heartlessly as I had.

'What do you *think?*' Sherlock snapped and strode past her.

After a moment of intensely looking him up and down, she decided, 'This Adler-woman took all your clothes? Seriously? Do you know what this looks like?'

I scowled at it being so obvious to her. Sherlock turned away to shovel papers on his desk.

'No, what do you mean?' he asked with disinterest.

'Never mind. Whatever you had with her is your business. I understand,' she stated provocatively with a wink at me.

He just went on ruffling through his chaos.

'Why did she...' Scarlett began, but then she walked over to him and brushed his hair from his temple. 'Oh,' she realised. 'She knocked you out. Did she take your phone?'

'Yes,' Sherlock retorted, going over to the fireplace. 'She thought I'd like to talk to Moriarty so she left me in Raum Q, and called him to meet me there on her way out. I woke up just in time to hear her phone call. Happy now?'

We were rather perplexed at this.

'Do you have any clue why she did that?' I asked.

'I've got about eight ideas, so far.' Sherlock murmured, still searching the room for something. Suddenly he picked up a letter. 'Maybe four.'

With the letter in his hand he went to his bedroom.

'John? Why is your blanket here?'

Scarlett and I exchanged an ironic glance. 'We thought we'd be safer in the bed of the great consulting detective,' I shouted over, and Scarlett giggled into her hand.

Sherlock came out of the room again. 'Both of you?' he asked with a stern look.

'Oh, for God's sake, she was scared to sleep alone. Can't you deduce that?' I shot back.

'Yes, usually,' he yawned. Then he simply went back into his room and closed the door.

We laughed out loud.

'I think I'm good to sleep upstairs. At least there's daylight now, so the snipers on the roof can see properly,' Scarlett smirked.

Secretly, I was a little disappointed, but I concealed it with a smile and opened the door to the stairs.

'Thank you, John. I won't forget you rescued me.' She winked at me and kissed me on the cheek.

Her lips felt so painfully familiar when I closed my eyes. She slowly wrapped her hand around my neck, and I knew where every of her phalanges would hit my skin before they did. I wished I could just turn around and kiss her, but then she let go and quickly ran upstairs.

* * *

Nothing happened for another three days. Our hands were tied. There was nothing we could do without the secret service noticing, which Sherlock wanted to avoid at any cost. There was also no news of Morecroft or his whereabouts, which was a bad sign.

John and I were happy to get some rest after *The Adventure of the Double Brother*, but Sherlock was boiling with tension. He tried to drown his desire for action in obtaining information instead. We hoped he wouldn't take any drugs again. John kept searching Sherlock's things and all his usual spots for any kind of secret supply, but there was nothing to be found.

It was during these days that I heard him composing for the first time. It was brilliant; long, graceful melodies with many compound intervals. *Is this the shape of his mind?* I found myself unable to be more in awe of anything than his music.

Meanwhile, Mrs Hudson regularly provided us with biscuits, which felt like they made up half of our living.

The flat was slowly but surely returning to its original state of mess. I only smiled at that, but John sometimes had outbursts of a compulsive sense of order, which were helplessly in vain. Something clearly needed to happen again.

Chapter 2

When I came down into the living room one morning, John and Sherlock were already having breakfast.

'Good morning, guys.'

They nodded with their full mouths. I sat down next to them and took a bit of scrambled egg onto the plate John had laid out for me. Sherlock constantly had his nose in a newspaper, blindly picking up his bites with a fork.

'What's the plan for today?' I asked.

'We could go shopping and get you some more clothes, since your luggage is still nowhere to be seen,' John suggested, and I blushed for a second. 'Sherlock has other things to do. He thinks it's safe to examine Barker, the body of one of Moriarty's dead assassins. He hid him at Salvatore's before Morecroft came in, remember? It's his idea of a nice afternoon.'

We both smirked at the consulting detective.

'What exactly is so important about him?' I asked.

'We think he was a double agent. MOD men killed him two weeks ago, but it was a little too easy,' Sherlock explained from behind his newspaper.

'I'm in,' I announced, swallowing the rest of my egg in one bite.

'Sherlock, a few days ago you said there was a message in that magazine. What was it called?'

'*The Strand*,' he answered my question grumpily. 'Nothing to be found there. I never understood why John subscribed to it at all. Ridiculous yellow press. Illustrated!' Sherlock snorted indignantly.

'I thought that was the trace they left you,' I averred.

'Maybe it was. All I can see there is that it had been bought two days earlier at a usual kiosk by a man who is about six feet tall and wore old black leather gloves,' he replied.

'Where did you get that from this time?' John asked with a raised brow.

Before Sherlock could explain, I interrupted him. 'Let me see, if I get it, too. Where is it?'

'Over there, in the shelf.' Sherlock motioned with a challenging smirk.

I swiftly wound myself out of the chair and went over to fetch it. Still standing, I took a look at it.

'Oh, the kiosk, I see. There are two buckles at the bottom and it's slightly lacerated in one spot at the side. The other is burnt off. That suggests it was stuffed into one of these metal display posts usually used at kiosks. I can see you discovered it on the day it was bought, because the pages are still sticky at the edge, suggesting it wasn't opened before it was burnt. There are very small patches of black leather around here, and no fingerprints, which means the man had gloves on that were so old the leather started crumbling already. But his gloves must have been wet, because there's a thumb-sized stain on the back, supposedly from the trigger or middle finger. Now you can estimate the height with a regression equation using hand length, gender, and approximate age. But you missed something,' I remarked coolly at the end.

'What's that?' Sherlock asked sceptically, without looking up.

'It hasn't been selling very well lately. This is the first copy sold at that kiosk, and it came out shortly before or at the beginning of the month. August issue. It's lacerated at the side, which means there were a lot of copies in the post. This one was the one in front; the copies at the back don't get lacerated as they don't get bent that much. If this was the frontmost copy, it was naturally the easiest to reach, yet it was only bought about four weeks after its release. There are even tiny traces of dust, sticky fabric fibres, on the top here. It doesn't look like a top seller to me,' I finished with a smirk.

Sherlock silently put away his newspaper, came over with swift, but smooth steps to glance at the magazine. He threw a shadow on it, but that didn't seem to hamper his sight.

'You're right,' he murmured, but suddenly his face lit up. 'That's it! The release date! It came out on the 25th July, as usual, and the next issue was out a day after this was blown up. Someone used it as a reference for a code! See, here's a quarter of a circle in felt tip. The addressee found the message and burnt it. For the answer, he will use the next issue, so the code has changed again. This is so neat!'

He leapt about the room like a dancer. I raised my eyebrows and gave John a surprised smile. He looked at me in utter disbelief. There were a hundred questions in his open mouth, the loudest of which must've been how the *hell* I had deduced something Sherlock Holmes had overlooked.

I walked over to him and slowly closed his mouth. When I let go, his jaw dropped again.

'John, you may close your mouth,' Sherlock remarked dryly from the kitchen. 'She's got talent, that's all.'

I had to suppress a grin. John was further than ever from closing his mouth. A little while later we found ourselves on the way to Salvatore's. Lestrade picked us up, but he only dropped us there as he had some other business for the day.

We deliberately ignored the sign saying 'Closed'.

Upon entering the restaurant, we almost tripped over the enormous mess. Chairs and stools were spread across the floor between half chairs and half stools, tables were lying on their side or completely upside down, while the table clothes were spooking around in between. There was a faint, almost magical glittering on the ground from glass candlesticks and vases shattered to pieces before treading on the fragments.

'Sherlock, is that you?' Salvatore stepped out from the kitchen. 'Ah, I hoped you would come! Have they arrested this fake brother of yours now?'

'No, they were *stupid*! They let him slip away,' Sherlock chafed with contempt, scanning every corner of the room. 'Did they take Barker?'

'No. I thought it best to stash him away in my big freezer in the basement after what happened the other day.' Salvatore rubbed his neck.

'Brilliant! Can we go and see him now?' Sherlock asked enthusiastically.

'Sure. Can I offer you anything before we go? A little snack for you and your date? All on the house.' The cook smiled.

'I-I'm not-' I started to stammer, but John interrupted me, taking my arm.

'He means me.'

'*What!?*'

'That's exactly what I thought the first time,' he grumbled.

'So, are you- do you usually go here with Sherlock? I-I never thought...' I was totally embarrassed now.

'No, I don't. Sherlock is not my boyfriend. Even if there were a swarm of people who wanted us to be, unfortunately we are not a couple. We just went here to solve a case once. But not even Mrs Hudson believes me after all these years. Do you mind if I change that?' he asked with a charming smile.

I just shook my head, so John turned to Salvatore. '*She's my date.*'

* * *

If I marked my calendar with superlatives, I would certainly have marked this day as the day of the most sheepish look I ever saw. And of the most spontaneous date I ever had, of course.

Salvatore turned from Sherlock to me, and from me to Sherlock, and then to Scarlett. His brows were drawn together into one dark line of a frown that promised an exploding brain any second. But that frown didn't keep its word, though it didn't leave Salvatore's face for the rest of the day. And the night, I'm sure.

I looked at Scarlett, only to see the mildly amused smile, the eagerly glowing cheeks and the gratefully surprised look I had always been so proud to be able to conjure on her face when we'd still been together. She started to chuckle and shake her head; then she looked at Salvatore and we burst out laughing.

'Well,' I said when Salvatore ceased to look frightened, 'can you offer us a table?' He threw a helpless glance at his messed-up restaurant.

'O-of course,' he grunted a moment later, climbing across the room to put up a table for us at the window, not without giving us incredulous looks in between. Sherlock swiftly went down the creaking stairs in the meantime. He seemed to have totally forgotten about us.

When Salvatore had finished building up a place to sit for Scarlett and me, I offered her my hand and helped her clamber over the ruined chairs.

'Milady,' I said finally, beckoning her to sit.

She smiled at me charmingly. 'Thank you, sir.'

Salvatore even forgot to bring the candles he always gave Sherlock and me. I think I shocked him more that day than the break-in at his restaurant. After Salvatore clumsily explained to us what his kitchen was capable of serving, I ordered two paninis.

'We've only just eaten, you little meanie. You're driving him out of his mind!' Scarlett reproached me, giggling.

'Don't worry. He'll get over it,' I assured her smiling proudly at my date.

For a moment, I forgot the years that had passed since Uni, and only Sherlock's throwing around of things reminded me that there must've been something afterwards.

A while later, Salvatore brought the food, and we started to eat.

'This is really good,' Scarlett remarked appreciatively.

'I'm glad you like it,' I replied with another smile.

'Thank you, John. This is so nice,' Scarlett said when she tried the salad, but it didn't seem like she was talking about the salad.

I took her hands into mine. Her beautiful, slender fingers. I caressed them with my thumbs, then drew them close to me and closed my eyes as I kissed them. When I opened my eyes again, she was smiling sentimentally.

'It's so sad I couldn't remember you were an old-school gentleman.' A tinge of melancholy shadowed her eyes. She took one hand out of mine, and briefly ran it over my cheek.

But as always when something was going really well, Sherlock ruined everything.

'John. John! Come over here! You've got to see this!'

I sighed my deepest sigh. The third superlative of the day.

'It's all right,' Scarlett said warmly, stroking my hand. I briefly smiled at her. Then we both rose and hurried over.

164

'There.' Sherlock pointed at a table which was broken in two. Just in between the two halves was another red thread message laid out for us.

THE LIBRARY – A CASE OF IDENTITY – ED

I skipped exclaiming 'What the hell?' and looked at Sherlock for an answer.

'Well, it seems we have another appointment to go to when we're finished with Barker,' Sherlock concluded calmly.

'Is that all?' I asked angrily, 'Can't you at least tell us who these messages are from? What they mean?'

Suddenly, Scarlett started panting, her eyes fixed on the thread in horror. She was seeing something we weren't. I turned her away from the sight of the thread.

'It's all right, Scarlett. There's nothing to worry about,' I murmured softly, but her eyes went completely blank. 'Look at me, look at me, Scarlett. Whatever it is, it's not your fault. Do you hear me?'

She shifted uncomfortably, looking past me as if she was only hearing but not seeing me. 'John, John, is that you?'

'Yes, it's me. It's all right,' I insisted, trying hard not to sound insecure.

Eventually, she loosened her grip, which had tightened around my shoulder.

'John, you're the best thing that's ever happened to me.'

Remembering my mistakes from all those years ago, I could only shake my head. 'I'm not so sure you would say that if you could remember everything.'

I didn't know what to do. I was desperate to kiss her, but I didn't want to take advantage.

Suddenly I saw Sherlock looking up from the message. 'What do you think you're doing?' he said quietly.

At first, I thought the indignation in his voice was aimed at our delaying the investigation. But I noticed he hadn't addressed this to me. He was looking intently at Scarlett, and I could help but feel a silent plea in his aura.

In abashment, Scarlett let go of me. I couldn't bear to look at her. My eyes were fixed on Sherlock, who was now casually picking up the threads to store them in his pocket. Scarlett turned her head.

'I'm sorry,' she said despondently.

'Don't be,' I replied, but she just shook her head and walked out of my arms. Out of my reach, into the bathroom, shutting the door behind her.

* * *

I looked in the mirror. *How could I put John in such a position?* It was my fault he didn't dare. *What must he be thinking now?* I wasn't the Scarlett from all these years ago, and none of my words could be entirely true anymore. There would always be something I missed, something I didn't know. Whatever I would say, it would all be empty. Above all, I shouldn't have looked back to see those grey eyes. *What was Sherlock thinking? What was I thinking?*

This couldn't be. With everything I must've done to John in the past, I couldn't let him alone like this. If words would only be lies, there would have to be something else to atone for everything. I'd need time to think and hope the right moment would come.

* * *

Punch him in the face! I thought. That was what he deserved. *How on earth could he ruin this moment?* But I couldn't punch him. Not out of compassion or friendship, but because then he would know what he had done. I picked up half a chair and hurled it into a corner. Salvatore came dashing out of his kitchen.

'Isn't my restaurant ruined enough?' he asked angrily.

'I'm only piling up the broken furniture,' I lied, throwing another chair half on top as an excuse.

Next Scarlett came back, still looking crestfallen. But when I thought of reaching out to her hand, I didn't feel like I was allowed to.

'We're going to examine Barker now,' Sherlock announced from the floor. I still wanted to punch him.

'But who is this message from?' Scarlett asked him sharply.

'I can't say for sure yet. Moriarty's men broke in here, but whoever left this message came afterwards. It's not one of them, but someone who knew their plans. You can see footprints of someone tiptoeing through the glass fragments, very careful not to touch anything. There's a traitor among Moriarty's lines, and he doesn't know yet. I think these messages will prove extremely helpful in our investigation. ED is the sender. Could be initials, but that would be obvious. Ed could be short for Edward or Edmund, first name or surname, but most likely a middle name or alias Moriarty doesn't know,' Sherlock explained in his quick manner.

'What about the message itself? What does that mean?' Scarlett asked.

'Maybe this person has delicate information to share, but is questioning our identities now that doppelgangers like Morecroft

167

are running around? We should probably bring our passports,' I suggested.

'Very good, John,' Sherlock said to my surprise. 'Really?'

'No. It's a book title, naturally - *A Case of Identity*. We're supposed to fetch it at the library. Which library, you may ask? The British Library, because that's where I always go. We're dealing with someone who knows our whereabouts, so this is where he'll hide it. A large volume, most likely - best to hide flat things in; documents, photographs. Smart guy. Can't wait to meet him,' Sherlock finished.

I felt sorry I hadn't punched him when I'd had the chance to.

An hour later, we found ourselves at Salvatore's flat in Brewer Street. I clenched my teeth the whole time, careful not to let anything slip out. My thoughts were all over the place, so I distracted myself with the task at hand - examining Barker.

Only once did I remember what Scarlett had said about cats falling in love. I wished I could dismiss that as her not knowing Sherlock well enough, but suddenly it didn't seem impossible to me anymore.

A moment later, someone rang the doorbell. Minnie entered the apartment, greeting everyone. To my surprise, she already knew Salvatore.

'O-of course. We often come here to hide dead bodies,' she stuttered with an amiable smile. 'No, actually it's delicate documents usually,' she clarified. 'And we get the food on the house!'

I smiled back politely, but I didn't know how to take Sherlock's keeping this a secret from me.

'Anyway, Sherlock, we hid the man that Morecroft killed; he's in Steven's office now. He was one of Moriarty's men, not Mycroft's. No passport or driver's license, of course, but we identified him as, er, Jonathan Small, an ex-prisoner. Shot right in the head. He wasn't carrying anything valuable and we couldn't find any obvious reason why Morecroft should kill him,' Minnie informed us.

'Oh, we'll find one, but let's have a look at Barker first,' Sherlock instructed.

Minnie helped Sherlock pull the body out of its bag, hauling it up onto the table. I was too numb to do anything. Scarlett didn't seem to have much of a zest for action either.

Sherlock had already begun scanning the body intensely while Minnie gave each of us a pair of latex gloves.

Barker was about forty-nine, tall and muscular, with brown grizzled hair, and showing signs of a beer belly. He'd been shot through the heart. They really *had* had it a little too easy.

Apart from the lethal wound, I recognised a few cuts at his side, and his hands were bloody as if he had fallen into a thorny bush. Then there was a strange mark on his left ear, like a black tattoo consisting of two dots and a hyphen in between.

'What does this mean?' I asked, pointing at it.

'Oh, that? We found it on each of Moriarty's men we had so far. We think it's Morse,' Minnie explained.

'It's for the different units in Moriarty's network. Barker belonged to a reinforcement unit, according to the tattoo,' Sherlock added.

'Dot-dash-dot is an R,' Scarlett muttered, and for another painful moment, Sherlock riveted his eyes to her in fascination. I turned away.

'What is ED in Morse?' I heard Sherlock ask her.

'I-I... I can't seem to... remember' she stammered.

'Something's blocking your memory! Think hard! What is it?' Sherlock sounded exceedingly human now. 'You know the Morse code. What is ED?'

Scarlett just stared ahead, dazed like her brain was too daunted at confronting this to compute.

Suddenly, Sherlock clutched her upper arms and shook her. 'What is ED, Lily?'

The words just stumbled out of her mouth. 'Dot – dash/dot/dot! L! It's my fault!'

She just stormed out, and to my dismay, Minnie was faster going after her than I was, so I stayed. *What is her fault?*

Sherlock's mind was racing now, I could see it. His eyes were filled with sparks of inspiration.

'What's going on, exactly?' I asked him.

'I said it already; Moriarty is planting information on her to use her as bait. If she knows Morse, what can she tell us about the sender of our messages, who is clearly part of his network? The information vital for this is blocked in her mind, though she is capable of the code. Why is that? Because it is linked to something painful in her past. Now, what is ED in Morse? E is a single dot, whereas D is a dash and two following dots. If you combine those two, you will get L which is the initial of the first name she has chosen not to be called by. There you find the link between the sender of our messages and her,' Sherlock finished drama-queenly.

I raised my eyebrows and sighed. 'She doesn't leave any trouble out, does she?'

* * *

'Those two can be quite exhausting, can't they?' Minnie observed with a cordial smile and a nod at Salvatore's window.

I nodded thankfully.

'Do you want to talk? About your memories?' She gave me a carefully questioning look.

170

'I don't know.' I sighed. 'How much has Sherlock told you already?'

'Oh, he never tells me much,' she said, blushing.

'He seems to trust you though,' I objected.

'Do you think so?'

I smiled and nodded. 'Well, if you really want to hear it, I lost my memory. Total retrograde amnesia. John and I studied together, and since I don't have any relatives, he agreed to take care of me when I got out of hospital until I could manage to live alone. We discovered that I was part of a criminal organisation before I lost my memory. Sherlock has the files, but he won't show them to me.'

'That sounds like him,' Minnie chipped in.

'Do you have any idea why he does that?' I asked.

'Sometimes I think he's afraid of failing. He wants to make sure that he's got it right one hundred percent. He's definitely a perfectionist. But then again, he hardly ever fails, and he knows it. Every time I'm convinced he's uncertain, he proves me wrong. It's strange with him,' she explained.

'But what did you remember then? It didn't just seem like recalling old memories to me,' she remarked coyly after a moment.

'I-I...' I came to a halt and leaned against the wall. 'It's... it was a... promise...'

Minnie soothingly stroked my arm. 'Whose promise?' she enquired carefully.

'I... promised him... to stay... because we... belonged together... but I promised... to save her... and I failed...' I panted.

'Who is he?' Minnie asked.

'I don't know, I don't know!' I cried.

'Can you remember who you wanted to save?'

At her words, Anne appeared just behind Minnie, reaching out for me, screaming, as if someone pulled her into her grave. My head grew and grew with her screams and her pain, which I shared for it being my fault. I wished my head would burst so her voice would vanish, but it didn't, so I was left to scream until my lungs failed me.

Chapter 3

Another scream snapped me out of my episode. It was Minnie. A masked man dressed in rags jumped at her from behind a car and sealed her mouth with his hand. She dropped her phone which I prayed she had called someone with already.

The man saw me lying on the ground. I tried to get up, but I still felt dizzy. I wasn't quick enough to avoid his foot hitting me right in the stomach.

The pain was excruciating. I saw red suns exploding in front of my inner eye. I had no breath to scream.

A second shadow joined the masked man. It flew over me, blowing a cold breeze into my face. There was a bump and a pained exclamation, then a crack.

'Brother mine, don't appal me when I'm at work.' That was Sherlock's voice!

I opened my eyes, and there he was: tall and fierce in his billowing dark coat. He was pressing the masked man against the wall, contorting his arm. When I sat up, my stomach felt like a bar of smouldering wood. I tried to speak, but only hot air escaped my mouth. Minnie slowly recovered from the shock and knelt down next to me.

'Lie down, lie down. You mustn't strain your stomach. We'll help bring you back to Salvatore's flat.'

She threw a long, admiring look at Sherlock, her eyes sparkling and her cheeks glowing. When she noticed me watching her, she grew pink in the face and looked away.

Sherlock pulled off the mask. To my astonishment, Mycroft's face appeared.

'Is this the right one now?' Minnie asked, and Sherlock nodded. 'What was he wearing a mask for then?'

'Do you honestly think I want everybody to know who I am? I had to rob a homeless person to get undercover! Moriarty has people searching for me!' He dismissively gestured towards me and murmured in Sherlock's ear, 'She's on our list. Don't you think it a little too barefaced to run around with someone we have been trying to arrest for years?'

I winced.

'Not at all,' Sherlock retorted, 'you're getting slow. She lost her memory.'

Mycroft turned up his nose at me.

'Oh, yes,' he twanged then with a condescending look. 'Nevertheless, I would like her to–'

'You wouldn't like anything, Mycroft. Now shut up and get moving,' Sherlock hissed, pushing his brother into our direction.

Sherlock extended his hand to me. I gladly took it, and together with Minnie, he helped me up. Once I was standing, Sherlock intensely scanned me without letting go of my hand.

His presence was pure thrill, and it was so strong it felt like the air changed around him. His lips twitched into an elated smile from time to time. When at last he looked into my eyes, it felt like they were plugged into a point.

Finally, he let go.

'Do you think you can walk?' he asked.

'Probably,' I estimated.

'Good.' Sherlock glanced around the rooftops in the street. We had to move quickly, despite the burning pain in my stomach. Minnie supported me all the way back to the flat. Sherlock kept looking into every possible direction, observing every corner, every shadow. Minnie's expression changed rapidly from admiring Sherlock to anxious awareness. It felt like ages until we arrived at the flat.

'Sherlock, why didn't you say what happened!? Why do you *never* say anything!?'

I was truly flattered that John simply overlooked Mycroft when he saw me. He seemed so careworn. Guilt ravaged my injured stomach.

'Didn't he tell you what I said to him? I was wondering why you weren't with him,' Minnie admitted in astonishment.

'Of *course*, he didn't. He just said, "Be right back," and went out.' John said furiously.

'I only told him Scarlett was having a panic attack because of her memories, but then Mycroft attacked us out of nowhere,' Minnie explained.

Sherlock was already dashing about again.

Mycroft lifted a finger and corrected her, 'I wasn't attacking you. I was merely trying to keep you from screaming and drawing attention to me, because as you may have heard, I'm being followed. I only defended myself against one of the world's top assassins.'

At the last word, a sharp memory overcame me. I knew it was a memory because it was nothing like my previous visions.

There. A body.

Right in front of me.

Dead.

A tall man of

forty years, in jeans and
a black jacket, grey hair and
horrified blue eyes. Shot in the
forehead. I
picked up the gun.
It was mine now
Nobody would know
And then I ran away.

* * *

She ran straight out, down the street, down Wardour Street, across Trafalgar Square and into the Strand. It was hard to keep up with her speed. She was ten yards ahead of me. I hoped to God I would catch up with her before something could happen to her. But she didn't slow down, and I could hardly speed up. There was no chance for me. Something else stopped her. I kept going, only halting when she hit a car.

'Oh God,' I exhaled, stopping on the spot. Slowly, she slipped off the engine bonnet. Adrenaline shot through my veins, and I rushed to her. The car had come from India Place, and it hadn't been very fast; it had come to a halt immediately when she'd run into it. The driver stepped outside the instant I reached Scarlett.

'Is she injured?' the driver asked, alarmed. 'Should I call an ambulance?'

'It's all right, I'm a doctor,' I assured him.

I held up her head. There were bleeding scratches in her face, but her neck seemed unscathed. I checked the rest of her body: her spine, her ribs, her legs, her arms. Nothing was broken.

'Thank goodness. I'm just glad I didn't speed up just then,' he answered. I gave him a forced smile.

176

'Scarlett, can you hear me?' I softly patted her cheek.

Her eyelids twitched, and after a moment she opened them. 'John? Am I dying? Am I dead? I think that's what they want,' she coughed, rolling her eyes deliriously. I leaned her head against my shoulder.

'It's my fault, I was too late. I'm so sorry. I shouldn't have let Sherlock go after you alone,' I maintained, but she put her finger on my lips.

'Can you try and help me up?'

I ran my thumb over her cheek. 'If that's what you want.'

I pulled her up to me slowly. Holding onto me, she eventually managed to stand.

'Do you feel any kind of pain? In the stomach or in your back?' I enquired.

'On the side, a little,' she admitted, 'but it doesn't feel like more than a bruise.'

She was holding her head.

'Do you feel dizzy?'

'A bit, but it's fading.'

I looked her over to see whether she was standing lopsided or in any other unusual way.

'May I?' I charily put my hand on her side, pulling up her shirt, after she nodded. The skin was swollen; it would surely grow dark purple in a few hours. Thankfully, I couldn't find any find any signs of internal injuries. Scarlett's grip tightened painfully around my arm as I was doing so.

Finally, I pulled the shirt back down. 'I think you're going to be fine. Are you still feeling dizzy?'

She shook her head. 'Thank you, John.'

'Don't thank me. It's due to the driver's quick reaction that you're still alive and barely injured.' I turned to the driver, embarrassedly scratching his head.

This was the first time I actually looked at him. He was rather young, tall, slender, had dark, tanned skin and short black hair. He wore an expensive white pullover and black trousers.

'Well, I'm glad that she's all right. Can I drive you anywhere?' he asked politely.

'No, thanks,' I declined, smiling.

'Please, let me know if I should have caused any harm that I can make amends for.' He handed me his card.

'Thank you, that is very considerate of you,' I remarked, clearing my throat.

'Why, certainly. Get well soon, young lady,' he replied, nodding at us. We also bade him goodbye before turning around to slowly make our way back to Salvatore's flat.

I had to support her quite a lot still, but I didn't mind. However, I was afraid she wouldn't be able to walk the entire way back. I called Sherlock, telling him to pick us up. He was reluctant at first; apparently Barker was very interesting to examine, but at last he agreed. I sighed, stuffing my phone back into my pocket.

Scarlett squeezed my arm.

'Don't worry, he'll come,' she assured me warmly.

* * *

It took a while until he did. We were sat on a bench in Wellington Street, not knowing what to do or say. One side of my head was burning and throbbing, my back was aching so much I couldn't lean against John.

I felt horrible that I had run away. I couldn't even remember the moment I had decided to do it.

John saw the pain in my face. He carefully ran his fingers through my hair, scanning every inch of my skin. He asked

178

again whether I felt dizzy, but I slowly shook my head. He checked if my nose was broken – it wasn't.

He looked me deep in the eye and ran his thumbs over my cheeks.

'Don't you run away again,' he sighed, his voice on the edge of breaking.

I shook my head with a smile and took his hands into mine.

'I promise.' I took a moment to continue, 'John, whatever happens to me, it's not your fault. If it's anyone's, it's mine, and if you knew what I saw when I ran away, you wouldn't care anymore anyway.'

'I don't care what you did before you lost your memory. To me, you're as innocent as when we first met,' he replied looking at me with sincerity.

For a long time, we fell silent. John's eyes glided all over the street, throwing very long looks at the cars passing by on the Strand. I could tell he was thinking of Sherlock, wondering when he might show up, if at all.

Suddenly, he opened his mouth, paused hesitating, but then said, 'I wish he wouldn't come–'

I couldn't let him finish, but took his lips to mine.

We both held still. I tried to take in every inch of his thin, strong lips to memorise and never forget them again.

* * *

It was strange to know how it felt to kiss her, knowing she didn't know how it felt to kiss me. She still had these incredibly soft and full lips, like a pillow you could sink into. They had a refreshing vibrancy, but at the same time the feeling of sinking down to troubled waters never left me when I kissed them.

Scarlett was a fascinating mystery.

I broke off the kiss to look at her. Her eyes were still closed, but she was smiling. This kiss had been so innocent, and yet a part of her innocence seemed to be motivated by fear of her own guilt. For a moment, I was worried history might repeat itself.

When she opened her eyes, I could see no guilt. I could see she was happy. If only for a heartbeat, I would do all I could, if only for that heartbeat.

'John, are you aware of the fact that your keys have just been stolen?'

Oh, one day I will kill him.

'*What* did you say?'

Sherlock was standing just behind our bench, his hands behind his back.

'I said, someone just stole your keys, didn't you listen?' he asked calmly.

I rose with a jolt.

'And who did it!? I suppose there's not enough time to tell me how you figured out this one, if I still want to catch the thief?' I snarled at him.

'Oh, there really is, you know,' he just started off. 'Your jacket is turned up at its side, but since you're a soldier you always carefully pull it straight. So, this time you haven't noticed its being pushed up which means you didn't do it. The only thing you keep in the front pocket of your trousers is your keys. The thief therefore must've known you do so, and since you don't look like you own a villa, he most likely even knows where you live and that there's something in our flat that he wants. We're dealing with a man with excellent training in quiet robberies, a keen eye, and a good informant, who actually happens to be me. Isaac happened to be in the area, so I texted him to fetch your keys and hide at our flat. He replied saying you were somehow engaged, so I said he should just take them from your pocket. It seems he did a good job.'

I punched him in the face.

'John!' Scarlett shot up.

'Can you believe his nerve!?' I shouted.

'Do you really think he's going to change if you break his nose? We've got enough things to worry about already,' she reproved me.

Then she went over to Sherlock who was holding his bleeding nose. She gave him a handkerchief.

'Dizzy?' she asked.

'It's not broken,' he answered with a charming ring to his voice, winking at her. I wished I had knocked him out.

He had parked Salvatore's car at Southampton Street.

'Where did you find Isaac?' Scarlett asked as we got in.

'At the Seven Dials. There's a pub at the corner called "The Crown" what an obvious name for a *secret* meeting point of the national secret service.' Sherlock shook his head with a superior smile. 'Since I had Norina do a bit of research in this area, it was child's play to figure out where they had brought him. I snuck in there and had a look. Where in a pub would you conceal a secret room, totally unnoticed by the customers? How do you ensure no one goes in there? The process of elimination led me to staff room next to the toilets. Wasn't a difficult leap.'

'And you just walked in there, and told them to release Isaac?' I asked disbelievingly.

'Oh, no, I had a huge fight with a horde of agents before I could rescue him. Well, of course, I *just walked in* - nobody was there. I had to knock out the janitor to nick the keys, though. The storeroom had a back door, only concealed by an apron. That told me they had only just left and meant to be back soon, otherwise they would have hidden it more thoroughly. I had to be quick. The room behind the storeroom was very big and there was a conference table in the middle. A lot of cardboard boxes were stacked by the walls. In one of them I saw an ear peeping out. When I opened it, Isaac fell out, snoring. We then hid in a shop across the street, watching the agents long faces when they came back. The only problem we have now is that since Mycroft was gone, the secret service have been doing what they want. Now that they distrust me, they also distrust the people I'm in contact with. They've started to shadow my Irregulars. That doesn't mean it doesn't work anymore; we only need to be more careful. Isaac will have to stay at 221C for the moment. I already arranged it with Mrs Hudson. I told him to go to the theatre first, so he can go incognito. They'll pull off a decent show. Maybe we'll still see some of it when we come home,' Sherlock finished, smirking.

'What did they want with Isaac in the first place? Why him and not Billy, or Finn?' asked Scarlett.

'Well, Isaac talked to Morecroft just after he went into Mycroft's role,' Sherlock explained. 'Of course, he didn't know who he was and told him where he could find me. Unfortunately for us, some agents saw him there, so he won't be able to show his face for some time.'

Sherlock turned into Rupert Street. Yes, I wanted to know all these things, but right now, my mind raced with thoughts about Scarlett and our kiss. *Is she really in love with me again? Has she made up her mind?*

She didn't seem quite certain about anything at the moment, and I couldn't blame her. So many things had happened since she arrived. Yet I couldn't keep my heart from wishing she'd make up her mind soon.

She looked at me and gave me her loveliest smile, taking my hand to squeeze it. She knew she wasn't ready to decide yet, but she would give me the strength to wait.

We came to a halt at Salvatore's flat a few moments later.

'So, what are we going to do now?' Scarlett asked, getting out of the car.

'Burn Barker,' replied Sherlock.

'*What?*' Either I had missed something again, or he was finally going nuts.

'I said, we're going to burn Barker, didn't you hear me?'

'Oh, right, of course. Obviously. *Seriously?* I thought he was important evidence against Moriarty!' I exclaimed.

'You're right: he *was.* But since he was a double agent, he was also important evidence *against* the secret service. They got wind of that and now they want the body,' Sherlock stated. 'I have all the information I need. We have to get rid of him.'

'Why us?' I asked. 'If they're getting in trouble over the evidence, they'll surely try to get rid of it themselves!'

'Oh, they would, but I don't want to give them the information on Moriarty, because then they'll spoil everything. Plus, if they knew that I saw the evidence against them, too, they'd try to get rid of me,' Sherlock answered as we went inside.

'How was he killed then?' I asked, when we stood above Barker's body.

'He wasn't just killed. He was executed. Barker owned Raum Q, remember? Where did he get the money from? I checked his income and it was hardly sufficient for Irene's standards. There had to be another source of money apart from Moriarty. As it happens, he was at the Crown the morning he died, which I can tell from the scent of his shoes. It's the same as the cleaning agent I smelled in the storeroom. Evidently, he'd been at one of the secret service meetings. It became fairly obvious where he got the money and why he bought Raum Q. Of course, the secret service knew about his double role, but Moriarty also knew, since he had a tracker, as I expected. This tracker has an implanted microchip, once you get into its system you can follow his route completely. He must have gone to some place he wasn't supposed to be, in the mind of our national intelligence agency, so they sent some MOD men to execute him as well as the other man, Baldwin, who happened to be his confidant, because he was having an affair with Moriarty's secretary. That was obvious when I first saw him. Not much to get out of him, though, because neither side trusted him. When Moriarty found out about the affair, he naturally informed the secret service of his relationship with Barker.'

Sherlock was rather proud of his elaboration.

Scarlett smiled at him.

* * *

'Where are the others, by the way?' I asked, looking around the room. There was no sound to be heard from the other rooms.

'Oh, Minnie called Steven. They're getting Mycroft somewhere undercover; a favourite place of mine. He'll be looked after. That's all for the moment. We need to get on with Barker,' ordered Sherlock.

'What about Salvatore?' John asked.

'He went back to his restaurant to get some firewood for our nice acquaintance here.' Sherlock nodded over to the body and strode across the room to fetch the bag it had been stored in. He beckoned me to lift the dead man at the shoulders while he gave John the bag and took the feet.

Barker's skin was ice-cold, its leathery texture leaving an unpleasant impression on my mind. I was glad when John slipped the bag over him. The sound of the zip cut through the room.

We got into Salvatore's car.

On arriving at his restaurant, we saw a huge heap of broken furniture in front of the building. A table half was hauled on top of the pile from inside. When Sherlock put his head round the door, a broken picture frame hit him right at his temple. It didn't seem to have much of a lucky day, his head.

'Good afternoon to you, too, Salvatore,' he shouted sarcastically, wincing as he touched his bleeding wound.

Leaving John to park the car, I went over to him and held down his arm. He wrinkled his nose in a peculiar way when he looked at me. The blow had made him a little unsure on his feet, I could tell. Sherlock briefly shook his curls in irritation. I brushed them out of his wound.

'If you keep collecting cuts on your face, you'll end up scarred like me.'

He smiled at my remark – predominantly, John would have said, but actually his eyes looked like they were reaching for the stars.

'I couldn't possibly gain your beauty,' he said suddenly, with a voice of satin. I didn't know what caused them, but this seemed like one of those moments where he would compose himself in a peculiarly elegant way and a spark of old-fashioned manners overcame him in fascination. His coat seemed longer, his jaw sharper, his hands stronger, and his whole body was pulsating with a countenance that was harder to keep. Considering the events of the following evening, I always found this the most implausible time for such a moment to occur. But I think it was because he was afraid.

I ran my fingers through his curls again, along the edge of his wound, wiping away his running blood.

Sherlock bent down and kissed my cheek. For a heartbeat, I could feel his full, keen lips on my skin, the tip of his nose at my cheekbone. When he let go, it felt like he ripped away the veil of his warmth to reveal the horror of my feeling unfaithful to John.

My hand slipped out of his hair.

Maybe I should have punched him too.

'Salvatore! We really need to get the stuff away now. John parked the car around the corner, he'll come in at the back window,' Sherlock shouted into the restaurant.

'Why should he?' I asked, offended and afraid at the same time.

'The street he turned into is being watched,' the consulting detective replied, his manner nonchalant once again.

He was allowing my worn mind to wonder whether I had only imagined what had just happened.

'No, Mary, no!' Anne's scream for her sister ripped me out of my thoughts, out of reality. Her cold fingers were at my neck, trembling and scratching my skin.

It was me who had made her hands so rough that they could cut me open now. She was charged for my crime.

I gasped for breath and ran into the house, wildly shaking my head to loosen her grip. But then, my foot got caught on something on the ground. I fell and my head hit something hard. Everything went black and when I stopped to listen for the noise of my body hitting the ground, I went into a red gloom.

* * *

At first, the sight of Sherlock cradling Scarlett on the floor filled me with red hot rage. In fact, he was just trying to wake her up from an episode, but I only saw that at a second look. I knelt down opposite him.

'What happened?' I panted, still out of breath from climbing in through the window.

Sherlock cleared his throat. 'She–' he hesitated, 'saw something again, and tripped over that chair.'

Hesitantly, he laid down her head and motioned towards me. Frowning at him, I pulled up her torso and took her head into one hand.

Sherlock threw a last deductive look at her, a tinge of anger in his eyes, as if he couldn't entirely figure her out. He exhaled and stood up, his nose twitching strangely once. Then he strode off into the kitchen to talk to Salvatore.

'Scarlett, wake up. We need to move or we're in danger,' I murmured.

She slightly moved her head. Her eyebrows were curled up into a pained frown, and her jaws were clenched.

'Get me some water and ice, please,' I shouted over. Shuffling was to be heard from within the kitchen and a moment later Salvatore appeared with what I'd asked for.

He shook his head, but offered, 'Can I help you with anything?'

'No, thanks, I'm fine here, but I think Sherlock might need a little help with putting the furniture into the car,' I advised him. He hobbled off.

Cooling Scarlett's temple, I put down the glass of water and dipped my fingers into it to sprinkle her face with it. She twitched, strangely shrugging her shoulders as if to cast off a shudder.

Suddenly, she shot up and burst out, 'Stop! Let me go! I couldn't save you! Anne, please!'

Then she opened her eyes and flinched at my sight.

187

I had thrown my hands up in shock at her cries, and now she was staring at me. It probably looked as if I was being held at gunpoint. When the shock in her face increased, I started to worry. Finally, her eyes shifted to something behind me, and I realised I couldn't take down my hands anymore.

'What do you want!?' Scarlett stammered at the person behind me. It was horrible only to perceive a presence, but not to see or hear anything of the opponent as we were all motionless.

A moment later, there were noises within the kitchen. Sherlock angrily shouted something, and I could hear the man run for it. He was so quick, I only got a glimpse of his black mask when he leapt through the window.

'Oh my God, John, I thought he was going to shoot you,' Scarlett whispered, then flung her arms around me. 'I'm sorry, I'm so sorry!' she whispered, her voice as rigid as ice.

'For what? It wasn't your fault, you did nothing wrong,' I averred, but she vehemently shook her head.

'Damn! They got away!' Sherlock swore, coming out of the kitchen. 'We have to be quick now. Get her into the car and help me to search the building for evidence. Salvatore will load the car and as soon as he's done, we're off.'

Slowly, I propped Scarlett up in my arms. Sherlock had already run off again. Tears were still glittering in her eyes as she placed her hand on my cheek. When I kissed it, a heavy sob escaped her, and I wondered if anything else had happened that could have shaken her conscience.

'Go, we've got to hurry,' she urged me then, and I nodded.

After I had sat Scarlett down in the car, I ran downstairs to help Sherlock who was weaselling about the place, but we didn't find anything that would explain the intrusion. He had already looked upstairs, and so we only checked the kitchen afterwards. Probably, someone looking for Barker again. The bangs of Salvatore loading the car with all the broken furniture were delighting the neighbourhood. When I got in, my head hit a chair leg, but eventually I found myself perched between pieces of wood of all sizes next to Scarlett, who didn't seem to have more space. She reached out and stroked my shoulder.

'Careful.' She smiled ambivalently.

Then we drove off.

A while later we found ourselves at Bedford Square Garden at the southeast side of the British Museum. Brazen as Sherlock was, he ordered Salvatore to drive right into its middle, because it had been raining for some time now, and nobody was there. There was a clearing in the middle of the square where we unloaded the wrecked furniture, buried Barker under it and set fire to it.

'Gareth? – Yeah, Lestrade, could you please keep your cops out of the area around the British Museum for a while? They can clear up the mess in two hours,' Sherlock commanded our favourite DI on the phone while we watched the flames reach for the sky.

I put my arm around Scarlett. There was a romantic touch to burning evidence against the British secret service, and the heat seemed to do her good. She grinned at me in silent agreement. Salvatore frowned.

'Do you know where Barker went already? Why the secret service followed him?' I asked Sherlock after some minutes.

'Yep, I do, and that's exactly where we're going now. It's round the corner. Gower Mews,' replied Sherlock, searching for something on his phone. We quickly got into the car and drove over.

We stopped in front of a yellowish brick house.

'What if there's someone in?' I objected, sceptically.

'There isn't,' Sherlock countered after a glance at the door. He pulled out a lock pick, and broke in.

189

Inside was rather dark and smelled of damp walls. Sherlock looked left and right, but even though there were closed doors on both sides, he seemed to know these rooms were of no interest, since he led us straight up the stairs.

On the third floor, a door to our left had been left ajar.

'It's here,' Sherlock murmured. Carefully, he snuck over with his typical cat-like moves. Pressing his body against the wall, he peeked into the room. He made no sound. Then, all of a sudden, he kicked the door open and marched in. Of course, we dashed right after him.

The room was empty except for a grumbling cat which I almost shot. Sherlock raised his arm just in time.

In the middle of the floor there was a huge red circle. Sherlock flung himself at the ground, smoothly catching himself before sniffing at it.

'Blood?' I asked.

He nodded.

'So what does it mean?'

'This is the hint I've been waiting for. The missing link! Oh, this is fantastic!' he enthused, standing up, only to get out his lens and kneel down again to go on and examine it.

'Sherlock, I still don't get it.'

'It's the reaction to Barker's death. He was a member of theirs. Neat idea. Large brush, natural bristles, 2.5 inches. John, do you have a plastic bag?' He chipped off a blood-stained piece of floorboard. 'We need to get this to analysis.'

His investigating ways still made me shake my head. He seemed to totally lose the connection to the rest of the world sometimes.

'No, I don't have a plastic bag, why should I?' I protested.

'I have one in the car,' Salvatore announced triumphantly.

'Great! Go and fetch it,' Sherlock ordered.

But as Salvatore left the room, something changed in Sherlock's face. He grew pale and alert, his eyes riveted to a point behind me. 'Lily!'

I whirled around. Scarlett was white as a sheet and her breath slowly changed to a pant. Her eyes were fixed on the red circle. She opened her mouth to speak but began coughing every time she was about to utter a word.

'What is it, Lily? Tell me!' Sherlock demanded fiercely.

For a moment, she looked like a doe staring down a car's headlights.

'G.G.' she exhaled suddenly. Then she fell into my arms, shaking.

'What does this mean!?' I reproached Sherlock, holding Scarlett tight.

'Initials. She knows the leader of the organisation,' he remarked already searching for something on his phone.

'What organisation? What's going on?' I blustered.

Sherlock briefly looked up from his phone, clearly annoyed. 'The Red Circle, criminal organisation based in Italy. About a century old, frequent connections to the mafia.' He went on searching again. 'Their trademark is a circle of blood around their victims' heads.'

He held out his phone to me. On the screen, I could see a picture of a large man lying stretched out in a dark room, a crimson halo around his head.

'This was meant for Barker. He was here just a few nights before this happened. Moriarty keeps in touch with the Red Circle, using them for his clients if he needs to. Barker was his messenger. The secret service didn't reckon with this complication, and I suspect the Red Circle didn't know about him being a double agent. When the secret service found out he was meddling with a third party, they had him followed to get at the organisation. He was keeping his information from them, so they located the place of his meetings with the Red Circle and went in on them here. You could see the marks of the shoes of about a dozen men storming up the stairs at the wall down there. Barker managed to escape, and the Red Circle swore to kill him, which is indicated by the quaint painting on the floor. Barker sent this man as a replacement, because he knew he couldn't much longer keep it secret that he wasn't only working for Moriarty. Now, we need to find out whose blood they used.'

After Sherlock's enlightening speech, Salvatore came upstairs with the plastic bag. Sherlock triumphantly placed his sample of the floor into it.

'Scarlett, it's all right, it's all right. You can stop shivering now, OK?' I muttered softly into her ear, but it was no use. *What does she have to do with the Red Circle? Is this a threat to members who left the organisation? Or is this some information Moriarty planted on her? Is he using her to lure us into his den; Scarlett leading the way, because he knew we'd follow her? But what will he do to her when she stops being useful?*

Suddenly I got rather worried. My hand went up to hold her head. Her neck seemed almost too weak to hold it.

'Sherlock, how did she know about the leader?' I asked.

'Oh, I thought that was fairly obvious,' Sherlock mumbled casually, inspecting the window.

'Not to me. If you ever care to learn that,' I retorted.

'Well, she was a member of the organisation,' Sherlock stated, swiftly turning around.

'What? I thought she was in Bolivia?' I protested.

'They have quite an international network.'

'How can you prove that?'

'It's in her files.'

I couldn't believe he just said that. *The nerve!*

One thing was for sure though. I would read those papers as soon as I could lay my hands on them.

Scarlett buried her head at the side of my neck. I wondered if she could feel my heartbeat.

'You'd better get her outside now. I'll come down in a minute,' Sherlock advised us, as if he cared. I more than liked to follow his orders for once.

Outside, I tried to cheer Scarlett up by strolling alongside the neat little shop windows in the street.

'Look, there's a little teddy bear. I think he likes you,' I remarked tenderly. 'See, he can't take his eyes off you.'

Scarlett made a shy attempt at a laugh. Arm in arm we were standing there for a while.

'John, I'm afraid you'll regret everything you said to me when you find out the truth about my life,' she suddenly said.

I took a long look at her beautiful troubled face, then shook my head. 'Look at the bear, no seriously, look at him,' I told her. 'Do you think he'd turn his back on you?'

She frowned.

'No, because he can't,' I continued.

'But that's because he's a toy. He can't move,' Scarlett countered almost reproachfully.

'*He* can't, because he's a toy, but that doesn't mean I *can*, because I'm not,' I replied.

A grateful and yet unbelieving smile overcame her face. The golden evening sun gently illuminated her face.

'You deserve a million kisses for this, John Watson. Will you be content with just one for now?' she asked with a voice of liquid silk.

Her lips were a blessing and a curse. I could feel the utmost extremes of a human life in them. As if to grasp her experiences,

I held her hands firmly in mine, and didn't let go when she took one of them up to place it on my cheek.

There was a placid smile in her face when I opened my eyes again. The sun glittered in hers, but their grey seemed to consist of fragments. I put my arm around her shoulder, and we went back to the house with the red circle. When I was about to enter though, Scarlett froze at the door, holding me back, looking over my shoulder in alarm.

'Is this Dr Watson?' growled a deep, rough voice behind me.

Scarlett nodded, slowly.

'I have information for you. In exchange, I want a safe place to hide from the secret service,' the stranger addressed me. I could hear him taking down a gun, and then taking a step towards us, but that was a mistake. Before I could turn around, there was a shot, and blood spattered on the street. The man stumbled and fell to the ground.

I rushed towards him.

'What information do you have? Tell me!' I demanded sharply.

'I- I... D-doy---le... was his n-na---me, Doyle was his name,' stammered the man before he passed out. The bullet had hit his lungs; blood was creeping out of his mouth.

'John, is he dead?' Scarlett whispered.

'Call an ambulance. Now. They can still save him. I only hope whoever shot him won't find him in the hospital.' I replied, trying to keep the bleeding at bay.

'I don't have a phone,' Scarlett objected hectically.

'Take mine.'

'Where is it?'

'Jacket.'

She instantly wrapped her arms around me to feel for my phone and dialled.

In the meantime, Sherlock showed up.

'Damn! They got away again!'

'Who?' I exclaimed. 'The guy who shot him?'

'Intelligence agents. They've been following him. He's one of Moriarty's men. They're definitely convinced I'm working with him now. They were too stupid to realise this man is no longer working for Moriarty. I told you there was a traitor among his lines. I doubt he left the messages for us though. If he had, he would've met us at the library and not risked his life on the streets,' Sherlock explained, looking the man over.

He was tall, probably in his late forties, had dark hair, a stubbly beard, and wore a grey denim jacket which was much too large for him.

'He's recently been abroad, slept rough for several nights on the run. Alcoholic. Betrayed his wife, got light-fingered and landed himself in trouble with Moriarty,' Sherlock murmured, but I didn't bother asking why or how *this time*.

'Did he say anything?' Sherlock enquired quickly.

'I don't really know whether I got it right, but he said something about a name. Doyle or Boyle? I think he said, "Doyle was the name." I wouldn't swear to it though,' I answered, conjuring up some thick clouds of thought on Sherlock's forehead.

Eight minutes later the ambulance pulled up next to us. Paramedics dashed out to haul the injured man up into the vehicle. Scarlett anxiously watched them while Sherlock paced and down the street, texting Minnie, probably telling to do an analysis of the blood sample. After the ambulance drove off, we got into Salvatore's car.

'Where are we going now?' Salvatore enquired.

'Baker Street. There's nothing we can do at the moment without a horde of agents following us. We have to meet Minnie at Cartwright Gardens on the way, so I can give her the sample. I told Lestrade to send his best man to the hospital so our informant will be looked after properly. I don't want him snatched away under my nose,' Sherlock clarified.

We drove northeast up Gower Street, into Torrington Place, passing Gordon and Tavistock Squares and then turning left into Cartwright Gardens, where Minnie was already waiting for us.

Sherlock swiftly stepped out of the car and handed her the plastic bag along with some confidential words I couldn't distinguish. She smiled, blushed and nodded avidly.

Chapter 4

Back at Baker Street, we spent some days in criminal quarantine. Sherlock kept pacing up and down the flat, waiting for news from the man who'd been shot, but when Lestrade finally called about him, it was to say the man had lapsed into a coma.

Scarlett and I meanwhile had a wonderful time, and watched a lot of crap telly, her head resting on my shoulder, except when Mrs Hudson was there. We tried to win the Nobel Prize in witty conversations, and enjoyed some dinners alone when Sherlock was thinking, aka not eating, in the evenings.

I filled Scarlett in about some of the cases Sherlock had solved with me, e.g. *The Sussex Werewolf,* or *The President Patient.* I told her about my career as a doctor, which hadn't been the most glorious one with Sherlock keeping me from work all the time. With all my might, I tried to distract her from all the terrible things she had seen and remembered about the Red Circle. She couldn't speak about it anyway. For once, I didn't care a thing about Sherlock's investigation.

Hence, I decided against reading Scarlett's file just yet. I knew she was scared of my turning my back on her. Although I knew that was never going to happen, I didn't want her to be worried and uncomfortable. After all, she was a different person now. When I told her I wasn't going to read it, she just wrapped her arms around me and kissed my cheek, which I believe was to say thank you for leaving us a small, untouched bubble of happiness for the moment.

I didn't ask her out, however. Not only because we literally couldn't go out, but because I could see she still wasn't ready for a relationship yet. Ever since Sherlock said that she'd lost her memory because of a traumatic event involving her boyfriend, I was worried I would hurt her making her remember. I tried to keep at least some emotional distance.

All the while, Isaac Houston lived downstairs at 221C, a flat Mrs Hudson had never been able to rent out. He felt like the king of France, because he had a roof over his head. There wasn't even a bed, but even the damp walls and blind windows seemed to be paradise to him. Moved by his happiness and astonishingly good manners, Mrs Hudson provided him with meals and a Lilo. She told him he was welcome if he wanted to stay sometimes in the future.

On Scarlett's request, he told us the story of how he became a part of Sherlock's Baker Street Irregulars. He had gotten involved with the wrong people, taken to drink and started to go to drug dens, which is where he met Sherlock – a fact he and I had quite contrary feelings about. Sherlock saved Isaac's skin in a brawl and then discovered that he had the missing piece of information in his investigation. After that, Sherlock had 'employed' him.

From Mycroft, we heard nothing. Apparently, his secret hiding place was secret enough.

The next issue of the *Strand Magazine* hadn't been able to prove Sherlock's hypothesis of there being a code based upon them. He was frustrated.

However, the appointment at the library with the mysterious messenger didn't *seem* to be very pressing in Sherlock's opinion, but of course he was dying to go there. I asked him if he actually thought the guy was going to show up, but Sherlock wasn't sure. When I asked him how the messenger was supposed to know if and when he was following the red thread instruction, he just said that the messenger probably knew more about us than when we go to the library. How very reassuring.

After about a week, Sherlock finally deemed it safe to go outside. Salvatore drove us to the British Library, after a, so far, quite exhausting day of being bossed around by Sherlock who couldn't prepare enough for the meeting. He'd been stressing as if he was going on a date.

We took a small detour in case we were being followed. All the way, Sherlock was grinning in excitement like a little boy. Scarlett couldn't stop smiling at him. His presence was so keen I could almost see it in the air around him. Considering everything that had happened before already, I couldn't imagine what was to top all that now, but Sherlock's whole demeanour told me we had something extraordinary up ahead, which was beyond everything I *could* imagine.

It started to rain.

Slowly, the British Library came into view at the end of Judd Street. Scarlett took my hand. This was a turning point in the mystery, and we all knew it.

When we got out of the car, the large, reddish-brown brick building stood unimpressed by the rain, imposing. Sherlock bid Salvatore goodbye, warning him to lock his flat.

The streetlamps lit up in the approaching darkness and the gathering of shadows. Scarlett looked up at the massive wall like Alice in Wonderland, who was painted on the sign identifying the British Library. I wondered if there were any white rabbits in there.

* * *

After a long moment of careful observation, looking out for the messenger or signs of anything odd, we went in. The entrance hall was so high and wide I almost wondered whether there was any gravity in this room. There were several spiral staircases concealed behind white walls wound around the steps. We took one of those on the right, ascending further and further into the library.

Immersed in the charm of the books stored in King's Library behind mere glass, I grew a little dizzy going up and up until we reached the third floor. Sherlock had spotted a fairly pretty female staff member sitting at a table with her laptop and made her out as his target.

Beckoning us to stand back, he approached her and said something presumably as charming as his smile. The woman seemed absolutely captivated.

In between flirting, Sherlock kept checking the entrance hall; it was four stories high and promising a fall. Comfortably, Sherlock now leant onto the golden railing in front of the woman. He started playing with a flash drive, which he had picked up from the desk. Then, seemingly accidentally, Sherlock dropped the thing into the abyss. The woman gasped, and Sherlock apologised. She grunted something which looked like asking him to stay and wait until she had fetched it, and rushed downstairs. With a grin, Sherlock waved us over and sat down at the table.

The laptop was still logged onto the staff member's account. John and I looked curiously over his shoulder as he entered 'A Case of Identity'.

'Damn!' Sherlock's fist came down hard on the poor desk.

No results found.

'*Why?* Why would he give us the title of a book that doesn't exist?' Sherlock scolded the computer and himself for not having thought of that earlier.

'Maybe it isn't a book title after all?' John suggested.

'But it *has* to be! There's no other–' Suddenly, Sherlock's eyes lit up and he jumped out of the chair. 'Brilliant, John!'

'Oh, was I right for once?'

'No, not really, but almost this time. It has to be a book that's not in the system, because it's a secret copy! Nobody knows of it, and where can you hide a tree better than in a forest? What a clever bloke!' Sherlock exclaimed, pacing off down the corridor.

'But how do we know where he put it!?' John shouted after him.

'He must have left another message!' Sherlock called back. 'I am on fire!'

Not every passage of the British Library was lit as brightly as the entrance hall that evening. I soon lost track of where we were. Sherlock's coat swept along the white walls as if across the pages of a book while he restlessly scanned every corner.

There was nothing to be found.

Through a wooden door with squares of glass, John and I watched him as he checked the reading room covering the fitting research areas. No luck.

Biting his lip, Sherlock exited the reading room, his dark hair curling up around his face, like dark storm clouds.

'You're not going to like this.' Without another word, he swept down the stairs, leaving us no choice but to follow. In the basement, he pulled out his lock pick to open a door labelled 'STAFF ONLY'.

John rolled his eyes. 'What are we breaking into now?!'

'The archive. Where they keep every piece of paper that has ever been printed in England. Well, one copy of each,' Sherlock corrected himself.

'This is a reference library, so I assume it will be noticed if you borrow something?' I spelled out John's lip-pursing thoughts.

Another broad grin spread over Sherlock's face. 'Exciting, isn't it?'

The lock gave a sighing click of submission, and Sherlock showed us into a dark and complex system of corridors with miles and miles of shelves lining the way.

'We have to spread out,' he announced when we reached a hall with about five parallel lines of shelves. 'I'll take the aisle in the middle, you take the ones at the walls on either side.'

John nodded to me, and I went to the left, while he took the right corridor.

This hall seemed larger than I expected. I kept thinking of the red thread messages. *If the sender had left another message here, it would surely look like the others, wouldn't it?*

However hard I looked, there was not a red spot to find. *Where did we find the other messages? Where did red threads appear at all since I arrived in London?*

The painful picture of the beheaded doll popped up in my mind. I gasped, trying hard to remember, ignoring the burning feeling in my stomach – flames rising up to swallow my consciousness.

That had been a warning. Or a threat. Either way I was to be beheaded. I hadn't yet thought it through so far, but now that I forced the picture to stay in my mind it all became horribly clear. Again, I gasped for breath, and came to a halt to hold on to a shelf so my legs wouldn't give way.

'Scarlett! Are you all right?' John shouted over. I wondered if my heavy breath was louder than I thought. Maybe the library was quieter.

'I'm fine, John, thank you,' I spluttered, trying hard not to pant. John and Sherlock walked on, and slowly their steps ceased to echo in my head. Somehow, it wasn't quiet though. *Is there someone else in the room?* The hall was huge; it was rather likely we weren't alone. But something about the noise I heard – a stealthiness, as though every sound was placed smoothly into the silence with care – set my nerves all on edge.

'Guys? Where are you?' I couldn't hear them anymore.

'Over here!' a faint voice called, but I was not entirely sure whether it was John's. Nonetheless, I went after it. The hall seemed endless, and the books seemed to close in on us suspiciously. I was now on the same corridor as John should be. But there was nobody there.

Nothing was to be seen – the light flickered – there was – something over there a white
note – a shred – of paper I
bent down, and picked it up – – –

It's not a book, idiot.

203

My muscles contracted. He was in here, the messenger. *Why would he insist on us finding the book when he is here in person? Sorry, the not-book. But what then? What could possibly justify all this trouble? A look into the future? Was he giving away plans? Sherlock said he was betraying this man, this...* I couldn't remember the name. *Or did he say that?*

My logic told me that if he actually did want to betray a criminal mastermind to us, he might not want to be seen. But he had given away his handwriting. 'Show-off,' flashed through my mind. Still, I couldn't help but feel he wasn't altogether well-disposed towards us.

* * *

'Sherlock, we've lost her!' I blustered when we finally reached the end of the hall.

'She's coming after us,' he said calmly as I went over to him.

'Do you see her anywhere?' I ranted under my breath.

He was seriously standing there, staring at the wall.

'Oh, no, she isn't. It's someone else.' he murmured.

Suddenly, he turned around and bent forward, listening intently. This was not a member of staff, judging by Sherlock's frown. I listened hard.

There was something peculiar about the steps we were hearing. They were too inconspicuous. Instinctively, my hand went to the pocket with my gun.

All of a sudden, there was a rushing noise. For a split second I saw a black shadow swishing through the air between the shelves – the next moment, the lights went out.

'Sherlock, did you see that!?' I cried, whispering frantically.

'Yes,' he mumbled.

I felt him walk past me. A cone of light popped up in the darkness, illuminating his way. At once, I followed him. The silhouette of his coat spinning along danced on the spines of the thousands of books to our left and right.

It was a game of shadows on both sides. We had often been in remarkable, even breath-taking situations, and I had written up quite a few of our cases, but I had never felt more like in a novel until this very evening.

Sherlock seemed to govern all the titles we were passing with his lashing shadow.

There was a swishing noise, hard on our heels. Yet when we whirled around, there was nothing. I wanted to call Scarlett, but I was worried she might give herself away to the mysterious visitor. Faintly, I could hear steps, smooth and quick like paws. *What was he trained to be?*

Out of the blue, a scream cut through the silence.

'Scarlett!' I cried.

A few shelves ahead there was another cone of light, quivering and slowly disappearing. Sherlock and I dashed towards it.

* * *

I ran straight into him. The messenger, it must be. He had me.

Seconds later, the lights went on.

I gasped. It was Sherlock. He was holding me round my waist so I wouldn't run away, presumably in case I was the anonymous correspondent. He left his hands there in case I was about to collapse from shock. I clung onto his coat and leaned my head against his chest.

'Found her,' he murmured with a tinge of bittersweet victory before releasing me.

I blushed terribly when I saw John standing behind him.

'Are you all right? Have you seen the man?' I asked quickly.

'At least you seem all right,' he replied.

I looked away.

'No, we haven't seen him. Have you?' he said a bit more kindly now.

I shook my head. 'I just heard something close by.'

John gave Sherlock a questioning look. Then I remembered the note I had found. Clumsily, I pulled it out of the pocket I had stuffed it into and forgotten later on.

'Here. This was lying on the floor over there,' I explained and handed it to Sherlock.

The detective looked at it with a frown only, but I could see in his eyes that the message was a blow to his stomach. His lids twitched and his pupils narrowed.

'He was expecting us,' he muttered, passing the note to John.

'It's not a book, idiot?' he read hesitantly. A complacent smile overcame his lips. 'I was right, wasn't I?'

But Sherlock wasn't listening anymore. He was already striding to another shelf to peek around the corner.

'Once in a lifetime, and still he won't acknowledge it,' growled John.

I gave him an understanding look.

Instead Sherlock, without turning around to us, made a vigorous gesture to silence us. I took John's hand.

Slowly, we followed Sherlock, tiptoeing over to a shelf even further to the left of the hall. Glancing down the aisle we could see the vague shape of a man standing in front of the shelf at the back wall, reading a book.

'Do you think he's our man?' asked John quietly.

Sherlock tilted his head to one side. 'Could be.'

As if on cue the light went out again.

'Who's doing this? It can't be him – there was no switch anyway near him,' hissed John.

'There are two people,' Sherlock replied under his breath. 'I thought as much.'

John sighed.

Sherlock extended his arm to shove us behind the shelf.

Nothing happened for a while, no sound, no move.

Then the lights went on again, as if nothing had happened.

'Shouldn't we go looking for our book that's not a book?' suggested John under his breath.

'No, we most definitely shouldn't,' replied Sherlock with a compelling smile. He led us into a darker corner and leant against the wall to search on his phone.

'You nicked her password, didn't you?' I reckoned, and Sherlock gave me an appreciative smile.

'I don't think we should do that now,' complained John.

'And that's exactly why I'm doing it. John, *you* should really know me as well as that,' Sherlock reproached him suavely.

Magazines |

he typed. Enter.

The plan of the library appeared, highlighting one hall in the archive.

'Oh...'

Yes, John, we are that stupid, I thought as he rolled his eyes.

The Strand |

Enter.

207

Again, John rolled his eyes. Of course, this was it. The exploding magazine.

But suddenly, Sherlock frowned. 'It's not here. The last issue in the archive is from 1950.'

I could tell he was truly puzzled by this. In a new tab, he googled the matter.

The Strand Magazine was a monthly magazine founded by George Newnes, composed of short fiction and general interest articles. It was published in the United Kingdom from January 1891 to March 1950, running to 711 issues.

Now John and Sherlock both looked like they had seen a ghost. It came round to me a second later: John had been reading this paper for years, and unless we were in a sci-fi movie, this was not 1950 anymore.

Suddenly, Sherlock's face illuminated. 'Oh!'

'What?' asked John.

'I was right! It's not in the system. Someone deleted it!' Sherlock exclaimed, jumping up.

John shook his head. The thought '*what a psychopath*' was all over his face.

Following a pompously smiling Sherlock, we made straight for the indicated hall nevertheless. I could tell from the width of his stride that he knew what he was looking for. The light began to flicker the moment we entered the magazine hall. I looked up at the ceiling. One lamp had been smashed and wasn't working at all, the others seemed to be in order, but were strangely swaying to and fro.

This is a carefully staged drama...

Sherlock took everything in with one glance before searching for the right shelf. John wandered along the shelves on the other side of the aisle, checking the inscriptions at their top. I instead walked off looking for possible clues the stranger might have left us. *If he helped us before, why shouldn't he keep doing that here?*

I would've loved to tell that man that his light show was ridiculously childish, annoying rather than intimidating, and I would have enjoyed it enormously to shout at the lamps, because they looked so involved in the conspiracy.

The moment I looked up, I noticed something in the corner of my eye: a light blue magazine, stuffed into the middle of the shelf to my right; an actual magazine between all the usual hardcover volumes containing the collection of one year.

Then I saw the red thread.

It was hanging from the top of the magazine, disguised as a bookmark.

'Guys!' I called out to them quietly, in case the stranger had followed us already. Sherlock was next to me in an instant. John was there a second later.

Carefully, Sherlock pulled the magazine from the shelf.

'This is in the wrong place,' he protested, looking at the book titles and the shelf mark.

'What's that about?' asked John.

'He wanted to hide it, from other people rather than us,' reckoned Sherlock.

It was not until then that we actually looked at the magazine. A cold, unmerciful shock caught us.

THE STRAND MAGAZINE

New Adventure of
SHERLOCK HOLMES
By
CONAN DOYLE

Sherlock's face almost visibly jolted backwards. This was a blow to his mind. He stopped breathing.

For a moment, his eyes scudded across the cover like those of a hunted deer. When he batted his eyelids hard, I could see he was questioning his sanity.

I knew how that felt to totally lose touch of truth and facts, to be ripped out of everything you know, to lose reliability to yourself, as if every rope tying you to your frame of life was cut off, every thought distorted by doubt and your soul floating in outer space.

For Sherlock, it was worse. His brain was his life; the validity of his deductions was the value of his life to the world.

If what he was seeing was true, it was impossible; it forbade his existence. This issue of the *Strand Magazine* from September 1891 rendered Sherlock Holmes unreal. This was beyond rational explanations. Sherlock appeared truly terrified – for the first time in his life John would later tell me.

He turned the magazine round and round in his hands, his lips pressed together in pain, cheeks quivering.

John and I exchanged concerned glances. It seemed like any moment Sherlock's head would explode. Finally, he opened the magazine.

'Is it genuine?' enquired John, desperately looking for a last reasonable solution.

Sherlock hesitated; then he exhaled, 'Yes,' admitting his defeat. The deer was shot.

Sherlock's voice sounded hollow as he read out the first lines, giving a voice to our ominous opponent.

'"My dear fellow," said Sherlock Holmes, as we sat on either side of the fire in his lodgings at Baker Street, "life is infinitely stranger than anything which the mind of man could invent."'

His voice trailed away as his mind wrapped itself around the meaning of the sentence and the implications of the strange messenger. He shuddered, then read on.

'"We would not dare to conceive the things which are really mere commonplaces of existence. If we could fly out of that window hand in hand, hover over this great city, gently remove the roofs, and peep in at the queer things which are going on, the strange coincidences, the plannings, the cross-purposes, the wonderful chains of events, working through generations, and leading to the most *outré* results, it would make all fiction with its conventionalities and foreseen conclusions most stale and unprofitable."'

'Who-who's writing this? I mean, whose perspective is this?' stammered John, with an uncomfortable suspicion.

'Yours,' said Sherlock coolly.

John was trying not to fall for the trick, but he was already upset to a degree which showed the severity of this realisation.

Sherlock scanned the page, his eyes seemingly losing their focus line by line.

I glanced at the text. He was not hallucinating as far as I could tell. The conclusion seemed inescapable: he was a fictional character.

'There must be an explanation, even if not a logical one,' I said to make him look at me, to loosen the virtual grip around his neck. 'Could a consulting detective maybe also deduce illogical things?'

Somewhere deep down in his eyes, I could see faint gratitude. For a second, a smile flashed across his face, almost unnoticeable. The deer started running again. The wound wasn't lethal.

* * *

What the hell does all this mean? This was an impudence beyond comprehension! Writing things in my name a century ago! *Why would anyone go to the trouble of faking an old magazine – it must be a fake – just to pretend we are in some story from over a hundred years ago? More importantly, why would Sherlock believe in such nonsense?*

Of course, it looked like a very *good* fake, *but why didn't he doubt it for even a split second?* He wasn't questioning anything anymore. He just accepted this absurd magazine as – *what? A threat?* This didn't make sense to me at all, as usual.

What was most frightening about this was the fact that it didn't make sense to *Sherlock*, and he seemed to have no intention of changing that as yet.

'Come on, Sherlock, brace yourself. Who put this magazine here?' I said, trying to make him think again.

At first, he appeared to be in a drunk-like state, but then the light came back into his eyes and he started searching the magazine for clues.

'This had never been in the library. It belonged to a collection of issues, a private collector in those days, and later his descendants sold it at a flea market. The collector preserved it in a folder, which is why it's in such a good state but,' he turned the magazine around, 'on the back you can see traces of a sticker, and there are some slight scribblings on the last page, which indicates it belonged to a child afterwards whose parents didn't see any historical worth in it. When the child had grown up, they sold it at a flea market. Where else could you sell such a thing anyway?'

'But what makes you think they sold it?' I objected.

'The way they treated it, they would have thrown it away otherwise. At the flea market someone recognised its value, probably a collector again, since it's been kept well afterwards. The scribblings are old and the trace of the sticker, too, since the fringes are smoothed over.' He thumbed through the pages.

'On the first page you can see a small note in pencil: £10. This was certainly not the original price, since that would've been a fortune in 1891. It also wasn't the price at the flea market, because that is negotiated and not noted, and the price is still too high for a flea market even decades later. The person who bought it there worked in a vintage magazine store, like the one in Brewer Street. Only collectors *buy* vintage magazines, so the following owner was another collector. Judging by your encounter with the exploding bin, the third collector is our man,' finished Sherlock.

'Do you think it was the man who gave me the guinea pigs?' I tried to think of myself as being clever to make the link, rather than failing to go after the guy that evening.

'It could've been him. But in that situation, I could hardly trust you as a witness. The human brain remembers very little of people and things it is not told to remember anything about or especially focussed on,' he explained.

As I opened my mouth to protest, he interrupted, 'Oh, you'd be surprised. It could've been anyone. An agent, an agent's messenger, that messenger's secretary, or the secretary's aunt.'

'So the secretary's aunt would try to show you that you were actually just a character from a story in a Victorian magazine? Of course!' I blustered.

'No, the secretary's aunt would only be the messenger's messenger, or a very cunning disguise,' he replied. 'Apart from that we don't even know yet whether those incidents are connected. It could just as well be that person was merely using the magazine for a code, and this is someone else's work entirely – someone who knows that you've been reading the *Strand*. Anyhow, we have to find out if there's more.'

'More of *this nonsense*? That's ridiculous!' I complained.

'John, this is a serious matter. We have to be careful about it, whether we believe in whatever this is or not,' Scarlett insisted.

I looked at the floor. *She doesn't believe such rubbish, does she?* I didn't dare ask.

The light flickered even more fiercely now. I began to wonder if it really was a technical defect. Before I could question it out loud, the lamps went out once more.

Chapter 5

'What do we do now?' I asked, hushing my voice.

'Wait and listen,' Sherlock murmured.

The darkness wore me out. More than once, it felt to me like figures were emerging from it, pushing it forward, closing in on me. Anne was behind all this, I was sure of it. She was definitely here.

My whole body was strained so hard, I felt like my muscles would tear up my skin any moment.

It was the darkness tore, and blood gushed from the fringes of the rip.

A sudden cold breeze hit my face and the light flashed.

'Now!' I heard Sherlock cry, and the next moment the steps of running men echoed between the walls.

I opened my eyes.

The light kept flashing and flickering, causing a dizzying shadow play.

John had run off, too, but apparently in a different direction.

Trying to follow all the figures, I jumped from shelf to shelf, but I was never quite certain who I was seeing. Once I thought I'd recognised Sherlock's coat, and yet another shape exactly like it appeared in a totally different spot the same second.

What can I do? No matter where I was, I seemed to feel someone's presence on my back, someone's step at my heels, someone's breath on my neck.

Still, I knew it was just panic wrecking my nerves.

I tried to rivet my eyes to the dark figures dashing about. Slowly, my ears started perceiving sounds again; I was getting closer to the action.

One figure caught my eye with a hypnotic undertow that made me follow it into a dark hall. I saw no face, nothing to identify the person running down the aisle, and I had no explanation but intuition as to why I was running after him. *Is it Anne?* No, I ruled out the thought. I was not having a vision anymore. *Who am I following then?* It wasn't Sherlock; there was no coat. *Could he have taken it off?* No, he was too vain. It wasn't John either though. This man was much too tall. *Has he noticed me following him?* I looked through the shelves to my left. Someone else was coming after him. So was this our strange messenger after all? Something told me, I knew this man. Actively. Not like a notion of recovering memory, but a definite awareness. *But who did I get to know recently?* I tried to peer through to the other person following this man. It was almost completely dark, but, still, I could distinguish the edge of a coat sweeping around a corner. So that was Sherlock. But then he ran off in the opposite direction. Now I understood: he was the one being followed. The person in front of me ran after him and I was right behind. One of the lamps flashed – I saw another person running, a fourth one, but it wasn't John. *So there are two strangers in here!* But as I was trying to piece things together, there was a bang and I fell over a pile of books before I knew the man I was following had knocked them out of the shelf.

* * *

I had completely lost track of Sherlock and Scarlett. At first, I had been following a black figure, but I lost sight of them when I discovered someone else.

There was a man standing inconspicuously at a shelf, and something struck me about his grey suit. It gave him an unnatural dusty air. He was about my age, but he wore a *moustache*. Maybe it was his pointy nose that upset me, maybe the fact that he was standing under the only working lamp in the room, using it to read *and* as a spotlight. He seemed as though he didn't notice anything going on around him. But he did. And I could see it.

Slowly, I approached him. For a moment, he continued to thumb through the volume he was holding, but then looked up at me suddenly. To my surprise, I found myself closing my eyes as a reflex. When I reopened them, he was looking at his book again. I made another step towards him.

'Doctor Watson,' said he in a clear, resonating voice.

I noticed my hands going to my ears to shield them. *From what?* I shook my head as wildly as I could, but when I finally looked at the man again, the lights went out. He left no shadow, no sound.

Rushing to where he'd been standing, I almost tripped over his book. A shudder went down my back. I had not heard it fall.

As I picked it up, the light flashed once again.

THE LOST WORLD

was the title.

But before I could read more, it was pitch-dark once more.

I dropped the book and ran down the corridor the man must have taken, but there was no trace of him anywhere.

* * *

'Help!'

Someone was holding me down. I couldn't breathe. I tried to move, to free myself, but my desperate grip caught nothing but air.

Suddenly, Anne's voice shot from the dark like an arrow into my head, 'You're my only hope! My life depends on it!'

I heard myself cry out to her, but I knew she was lost, and I had failed.

The light started flashing and flickering again. I opened my eyes.

To my great shock, a masked man, dressed completely in black, was bending over me, clutching my upper arms. His knee was pressing down my torso; my writhing and wriggling was of no use.

'Help!' I screamed again, already wondering why he hadn't bothered to keep me silent. My nose had to pay for the scream.

* * *

I had no idea where she was.

When I heard the second scream, I was almost sure it was Scarlett. It came from so far away, and there were so many doors I could take. Left, right, left, right.

I rushed to the door to the right, hoping it would bring me back to the others, and indeed, someone immediately ran into me. *Bloody hell!* He completely knocked me over. I hadn't even seen him coming, although here the light was less temperamental. *If we only knew who is behind this temperament.* And now the guy was off into the darkness of the hall I had come from.

Standing up, I scratched my head, considering my chance of catching up with him. Weighing it in my head, I started running in the opposite direction – towards Scarlett.

* * *

Next, somebody else's nose paid with a crack. The man sitting on me backed off, clutching his nose with one hand, the other braced in a fist. Shielding my face with my arms, I tried to get up looking around me. Sherlock was holding his stomach, his glove dripping with blood from the punch he had thrown at the opponent.

As the two men began something that looked like a mixture between a dance and a boxing match, I tried to ascertain how not to hit the wrong man in the dim light. Just when I raised my arm, however, Sherlock's leg shot forward and felled the opponent with one single blow to his knees. He proceeded by taking some books out of a shelf, smashing them at the masked man's head. The man lay sprawling on the floor, knocked out.

'I never thought books could be used as weapons,' I admitted appreciatively.

'Oh, they can,' Sherlock replied, in a voice a lot more serious than I felt comfortable with. 'Are you all right?' he asked, wrinkling his nose as he looked at mine.

'I'm fine,' I said unconvincingly.

He bent down to closely inspect my face, looking deeply into my blinking eyes. 'Dizzy?'

'A bit,' I confessed.

Sherlock took off one glove. Carefully, he placed two fingers on my nose and felt for a fracture. I closed my eyes in awe of his touch.

'It's still in one piece,' he concluded after a moment.

I opened my eyes and smiled.

* * *

What was that? There was constant noise around me, but I was never quite sure whether they came from me or elsewhere. *Can sound echo from books?* I doubted it.

The aisle seemed endless as I ran along the shelves checking every space between them. I ran left and right, checking the parallel aisles. *If they were in this room, surely I would hear them now, wouldn't I?* Steps. My steps, my breath. Voices. *Was that Sherlock's voice?*

In the hall to the right there was a loud bang, as if a shelf board had given way under the weight of its books.

I just hoped I was in the right room. My orientation had totally left me, and I had no idea what could have happened to either Scarlett or Sherlock. I didn't dare to think of who they could be facing at the moment. *Will I be in time?*

*** *** ***

With a lissome move Sherlock knelt down next to the man, tightly tying his hands with his scarf. Then, he called Lestrade.

'Yes, the British Library. There's someone for you to arrest here. Make sure you get all the credit – it's a big fish.' Sherlock smirked and hung up.

He leaned the man against the wall, only to start burying him in books.

'Will you help me? My scarf won't hold that much,' he estimated, and smiling I rose and grabbed the books that were left in the shelf.

When we were finished, we were both laughing.

'Time to reveal the big fish face,' Sherlock chuckled, and pulled off the mask.

*** *** ***

'Sherlock!'

When I saw them, I exhaled in relief.

'John!' Scarlett called gladly.

Blood was running down from her nose, but apart from that both she and Sherlock seemed unharmed. They were sitting by a huge heap of books which, as I approached it, appeared to have a head. An actual head, sticking out of it. I blinked a few times.

It was Morecroft!

'Where the *hell* did *he* come from? Is he our mysterious messenger?' I asked.

'He's not. He had a meeting here like us, but apparently his date didn't show up,' said Sherlock gloatingly, holding up a typewritten note.

```
Six o'clock, same place

              - Windibank
```

'What does that mean?'

'I haven't the slightest yet, John,' Sherlock confessed. 'We have to go after the other fellow now. I think he'll be able to tell us more.'

They both rose.

'Are you all right?' Scarlett asked me.

'Yeah, I'm fine, but you don't seem very much like it. Is your nose broken?' I handed her a handkerchief.

'Thank you. It's okay, Sherlock checked,' she replied, wiping away her blood.

Once again, I felt a huge desire to punch him.

'Did you think to call the police for once!?' I barked at him.

'Oh, yes. Lestrade is on his way,' Scarlett informed me.

'Good!' I was surprised.

Morecroft groaned, and I just knocked him out again.

'Just to make sure he stays where he is. I don't actually trust your literary construction,' I explained, and Sherlock grinned.

'All right, now we'll stay together and search the halls systematically. John, did you see anyone on the way here?' Sherlock enquired.

'Someone knocked me over when I entered this hall. He ran into that one.' I pointed in the direction of the hall I had come from.

'Good, then we'll go over there now. Each of us will take one of the aisles,' Sherlock instructed, and we did as he said.

Just before we spread out, I had one more question though. 'Sherlock, are we looking for our messenger now? Do you think that was him?'

'Yes, it was,' he replied with a smirk, and off we went.

Only one lamp in the whole hall was working, spreading a foreboding gloom between the shelves. Quietly, we snuck forward.

After what felt like an eternity, we had crossed the entire hall without noticing any movement other than our own. On Sherlock's nod, we went across the terrace where a chilly wind blew against our faces.

We entered the next hall.

To our surprise all the lights were working here, except for one, which was in the corner on the opposite side; it was flickering heavily. Slowly, we moved towards it.

Suddenly, as we drew near, we saw a man in the shadow. Sherlock dashed forward, and Scarlett and I followed at his heels.

Of course, the stranger immediately ran for it, but this time we were faster. He ran down the aisle, through the door, burst into the almost deserted entrance hall and then vanished around a corner, running down the stairs back into the basement. We followed hard on his heels, only to see his shadow on the doorframe of the locker room.

'There's no escape for him there - it's a dead end!' cried Sherlock, and we all rushed after him.

Finally, we would catch our messenger. We turned the corner as we reached it and stopped dead.

There was nobody there except for a man in a white pullover leaning against the red lockers, reading a book. That couldn't be him; the man we were chasing wore wearing dark clothes all over.

Sherlock's face was empty.

The man didn't look at all disturbed, nor was he out of breath. Something else about him, however, seemed to trigger warning signs in my brain.

'Can I help you?' he asked politely.

When he looked up, it hit me: it was the driver of the car Scarlett had run into.

Chapter 6

For the rest of the evening, Sherlock looked as though he himself had been turned into a ghost by the mere presence of the man named Ignatius Thurston. I don't know what had gotten into him when he'd just grabbed the man by the collar and shaken him, shouting questions at him until we questioned both their sanities. I suppose it was an attempt to survive.

Scarlett and I had managed to pull the two apart with somewhat of an effort after some time, telling him we knew the man, though that hadn't exactly lightened our hearts. Naturally all our excuses were of no use after that, and Mr Thurston could – which made it even worse – not tell us anything about a running man in dark clothes. He had neither seen, nor heard anybody, being totally immersed in his book.

Yet, he'd seen us and the fact that he'd hit Scarlett with his car didn't make him a particularly trustworthy witness in my eyes.

Now, we were on our way home, and Sherlock didn't utter another syllable. Lestrade had successfully arrested Morecroft, to our relief, but even that didn't take the gloomy veil of the events in the library from us. The feeling that this was foreshadowing an impossible, incomprehensible case coming upon us, a game we seemingly weren't able to win by any law of reality, kept us in silent, but imminent fright. I still refused to believe in any supernatural nonsense, but from whatever angle I tried to look at it I didn't feel well in my own skin.

When we got out of the cab at Baker Street, the air was cruelly cold, yet it somehow reminded me of my existence.

I helped Scarlett out of the car, worried her nose might be worse than she expected. She thankfully took my hand and kept holding on to it until we'd safely made it up the stairs.

All the while, Sherlock looked like he'd been smashed into a cliff, face forward. He was clutching the *Strand Magazine* that had caused us this enormous shock. Searching for the keys, his hands were shaking, so I quickly fetched my own and let us in.

A giant chaos jumped at us the moment I opened the door almost literally pushing us outside again. Isaac sat in a corner, quivering and crestfallen. Sherlock dashed over to him.

'Isaac, what did they take? What were they here for? Did you see them?'

The boy sadly shook his head. 'I have no idea. Someone knocked me out when I was standing at the window, but I couldn't see who, or how many. I didn't wake up until they were gone!'

'Well, maybe that saved your life. There's a fair chance they might've killed you if you had seen anything,' Sherlock tried to soothe the boy.

Isaac looked properly terrified now, so Sherlock helped him up and told him to go to the kitchen and eat something. The new mystery seemed to reinvigorate his spirit. The next moment, the detective was running to and fro in the flat, looking for clues and trying to find out what had been stolen, while I scuttled after him to tidy up what he threw into the air. That was about everything, so I had quite a job to do, but that also meant I tidied up about everything.

In the meantime, Scarlett made tea for all of us. When Sherlock yelled, there was a splash and she came scurrying in with an indignant face.

'Couldn't you have found out what they stole a minute later?' she asked, raising her brows. I just looked at her with both frustration and admiration at her realising what had happened earlier than me, who was standing right next to Sherlock.

'Well, what did they steal?' she enquired after another moment.

'Your files,' Sherlock grumbled. He clasped his face with one hand and ran it downwards until the tips of his fingers were at his chin.

Only then did I realise. 'What!? Where did you put them? When almost everywhere in our flat is as good as a silver plate? *You*, the great Consulting Detective!? How am I supposed to resist the temptation to throw you out of the window now!?' I bellowed at him.

'Like everyone else does,' Sherlock murmured.

He seemed unimpressed at first glance, but looking closer, I could see if not my words then still the fact itself had paralysed him. Yet, I was too angry and too worried about what those people might do with the papers to try and soothe him. It was all I could do to stop myself from continuing my rant by going out of the flat and down to Mrs Hudson's.

* * *

This was bad news. Really bad news. I felt a queasy pain in my stomach when I looked at Sherlock's face. *What will they do to the files? Will they give them to the police? Could I still be convicted for them? What would happen to John and Sherlock for retaining them? Will someone try and blackmail us?*

227

It was horrible not knowing what those papers said. Losing the memory of your own life was one thing, but losing that of the lives you've ended is quite another.

Once John had left, Sherlock squinted and raised his hands to his temple. I poured him a cup of tea and brought it over to him.

'Don't blame yourself. That won't help us, even if you deserve it. It might be your fault, but you're also the only one who can sort this out again.'

He pressed his lips together, frowning, and took the tea. For a long time, there was silence, then he sipped a bit and put the cup down on the table without looking.

'Why now, Sherlock? What is in those files?' I asked quietly.

'The usual stuff. You were a member of the Red Circle,' he stated seemingly carelessly.

'How many people did I kill?'

'John would kill me if I told you.'

'He's not here.'

'Twenty-three.'

'Oh, God.'

'Oh, yes. John is right sometimes, isn't he?'

Sherlock took a big gulp of tea this time. When he put it back, he was probably wondering why there was no alcohol in it when he needed it. Still the idea seemed to repel him again at once.

'I feel like a puppet,' he confessed suddenly. 'A puppet that doesn't know where its strings converge.' Someone had taken the light from his eyes.

'There. Thousands of strings. At your disposal.' I ran my fingers through his hair. He did not smile, nor did he stop to frown. Almost without me noticing it, my face moved close to his, or did his to mine? My hand was still in his cold hair. His dark curls coiled up around my fingers so effortlessly. As if they wanted to keep them. I could feel his warm breath on my lips as he was looking down at me.

'What would you do if you were in the stories with us?'

'Try and break out,' I replied with a rebellious smirk.

'It might kill you,' Sherlock warned me, knowing that it wouldn't stop him.

'I'm already trapped in my old life. Whoever is trying to make me remember it has power over me, and once I do remember, there'll be no escape.' I ran my thumb over his cheek, and he closed his eyes. 'Don't ever let them do that to you,' I insisted.

He squinted, then opened his eyes again and turned around to his desk, from which, with a cry of triumph, he drew a piece of paper.

'I knew there was something else!' he exclaimed, dashing over to a shelf. I shook my head and smiled.

He opened a book, scribbled something onto the paper, and then made for the door. 'Billy will help! Tell John I'll be back in half an hour!'

And gone he was.

* * *

Mrs Hudson looked in no way surprised that I came.

'If you'd come home at a decent time for once, you would've caught them in the act,' she snapped.

I was rather taken aback at first, but then I saw the biscuits on the table. 'Did you expect us to come downstairs?'

'Oh, not exactly. Let's say I had a *feeling* you would. Now, don't look so frightened and eat your bloody biscuits before you starve from shock,' she grumbled, sitting me down at the table

229

and closing the door. 'That boy asked for a meal already when he came up, so I thought I'd better get some biscuits, too.'

'Oh.' I had already forgotten about Isaac. 'Well, is your oven all right again? Has it made any trouble since you cleaned it out? It barely smells of smoke now,' I enquired innocently to change the topic.

'Oh, I have a nose, too, my dear – you don't need to be that polite with me. I know it still stinks, but at least I can use it again. How is your girlfriend?' she just asked with a cheeky smile.

Now how did she get that impression? 'Well, she's not... actually my girlfriend... anymore,' *Oh John Watson, pull yourself together!* 'She's er... hey!'

Of course, Scarlett came in that moment. *Always! Always at those moments!*

'Hey,' she piped, tentatively putting her head round the door. 'Sherlock's, um, gone out for a moment, and I smelled biscuits.'

'Oh, do sit down, dear. If John doesn't eat *you*, I daresay you can still get some,' Mrs Hudson replied heartily.

Scarlett sat down on the chair Mrs Hudson pulled out next to me. I could've punched Mrs Hudson for her knowing looks and smiles, but she wasn't Sherlock, so my manners were stronger than my anger.

Scarlett didn't notice. She was busy picking the right biscuits and eating them without spreading crumbs all over her shirt.

Mrs Hudson noticed the tension in the room and felt an urge to say something. 'So, how was your day? How is Sherlock's investigation going?'

'Quite all right, thanks for asking.' I spun round at Sherlock's voice.

He was smiling as he stooped through the door. 'I found Billy, Lestrade just sent him round to me. I gave him an address which I got at the Crown, so he can go and search for the files there,' he explained, sitting down next to Mrs Hudson. He put one arm around her shoulders and stuffed a handful of biscuits in his mouth with his free hand.

'Oh, the files!' exclaimed Mrs Hudson. 'Let me go and fetch them.'

I couldn't believe my ears, but the next moment the old lady produced a set of papers from her fridge.

'Mrs Hudson, you're a saint!' Sherlock cried, lifting her high into the air as she came back.

'Oh, I don't know if that was necessary,' answered our landlady with a flattered smile when he put her down again. 'I just thought they might be safer down here when I tidied up your flat a little bit yesterday.'

* * *

I didn't know whether I should be happy about it. Sherlock was happy, and John seemed really annoyed, but relieved at the same time. Mrs Hudson looked like she had no idea of the whole business, but she must have had a look at the files at least or she wouldn't have brought them downstairs.

Now, there was one thing in the world I wanted: to read them. I wanted to face it. I had killed twenty-three people, and I was ready to take responsibility for it. There was no excuse for me. I didn't want to live the life of an innocent human being if I didn't deserve it. And a simple temporary amnesia was nothing which could earn that in my opinion. I would remember everything sooner or later anyway.

It felt so wrong to keep abusing John's generosity while he didn't even know what I had done when, in fact, he and Sherlock were in danger of being arrested because of me.

And there they were, those spitefully white papers, in Sherlock's hands. Suddenly, I felt a harsh resentment rising in me, and my muscles hardened.

'Give me the files.'

Sherlock looked surprised. 'I'm sorry?'

'Give me those papers,' I repeated.

'No.' He saw the menace flickering in my eyes.

'I. Said. Give. Me. The. Bloody. Papers.'

He shook his head. 'Keep calm. I can't. And I won't.'

Now fury was boiling inside me. I had a right to the files. They were my own files, and nobody was allowed to keep them from me. I wasn't going to wait any longer. And I could see there was no way of persuading the man holding my files with words...

Before I knew it, I was at his throat.

* * *

'I had it all under control.'

'No, you didn't! She could've killed you!'

'No, she couldn't.'

'You were utterly defenceless!'

'She didn't mean to.'

'By this point, we know that's no guarantee! What if she had one of her visions again?'

'She didn't. She just wanted the papers.'

'Then why didn't you give them to her!?'

'Because they might drive her insane.'

'How would you know!? *You're* the insane one here!'

'I'm not the only one apart from her.'

Sherlock had carried away several bruises and a sprained finger from his combat with Scarlett. She had slammed him against the wall, turned his arms on his back until his face was red, and tried to wrest the papers from him.

My helpless attempts at pulling the two apart had been so in vain that Mrs Hudson had intervened with a frying pan. I almost felt like using it on her when she knocked Scarlett out, but she was up again before I could deprive Mrs Hudson of her weapon.

Now, Scarlett was shaking in Mrs Hudson's blanket on the sofa downstairs, while I was giving Sherlock some unwilling medical attention. I was aware of the fact that he had enjoyed her attack including the pain it had caused him. He was feeling something again. Only at my last remark, the focus faded from his eyes a little, and his thoughts seemed to wander off into unknown grounds beyond his sanity.

'Why *really*?'

Sherlock curled up the bridge of his nose at my question.

'What's the real reason you're not giving her the papers? It's not just your concern about her mental wellbeing, is it?' I asked him. I knew him far too well not to notice he was concealing something. It was something around the corner of his lips, an itch telling of the impulse to show off, which he resisted.

Finally, he gave in. 'I don't trust those files. She might remember false things on reading them. There have been psychological experiments which prove you can make people remember things they never did in their lives with as much as a photoshopped image if only the illusion seems authentic. It was far too easy to get to the papers. Either they are a fake, or they're not really hers. Whether or not it was Moriarty's intention that we should read them, he definitely hasn't got a problem with it if we do. In any case, it's a trap. To me it looks as if he was trying to pull us down with her. The files might distort her memories, and induce her to give false evidence against herself.'

I was totally petrified by this. Not only that the profoundness of his reasoning was way beyond what I could have imagined, but the graveness of the situation Scarlett was in hit me like a lightning bolt, opening my eyes to an avalanche of rocks about to thunder down on us. I had just gotten her back. *Am I going to lose her again so soon?*

'There's nothing to frown at, John.'

Just this once, Sherlock's calm, knowing words would save my sleep. But though God knows it was so seldom and unlikely that I had to think twice before I could believe my ears every time it happened. This was one of those moments.

* * *

That night I had horrible nightmares. I killed people, they killed me back.

I woke up.

There were no faces, just blood on my hands, and it stuck to them even when I got up. It wouldn't be washed away. I felt the water pouring down on my hands, but instead of cooling them, it boiled up the blood to scald my skin. And when I looked in the mirror, I realised that not I had been killed in the dreams, but someone I should have given my life for.

'Scarlett?' I woke with a start when John touched my hand. 'Sorry, I didn't mean to scare you,' he apologised, stroking my hand.

I ripped it out of his grip and stared at it in horrible expectation. It was perfectly clean.

'Sorry, again,' he said, raising his arms and taking a step back.

'No!' I grabbed his hand, realising what he must think. 'I'm sorry. This had nothing to do with you. Just bad dreams. Stay here, will you?' I asked feebly.

He nodded with a hesitant smile and sat down at my bedside.

'Did you sleep well at least?' I tried to make conversation.

'Oh, me, er, like a baby.' He seemed just casually indifferent, but I could feel there must have been something making him uncomfortable. When he looked away though, I thought it better not to press him on the subject.

'How's Sherlock doing? Did I kill him after all?' I had seen him dead a few times now in my sleep, but I couldn't believe the ease with which those words dropped out of my mouth.

When I had attacked him, I had allowed my fighter's instincts to come out in rage over my files and the desperate longing to know the truth. I was constantly afraid of myself, but even more about the parts I had no inkling about than of the things I knew already. It had been a rather narrow escape from me turning into my inner monster when Mrs Hudson had knocked me out. A moment longer and I might have given in to another vision of Anne forcing itself onto my mind. Now that I was remembering his head quiver from my grip I could see it stop, and with it stopped my breath.

'He's... er... fine,' John stated finally, setting my breath in motion again. He was looking at me in both concern and slight disappointment. 'You didn't hurt him very much, just a few bruises, nothing he couldn't afford to be thrilled about.'

I could hear how difficult it was for John to acknowledge this. But before I could start to reproach myself for bringing him into this painful juxtaposition, he went on, 'Sherlock's having breakfast at the moment, by the way. If you'd care to join us...'

I nodded vigorously with a smile and John smiled back for a moment. Then he looked away again and his smile slightly froze when he added, 'He's still convinced you wouldn't have killed him.'

'And you don't agree,' I replied understandingly.

John shook his head – as though not to say no – and looked up at the sky we couldn't see above the ceiling. 'I loved you, Scarlett. I always did. I mean, I had other women after you, but I never forgot about you.'

It was hard to hold back the tears about the loss of my memory here.

'Sorry, I-I didn't mean…' John stammered, giving me a handkerchief.

'It's all right, forget it – no, damn it, don't forget it! – just say what you were going to say,' I nearly sobbed.

'Well, there was something you always said. "The clouds will move south with the birds one day." It was from a poem you'd found in your letterbox. And when I asked why the clouds should do that, you would say, "Everyone needs a holiday now and again."'

John had to smile at this memory, and I tried to remember his face at my saying this, but instead a sheet of paper with blurred scribblings flashed across my mind, and a silent scream shot up in my conscience.

I tried to rivet my eyes to John's face and to my astonishment, the impressions vanished.

'All I'm trying to say is,' he continued then, 'you were the one who knew there always was a way out.'

I just wrapped my arms around him.

He gladly returned the hug.

'John, will you promise me one thing?'

'What's that?' he asked suspiciously.

'Don't ever let me kill you.'

He gently laughed. 'I'll do my best.'

I moved back a little to look at him. 'Aren't you afraid of me at all?'

'If I were afraid of killers, I wouldn't be living with a private detective,' he replied and we both had to laugh.

Epilogue: Where Our Silhouettes Have Gone

When you read this, it will probably seem strange to you how we did not see it all coming. When you read this, you will probably ask yourself how we had escaped our Victorian shadows for so long.

When you read this, I can see it will puzzle you that we walked into your modern day and forgot about ourselves. Sherlock Holmes is not easy to overlook in Baker Street. His silhouette is everywhere.

You probably know all the stories, had a famous actor read them to you, perhaps. You probably saw some films even, attempting to depict the life of the greatest detective who ever lived.

You probably know people who have Sherlock on a T-shirt.

If you've searched up my name, you will have found dozens of people claiming my voice. If you went on Google images, you would find dozens of faces attributed to me, some of which you will dislike because they don't look the way you imagine me.

In the end, the same happened to Scarlett's face, though you may not remember yet, but it will come clear in time. Like us, you will wonder how you could not have recognised her. If you found all the clues, you will know her already. If you haven't, you will find out the same way we did.

Once you've had a drink at the Conan Doyle in Edinburgh, you will know people don't overlook the golden letters outside the pub. Once you've walked through Meiringen in Switzerland, you will have seen all the people in deerstalkers pointing at the mountain side. Once you've been to Baker Street, you will have seen the countless letters to Sherlock Holmes by people who believed he was real. They still arrive, don't they?

The truth is I cannot prove to you who was first. The stories, or our lives. I cannot prove to you what they did to us, how they plotted against us, or why our only defence is to write it down. All I can do is ask you to read what we have to say and believe us.

~John Watson

Orange Pip Books

OP is the sassy younger sibling of world's largest Sherlock Holmes publishers, MX Publishing. We were created in 2019 with the idea of bringing some of the light hearted fun to the Holmes family Canon, as well as looking to publish more inclusive storylines including LGBTQ+ and BAME characters.

www.orangepipbooks.com

Also from Orange Pip Books

Adventures of a Teenage Detective – Violet Jolmes and

The Agent's of H.I.V.E. – Volume 1

Violet Holmes is not an ordinary teenager because, well, nothing is ordinary when you're the adopted daughter of the great Sherlock Holmes. Having been home schooled for her entire life she has decided to take the plunge, at 14, and attend Bardle Secondary School to study for her exams. But after a week, she notices that the school hides a deep secret, and she's determined to crack it wide open. Are the current spate of school thefts the work of criminal masterminds? Is there really a secret society behind closed doors? Can a girl like Violet make friends and fit in?

The Disappearance of Inspector Lestarde

Dr. John H. Watson is a man of medical science, a man of action and a man of letters. His life has been one of adventure and romance. In 1894 he finds himself alone following the death of his great friend Sherlock Holmes three years earlier and now the passing of his beloved wife, Mary. His loneliness is all encompassing and only a true friend can help him to see there is still reason to continue living. But when that friend, Inspector G. Lestrade of Scotland Yard suddenly and mysteriously disappears, Dr. Watson takes it upon himself to discover the reason for the abduction.

Also from Orange Pip Books

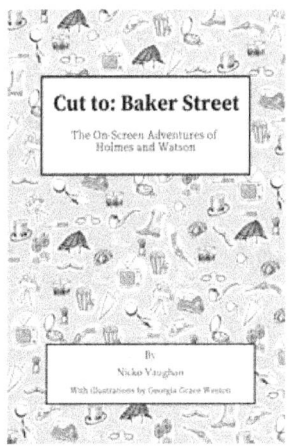

Cut To Baker Street - The On Screen Adventures of

Holmes and Watson

It is well documented that Sherlock Holmes is the most depicted literary character on screen; he even has an entry in the Guinness Book of Records to prove it. This reference guide covers depictions of the world's most famous detective, and his faithful companion, from the first silent film Sherlock Holmes is Baffled (1900) to the Will Ferrell, John C. Reilly comedy Holmes and Watson (2018).

As well as cinema and television portrayals, this book by Nicko Vaughan (Author of The Wordy Companion: An A-Z Guide to Sherlockian Phraseology) also covers documentaries, animations and web series adaptations alongside début feature artwork by graphic artist Georgia Grace Weston.

www.ingramcontent.com/pod-product-compliance
Lightning Source LLC
Chambersburg PA
CBHW071302250626
47159CB00004B/1271